MANY THE MONSTERS

ASHLEY MUSKETT

Book Cover by Brittany Evans of BEDesigns

First edition 2026

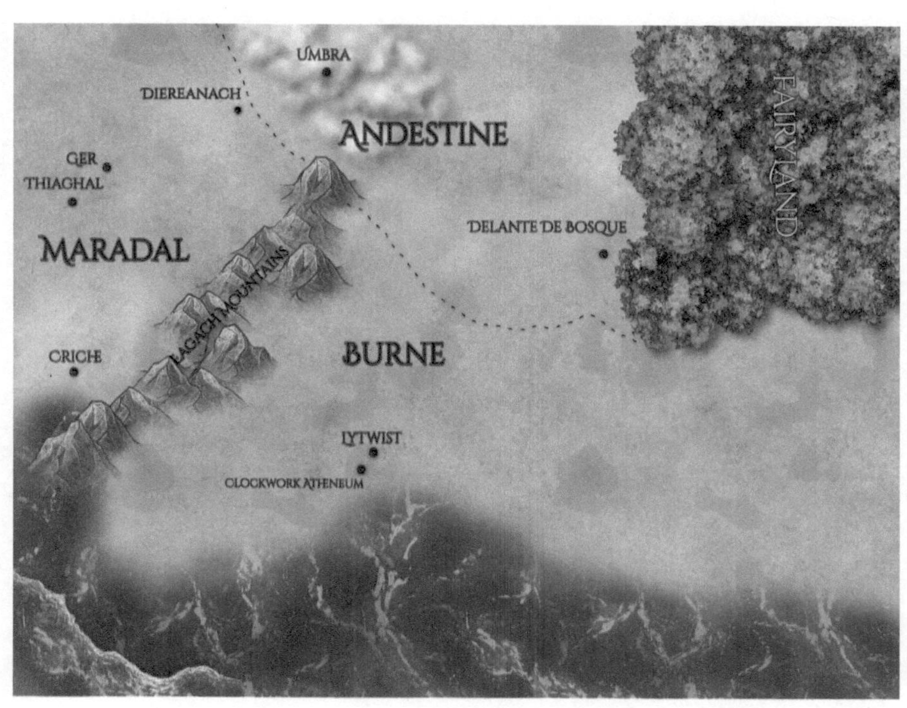
UMBRA
DIEREANACH
ANDESTINE
GER
THIAGHAL
MARADAL
DELANTE DE BOSQUE
FAIRYLAND
EAGACH MOUNTAINS
CRICHE
BURNE
LYTWIST
CLOCKWORK ATHENEUM

To Peter. My debilitating anxiety about anything bad ever happening to you when we were in college was a huge inspiration.

"There is a many a monster that wears the guise of a man; it is better of the two to have the heart of a man and the form of a monster."

- Jeanne-Marie Le Prince de Beaumont, Beauty and the Beast

1

A sense of surrealness washes over me again as I look down at my sleeping wife. Calla. *My wife.* It doesn't seem possible that I'm actually married to the woman asleep beside me. I feel so close to her, and yet the events of the past few days remind me how little I know her, how short a time I've known her. Her breath rises and falls. Even though she's sleeping, she doesn't look peaceful. I don't think I've seen Calla look truly at peace even once in the months that I've known her. When she sleeps, I watch her, the gentle movement of eyes behind closed lids suggesting a vivid dream that I know she won't tell me about. Calla, I'm learning, has endless secrets. For just a second, I have a horrible feeling of dread as I watch her, which makes my entire body run cold. At the same time, I gently brush some of her long brown waves out of her face and set one of my hands on her bare shoulder, the tips of my claws just barely resting on her shoulder blade. Some of my inexplicable dread fades away at the solid feeling of her body under my clawed hands, and the gentle rise and fall of her breath.

Not for the first time, I think that Calla may be the most beautiful woman in the world. A woman of constant contradictions, she nestles into the comfort of my body as if she's cold; her skin, meanwhile, radiates a feverish warmth. I tell myself that whatever danger I think I'm sensing right now is foolish. I try to tell my muscles to unclench, to relax, to go back to sleep, to stop staring at her and trying to unravel the thread of her sleeping thoughts. I mentally will Calla's muscles to relax, too. I never realized before we were married, before Calla slept against me every night, that her muscles always felt coiled and ready to snap. She sleeps with her arms curled close to her body, bent hands tucked under her chin. I drag the nails of my claws gently up and down her arm and feel her muscles relax just the tiniest fraction as she lets out a long breath. I try to relax my muscles just the tiniest bit too- but as I fall asleep, I can still feel the whisper of dread, burrowed deep in my stomach.

1 Year Earlier

It's close to 2 am when I make my way downstairs for yet another emergency household meeting. I would be irritated if I weren't so tired. I sluggishly wind my way down the hallway from my room, down a grand staircase, and directly into our comfortable main sitting room. My mother will be frustrated at my lack of urgency, but I'm frustrated at yet another unnecessary late-night meeting. It's hard to imagine that I'm going to hear anything about The Inimical at this meeting that couldn't wait another four hours, unless he's literally at the front door. There's a fire going in the fireplace already, courtesy of Mom, even though it's the middle of the night. It illuminates the green plush sofas, brown armchairs, and brown rug of the sitting room in a warm, flickering light. It might have been a cozy winter evening if it weren't 2 am. My kind-of-cousins Bevin and Madeliza, the children of my mom's late best friend, are already here. I can't stop myself from doing a double-take at Maddie. Growing up, Maddie and Bevin always looked similar, with matching strawberry blonde hair and blue eyes, but lately Maddie's hair is somehow a shocking silver color. Over the past summer, it seems like she's grown a foot into a long, gangly teenager, well surpassing Bevin, who, in her late 20's, has always been short and round. Maddie is stretched out in front of the fire, sketching something in her sketchbook. I nudge her side with my foot as I walk past her towards the armchair.

"Shouldn't you be in bed, Mads?" I say.

"Speak for yourself," she says, smiling. "I was the only one who was actually still up when the message was delivered."

"Aw, Mads," I say, my heart sinking, "I didn't realize you got the message first. You alright?" Her smile fades, but she keeps her eyes on her sketch book and nods. I drop into the armchair closest to the fire and make eye contact with Bevin, who gives me a half smile. She's sitting on the plush sofa next to my mom, Laurel, with her arm wrapped around my mom's shoulders. Mom has clearly been crying. I should comfort her, but I can feel my frustration with this conversation already, and I'm worried that if I open my mouth, I'll say something I regret. Aydin, my actual cousin and best friend, stands up, closes the door, and vaults over the back of the sofa to sit next to Bevin. Aydin's dad is my dad's older brother and after Dad died they moved away pretty quickly, I think to escape the sad memories. His parents moved to Criche, a quiet town even smaller than Thiaghal. They sent Aydin back to live with us when we were teenagers to be around more people his age and he's been here ever since. We all have.

I realize by taking the armchair I've positioned myself so they're all staring at me, which does nothing to help my growing frustration. I decide to try to control the situation while I still can. I take a deep breath and stand.

"The Inimical?" I say. Aydin nods, and I quickly continue before Mom can take control of the conversation. "When?" I ask.

"Aunt Laurel says that she just got word that Bierne is gone," says Aydin. I cut my eyes over to my mother, whose lips are pressed together in a grim line. My stomach twists as I watch her face, hoping she gives some feeling away, but she's still as a statue. I want to know that she's coping with the news and not about to have a catatonic episode. Bierne was the last cursed beast in all of Maradal. Actually, the last one anyone knows of anywhere, that is, besides me.

"So," I say, "We know for sure that Bierne is gone? He isn't just traveling? Or . . ."

"He isn't traveling, Tyre," says Mom. "He hasn't gone anywhere for the past year."

"Since his unfortunate run-in with a fairy," says Aydin, "that resulted in him being turned into, well . . ." Aydin gestures in my general direction, referring to my appearance ever since my own unfortunate run-in with a fairy. When I was 11, I wasn't appropriately charitable to an old woman who came to our door offering to sell us a barrel of apples, and she decided that I was unfairly judging her for being ugly. She transformed into a fairy woman and cursed me to remain a horrible beast until someone could fall in love with me, breaking the curse with true love's kiss. Truthfully, I hadn't even really registered what she looked like; we just didn't need any apples. Since then, I've looked like a mixture between a bear and an, I don't know, an antelope maybe? I can walk on two legs or four, I have antlers for some reason, lots of fur, and claws where most people would have fingernails. There are other people, like Bierne, who have been cursed in similar ways, and in my hometown of Thiaghal, old fears of monsters and magic run deep. The day I was cursed, my mother moved my room as far into the house as possible in case word got out about the curse and an angry mob descended on us. In a way, my mother and the rest of my family haven't stopped hovering since. Never mind that part of being a cursed beast is superhuman strength, speed, and accelerated healing from injuries.

"Maybe he just got sick of living in hiding," I say.

"Tyre," says Mom, "could you please not. Not tonight." I take another deep breath and unclench my claws. I stare down at the fur on my hands and try to even out my breathing. It isn't Mom's fault that I never leave this house. Sure, maybe when I was first transformed at 11, it was her fault for hiding me away. As a teenager, one could argue that keeping me hidden wasn't the best way to acclimate the town to my new appearance. Now I'm nearly 30, well into adulthood, and I could leave this house, consequences be damned, but when I look at my mom and know the intense anxiety she would feel, I can't do that to her. Not after everything she's lost. It isn't fair for me to take it out on her. If I'm honest with myself, I talk about having a right to go out into the world, but it's hard to do something I haven't done since I was 11.

"The Inimical is a serious threat," she says.

"For fuck's sake!" I yell. So much for my good intention of not losing my temper. I feel Bev and Aydin turn their eyes towards me. Aydin looks reproachful; Bevin is trying not to laugh. I don't look at Maddie, but I'm sure she is too. Even Mom cracks a smile. I can almost see her roll her eyes like she did when I was a kid, constantly stating my opinion as fact. Proof that, despite the fact that I have antlers, I'm surrounded by people who will eternally see me as harmless. The thought is steadying somehow. "Sorry, Mom," I say, "I just mean, do we really need to keep calling him 'The Inimical'?"

"Well, what do you want to call him?" says Aydin, smiling now, too.

"Let's call him 'Mark'," says Bevin. Maddie snorts and adds a line to her sketch.

"I'm not calling him Mark," says Mom. Somehow, my outburst has taken some of the edge off the conversation. It's enough that I don't immediately bristle again when my mom says, "We need to discuss your safety."

"Mom."

"Tyre."

"Everything will be alright." I get up and put a hand on her shoulder, as she wraps her hand over mine. "I'm safe here. I'm safe anywhere. Look at me." I hold my arms, which are notably covered in fur and end in clawed fingers, out to their full length for dramatic effect.

"We don't know that," she says. "We don't know that at all. Bierne was cursed like you, and look what's happened to him."

"We don't know it was Mark that did it," said Bevin. "What's the full story? Did his family wake up to an empty bed?"

"Apparently, strange men came in the night," says Maddie from the carpet. "They requested shelter, and you know it's frowned upon by the faeries to refuse shelter to travelers, so Elena, Bierne's mother, and her husband, Bierne the elder, let them in. All they remember after that is that they felt very unwell, fatigued, and fell asleep. In the morning, the younger Bierne was gone."

"Well, I can solve that," I say. I feel all eyes turn to me. "I'll just refuse shelter to any travelers. What else could possibly happen?" I hold out my claws again for emphasis. "It's a silly superstition, anyway. The fairies work at random, not based on human hospitality conventions."

"This is serious, Tyre," says Aydin.

"I am being serious," I say.

"They would have forced their way in," says Mom, "if they hadn't been let in. Elena and Bierne the elder would have probably fallen asleep just that much sooner." Silence falls over the room as we all stare at each other for a moment. Mom sighs, "Well . . . you know what I think." She crosses her arms and stares at the table.

"Mom," I say as gently as I can, "I can't have his conversation anymore. I've already told you that—"

"That what?" she cuts in. "That you have no interest in changing out of this strange beast form that you're cursed to? That you're never going to go back to looking like the little boy I raised? That you're content to live a life of seclusion in this castle, barred from the world? That even though The Inimical—"

"Mark," mouths Bevin so only I can see. I mercifully keep a straight face.

"—is clearly collecting people cursed by fairy magic for who knows what purpose, you won't even try, *try*, to break the curse?" Mom finishes speaking and wipes a tear from her face.

"Mom," I say, while I give her shoulder another squeeze, "I didn't say I didn't want to, I just said it wasn't a priority for me at this time." Mom throws her hands into the air in frustration. "And," I continue, "even if I did want to, we don't even know how."

"We do know how," says Mom. "The fairy said very clearly that a young lady needs to fall in love with you to break the curse."

"Bevin loves me," I point out.

"True," says Bevin.

"Me too!" chirps Maddie from the carpet.

"Yes," says Mom, "but last I checked, Bevin wasn't *in* love with you. Unless there's something that I need to be made immediately aware of?" She looks back and forth from me to Bevin as we both shake our heads 'no.' "And," she continues, "Maddie, you're 15, so you're not allowed to be in love with anyone." Maddie rolls her eyes. "Furthermore, even if Bevin were in love with you, Bevin knew you when you were more conventionally attractive. I'm not sure it would count."

"I pity the men with steady girlfriends who are uncharitable to fairies, am I right?" says Bevin.

"Oh, I don't know," says Aydin, "I'm not convinced that knowing them before immediately disqualifies you. You'd still have to accept their new form."

"Children!" says Mom. Bevin, Aydin, Maddie, and I are all immediately quiet. "We're not debating the finer points of the rules of curse-breaking. Unless they're suddenly relevant?" She looks again from Bevin to me, and we again shake our heads 'no.' "As the matter stands," she presses her hands against her temples, "we need to get another young person, young lady, in the castle and in love with Tyre. Then the curse will be broken, and he'll stop being a possible target of The Inimical."

"Mom," I say, "everyone in here," I sweep my hand across the room, "is used to me. You can't actually think that anyone from Thiaghal, or even all of Maradal, would want anything to do with me. Don't most of them think I died?"

"Don't be ridiculous," she says. She sniffs and tucks a piece of hair behind her ear. "That is a ridiculous rumor started by ridiculous people. You have power and money, I find it hard to believe that there isn't a young lady who would be interested in you."

"Because that's who we want," I say, rolling my eyes. "Let's go public with what I look like, confirm all the rumors, and bring in all the women after money and power. I'm sure my true love is there somewhere."

"They'll come for the money and power, but once they see what a good heart you have . . . "

It's pointless to argue with her. We've talked in this circle before, and it's no use telling her that anyone who intends to merely tolerate a monster in order to gain money and power is highly unlikely to break the curse. I make eye contact with Bevin and Aydin, willing them to read my mind and help. *Anything*, I think, *say anything. Just get me out of this endless conversation and back to bed*. Aydin finally obliges.

"We cannot entertain suitors for Tyre," says Aydin, standing up.

"And why is that?" says Mom, turning to look at him.

"Because, um. Well, you see. Because . . . " I groan internally. Poor Aydin. Such a good friend. Such a bad liar. "Bevin really is in love with Tyre! I cannot stand by idly while she's too shy to be honest about it." He walks across the room and knocks a chair over for dramatic effect. After a full five seconds of silence, he slowly picks his chair back up and sits down. At first, I think my mom is going to yell, but after a minute, she laughs.

"Will you four ever stop being silly?" she sighs. "Back to bed. All of you. If this pack of almost 30-something's . . . "

"Hey!" interjects Maddie.

"And one teenager," Mom amends, "can't be grown-ups, get out so the grown-up can think." Under normal circumstances, I might have tried to stay and comfort Mom. Even with all my frustration about how she wants to handle Mark, I can't stay mad at her when her face is still puffy from crying. I might at least try to have a conversation that would reassure her, but I've had this conversation before. Several times. Nothing new happens, and nothing changes. I give her shoulder one last squeeze, and slowly, Bevin, Aydin, and I shuffle out of the room. Maddie remains where she is, sketching by the fire, which I'm glad about. Mom shouldn't be by herself. The large oak door swings shut behind us, leaving us in the silence of the hallway. I let out a long sigh and sit down with my back against the closed door.

"Hey," says Bevin, as she and Aydin sit down next to me, "you alright?" She reaches out and puts a hand on my knee. With just Bev and Aydin, I can feel what I can't let myself feel in front of my mom and Maddie. The Inimical appeared out of thin air only two years ago. So short a time, but in that time, he's taken control of the entire city of Umbra in our northern neighboring Kingdom of Andestine, and then people like me, anyone cursed or gifted with fairy magic, started disappearing. The Inimical has only gotten more powerful with the cursed wall of impenetrable fog he casts, taking over more and more land. Once the fog spread over your home, or neighborhood, or town, that was it, and you were never seen again. No one in, no one out of anywhere that the fog covers. For what feels like the hundredth time I wonder *why*? *Why is The Inimical, whoever he is, doing this?*

"Do you think it's true?" I say. "What people have been saying."

"What? That The Inimical is the first and only mortal man to figure out how to use magic and does so by draining the magic and life out of anyone cursed or blessed by fairies?" says Aydin. Bevin shoves his arm.

"Yes," I say, "that."

"I don't know," says Aydin. We all sit in silence for a few minutes.

"I'm not in love with you . . . " says Bevin.

"Thanks, Bev. You really know how to cheer a guy up," I say.

" . . . but I would marry you if I thought it would keep you safe from The Inimical."

"Thanks," I say. "Let's just call him Mark."

***

I toss and turn that night, trying to fall back asleep. I finally drift off, but the line between sleep and wake is blurred.

"Tyre." Aydin's voice echoes around the walls of my dream, but in my dream, I'm talking to my dad. He's trying to tell me something, but when I reach for him, my hand slips through him. I know I won't be able to hear him unless I can touch him . . . or I won't be able to hear him anymore if I touch him? It's hard to tell. When my hand passes through him, he shakes his head frantically, 'No.' So I'm not supposed to touch him then? "Tyre." Aydin's voice echoes from somewhere again, and I'm becoming more and more aware that I'm asleep. The dream is fading away.

"Dad!" I reach for him again, but he jerks back and finally speaks.

"Don't touch," he says, "not after the blood." It's so good to hear his voice again that I don't care what he's saying. He could tell me to ride a magical worm naked through the campus of Clockwork Atheneum, and it wouldn't faze me. "Tyre," he says again, but this time with Aydin's voice. Suddenly, I feel a warm hand on my shoulder and a searing burn across my chest. I jerk awake and yell.

"Whoa, sorry!" says Aydin. I rub my eyes and look around, trying to reorient myself and catch my breath.

"It's alright," I say as I rub my eyes and reach for the bottle of water next to my bed. Suddenly, I realize my chest is still burning. I clutch at the burning spot and find my hand wrapped around the family medallion my dad passed down to me. The second I touch it, I gasp and pull my hand away, which leaves it to drop back on my chest, burning the same spot again. I suck in another breath, reach up to yank the medal from around my neck, and throw it across the room where it clatters to a stop next to the fireplace.

"What?" says Aydin, looking back and forth between me and the medallion. "What's up?"

"It . . . it burned me . . . " We both stare at it lying on the floor for a full second.

"Has it, uh, ever done that before?" says Aydin. I just keep staring at it with a blank look on my face, which I can only hope answers his question. Aydin slowly walks over and kicks it, and we both watch, waiting to see if it will, I don't know, combust? I get out of bed too and give it a kick for good measure. When it still doesn't do anything, I bend down and touch it gingerly to find it has returned to normal temperature. Aydin and I look at each other and shrug. He's still in his pajamas, and his dark hair is standing straight up like he's just tumbled out of bed and right into my room. Like most people in Thiaghal, Aydin has pale skin that's a sharp contrast to his black hair, and he looks like a ghost in the eerie moonlight from the window. Growing up, my mom always said that Aydin and I looked like brothers. We probably still would if it weren't for the curse, although there are probably still some similarities with my dark fur. Sometimes looking at Aydin is eerie, like looking in a mirror of what could have been. I stand up and place the medallion back on.

"Anyway . . . " says Aydin. "I heard you talking in your sleep. Figured I would check on you after our fifth midnight meeting of the month and see if you were alright."

"Thanks," I say, rubbing a hand over my face and sitting on the edge of my bed. "I don't know why we keep getting updates about Mark in the middle of the night, but it seems like Mom continues to feel like we need to talk about each of them immediately." Aydin sits down next to me and flops backward. "Dreaming about my dad again," I say as I flop back next to him.

"The same dream?" he asks.

"Yeah, the one where he warns me not to touch something after some kind of blood. I can't make sense of it."

"Any luck with his old books?" says Aydin. I glance over to the pile of textbooks on my bed from my dad's time as a student at Clockwork Atheneum. I've been looking through them for any notes he might have made about magical dreams, but most of his research seems to be about the magical properties of dragon-made gold.

"No," I say, letting out a long breath.

"Any chance it's just a dream?" says Aydin. "You have been under more stress than usual lately."

"Maybe," I say, unconvinced. I've had dreams before, even vivid ones, and they've never felt quite like this. However, it's the middle of the night, and Aydin is making a huge effort to keep from falling asleep. I watch his eyes flutter open and closed next to me in bed. My reasons for thinking these aren't just normal dreams can wait until another time.

"Aydin," I say, reaching over and shaking his shoulder.

"I'm awake," he says, startling and sitting straight up.

"Yes, I see that. Go back to bed, Aydin, I'm good." He nods slowly and claps his hand on my shoulder before half sleepwalking back to his room.

2

The first snow of the season covers the ground a week later. The most recent sighting of Mark is all but forgotten by most people in the house, although probably not for Mom. For years, Mom was the governor of our tiny town, Thiaghal. There are five different provinces, each with a central town, all of different sizes. Maradal and Thiaghal's province is by far the smallest. The people of Maradal tend to be solitary. It's not in our culture to be overly social outside our close family groups, and our geography doesn't really help with that.

Thiaghal is cold most of the year. We're lucky if we get even a month of weather warm enough for our garden of imported Andestine roses to bloom. Most of the provinces are cut off from one another by mountain ranges that are dangerous to cross. We don't have a centralized government and operate more like an alliance of smaller countries than one big one.

Each province is governed by an elected governor, but there's very little that the people of Maradal, or at least Thiaghal, dislike more than change. The election is a formality. No one ever runs against the currently governing family, and the position is handed down from parent to child, the same as any monarchy I've heard of, no matter what. In my case, that remains true even if there's rampant (and entirely correct) suspicion that the son of the current governor, who hasn't been seen since he was 11, has been changed into a monster by fairy magic.

My mom stepped down two years ago, and I was elected governor at 27. I took the job as governor as expected. Maddie asked me once if I liked it, and I surprised myself by realizing I didn't have an answer. It was like asking if I like breathing, if breathing were attached to the crushing weight of responsibility for the physical and emotional safety of everyone in this house. It's never occurred to me not to do it. Since Maddie asked, it *has* occurred to me that I don't like it that much. But what else can I do?

It's amazing how much governing can be done entirely remotely, which means I stay here, just a favorite Thiaghal myth. Mom still insists she attends the yearly council meeting of the five governors of each Maradal province as my proxy, and everyone is too polite, or too deeply committed to minding their own business, to ask questions to our faces. I still do see the smaller Thiaghal council on a fairly regular basis when we meet at the manor house, so they know what I look like. Somehow, this doesn't seem to have impacted the rumors about me one way or the other. The small Thiaghal council all seem fine with me, with one notable exception being Sheriff Murchad. Murchad has made it abundantly clear that he doesn't trust anyone touched by fairy magic and that he thinks I'm an animal and not a person. Can't win them all, I guess.

On this snowy morning, I plan to do what I always do. Go to the kitchen for breakfast and head to my office to wade through memos, business license renewal applications, and various minor citations ahead of our weekly Thiaghal council meeting. For just a second, as I look at the door, I feel a surge of anger that has nowhere to go. I can't direct it at my mom, even though she taught me to fear the world, because she's lost too much for me to be angry at her. I can't direct it towards Bevin and Aydin because it isn't their fault that they're free to travel, shop, and dance in town, and I'm not. It's not even towards my dad, who died and left me in charge of this massive house and these traumatized people. It stays where it is, swirling in my stomach in an endless knot that I've become good at ignoring. Maybe I'll see if Mads wants to build a snowman later as a distraction. As I'm unlocking my office door, I hear,

"Tyre!" I turn and see Mom walking down the hall towards me.

"Hello, Mom," I say. I shake myself out of my thoughts and manage a smile as she reaches up and smooths a piece of fur behind one of my antlers. "Alright, enough, Mom," I say as gently as I can, moving her hands away from my head. "I'm just going to get started for the morning." I gesture towards my office door with my head.

"It can wait," she says. "Come with me."

"Why? What's going on?" I ask. "Is it about Mark?" I feel my stomach squirm, but manage to push away the feeling by reminding myself that I'm a 6'5" monster.

"In a manner of speaking," she says.

I turn and follow her down the hallway. It's a few minutes before I realize we're headed back towards my room. Why? Before I can wonder for long, I have my answer. Mom pushes open the door to reveal that, in the 30 minutes I've been at breakfast, she's filled my room with an explosion of formalwear.

"Mom, what . . . ?" I start.

"We are having a party," she says. "The party we would have had for you when you turned eighteen under different circumstances. We should have just gone ahead with it then. If we're ever going to stand a chance of breaking the curse, you at least need to meet the young ladies of Maradal. I am tired of being talked out of this."

"Oh, Mom . . . " I feel my stomach squirm again, only this time, reminding myself that I'm a 6'5" monster only makes it worse. "Mom," I say again, "you know this is a bad idea. Be reasonable. Do you really want to give the entire country a good reason to gawk at me?" She makes a clicking sound with her mouth and turns to fix the tie on one of the suits. "And," I continue, "it could be inviting danger. I don't know if it's the best idea to have the castle open just now. Think of what could go wrong, for all we know, Mark could send his magic in with the crowd."

"The Inimical is exactly the reason that we're doing this. I'm tired of doing nothing. It's a risk we need to take."

"It's not just Mark, you know. Ordinary people might try to kill me, too, if given the chance. Do you really want to open the doors to an angry mob?" Murchad's poorly concealed hatred of me crosses my mind.

"There will be plenty of security precautions," she says. "I'm tired of doing nothing, and I'm tired of being talked out of this. Start trying on suits."

***

"She's delusional." I kick a rock hard down the path outside. Bevin, Aydin, and I are out walking in the twilight later through what would be a rose garden if it were Maradal's one month of summer.

"She's worried," says Aydin. He quickly ducks under a snow-covered trellis, barely missing a patch of snow falling from it to the ground.

"Who knows?" says Bevin, "The party could be fun! If you know, no one tries to kill you with a crossbow."

"That's what she doesn't understand," I say. "She doesn't go into town like you two do. She doesn't hear the talk." I look towards the wooded part of the castle grounds, and the three of us stand in the silence of freshly fallen snow. "I'll be back in a minute," I say, finally.

"You alright?" says Aydin.

"Yes," I say. "I just need to talk to someone." I gesture towards my dad's medallion hanging around my neck. Bevin and Aydin both nod in understanding.

"See you inside then," says Bevin. "We'll heat up cream for hot chocolate."

Once they turn and head back to the house, I take off running. I start on my feet, but eventually I fall into the rhythm of running on all fours. This is another perk of the 'curse.' I could never have run like this in my old shape. I fly through the forest with trees and leaves flying past and cold air filling my lungs. Finally, I see my destination ahead. I slow until I see the light of the clearing where the oak tree waits.

***

It's dark when I finally make my way back to the house. I enter through the front doors, but instead of turning left to the sitting room, I keep on straight and turn down a flight of stairs leading into the relatively small kitchen with a square wooden table and another large fireplace. We have a dining room off the living room, but I can't even remember the last time I was in there. We always sit here where it's warmer. "Feeling better?" says Bevin. I walk into the kitchen, shaking snow off my coat as I go.

"Much," I say. Aydin smiles and passes me a hot chocolate. The fire is crackling in the kitchen fireplace, casting soft light around the room. We sit in silence, sipping our hot chocolates and listening to the fire.

"Well," says Bevin, finally, "I think I'll go to bed . . . " A loud bell suddenly rings, filling the kitchen with noise. We all look at each other, frozen. No visitors are expected at the house tonight, or ever really.

"It's probably nothing. Maybe Murchad, with something urgent," I say. We've all been on edge with The Inimical's fog and disappearances approaching Thiaghal. It isn't so unusual that someone would visit here passing through, but we all jump again when the bell rings for the second time. I'm standing up to answer it when Mom rushes into the room.

"You're not here," she says to me. I open my mouth to speak. "You're away. Staying with Aydin and his family in Criche."

"Is it . . . ?" begins Bevin.

"I think so," says Mom, "It's someone who says they're traveling, looking for a place to stay, but I can't see their face. They're wearing an enormous dark cloak." Bevin presses her hand to her mouth and nods, eyes wide.

"Bevin," she says, "you need to come with me to help serve warm drinks and get this person settled into a room."

"No!" I say, grabbing Bevin's arm and pulling her back.

"We don't have time for this," says Mom. "We can't be sure it isn't fairies, and lord knows we've had enough trouble with fairies."

"Let me go. I'd love to meet up with another fairy," I growl. "You know the hospitality thing is a myth, just send them to town. They can find somewhere there."

"Don't be ridiculous," snaps Mom. "What if it isn't fairies?"

"I say we fight! I'm tired of sitting and waiting for Mark to show up. If he's here, let's bring the fight to him. We should have taken the fight to Mark a long time ago. I've already said that."

"I've already told you," she says, "that we don't have the power to take on an enemy with strange, unknown resources. We need to get a better idea of the situation and keep you safe in the meantime.

"Too late," I say, "they're apparently here! The fight has come to us."

"This doesn't have to be a fight. Please," says Mom. "I can't lose you, too."

I'm about to roar in frustration when I realize that the unknown visitor would probably hear me. I think about Maddie asleep upstairs and slowly let go of Bevin's arm.

"I'll be fine," she says. She disappears out the door following Mom. Aydin and I pace in front of the fire. After a few minutes, I can hear a muffled conversation above us in the sitting room.

"Something's wrong," I say.

"What?" says Aydin. "I don't hear . . . "

"I have better hearing than you do." I twitch one of my ears forward. I hear a chair scrape against the floor suddenly as two feet hit the ground. As if someone has jumped up. Then we both hear it, raised voices coming from the room above us. An argument. Then a scream.

"Bevin!" we both shout simultaneously. I spring towards the door, and by the time Aydin and I burst into the sitting room, all is quiet. Mom and Bevin are sleeping in the two chairs by the fire.

"Hello, Tyre," says a voice behind me. The door suddenly slams as Aydin and I spin around. Standing in front of us is . . . something. It speaks like a human being, but it clearly isn't. It's impossibly slim, and it has no body parts I can identify as human, at least as far as I can see. Everything is obscured by an enormous black cloak and a wide-brimmed hat. Aydin, ridiculously, steps in front of me.

"I'm a seven-foot-tall monster," I whisper, "I think maybe I should be in front of you."

"You're 6'5" at best," Aydin whispers back. Before I can answer, the shape speaks again.

"I'm here to collect you," it says. "I have orders to bring you with me." Before I can react, Aydin is thrown out of the way.

"Aydin!" I try to run to where he landed, but a golden rope has tied itself around my ankle. I feel it tug, and my feet go out from under me as

I fall backward. I reach down to tear at the strand, but before I can get to it, another fastens itself around my wrist. A shining, golden light is filling the room. It's actually beautiful, and it's warm and calming. I can feel my heart rate slowing and my eyes closing. Suddenly, the medallion around my neck burns white hot, the same way it had a few nights before. The sudden pain jolts me awake. I can see the shape preparing to throw another gold thread around my legs. I stand as best I can and launch myself forward at the shape, grabbing at its neck with my teeth.

"Tyre! Tyre!" I don't know how long it's been when I feel two pairs of hands on my shoulders, jerking me backwards. Suddenly, I realize that I'm fighting with nothing but an empty cloak.

"What? What happened?" I ask as I look around, breathing hard.

"It's gone." I look up and see that Mom and Bevin are the ones who pulled me backward. Maddie is standing behind them, looking like she's going to cry with a crumpled piece of paper clutched in her hand. She must have been up sketching and heard the noise.

"I don't know what it was," says Bevin, "but it's gone." Mom wraps her arms tight around my shoulders and holds on for dear life.

"I'm fine, Mom. Really," I say. There's a groan from across the room.

"Aydin!" Bevin jumps up and runs to where Aydin was thrown. She carefully helps him to a sitting position.

"I'm alright too," he says. He stretches his arms carefully. "Definitely alright." Bevin sighs and drops to sit on the floor next to him.

"What was that?" she says. Cautiously, we make our way over to the cloak. I can feel Bevin, Maddie, and Aydin's eyes on me as I look down into the enormous cloak. In the center lies a broom broken in half.

"It . . . it was a broom?" I say.

"I don't like this," says Mom. "This is strange magic." I have to admit, I don't like it much either. I scoop up both halves of the broom and toss them into the fire.

"There," I say. "That takes care of that." *For now*, I think. For Mom's sake, I manage not to add that out loud. I take a deep breath and look around, and am suddenly overwhelmed by the feeling that I can't have all these worried eyes on me for another second. "I'm going to bed," I say. As I walk out of the room, I feel everyone's worried eyes follow me, except for Maddie, whose eyes are tear-filled but locked on the paper in her hand.

It's my fault, I think. If I weren't like this, Maddie wouldn't be scared half out of her mind in the middle of the night. I squeeze my eyes shut and press my hand to my temples. By the time I reach my bed, my head is pounding, and I drop into yet another night of restless sleep.

3

The next morning, Mom is in full swing with preparations for the party. The previous night's events have only strengthened her resolve to break the curse as quickly and effectively as possible. I watch as streamers are put up in the ballroom with an almost manic sense of purpose. Bevin and Aydin go into town to talk with vendors about food, and Bevin needs a new dress. I tried to go with them, but I always stop myself. I'd love to say that I'm stopped by my mom, but if I'm honest with myself, it's only the knowledge that most of Maradal is horrified by me. All meetings and all work have been canceled and halted. The party is in two weeks, and every single person in this house has been corralled into frantic preparation. I watch as a chocolate fountain is placed on the side of the hall. That, at least, is something to look forward to.

I feel like a teenager again, walking my childhood home, avoiding Mom, and generally trying to be unhelpful. Around noon, Mom tracks me down in the library and asks me to go to my room and not come out until I've picked out something to wear. I see the circles under her eyes, undoubtedly due to a sleepless night, and a wave of guilt stops me from arguing. I go up to my room, but this is the kind of task I need Bevin for. Eventually, I settle on something blue. No one will be paying much attention to what I'm wearing anyway.

Everywhere I go in the house, there's preparation: cleaning, cooking, decorating. Everywhere, the extra staff that's been hired look at me and whisper to each other. They, unlike Mom, know that this is, at best, a joke and at worst a disaster. They're apparently meant to be a test of how the rest of Thiaghal will respond to the confirmation that I exist, and so far they've all responded with silent suspicion. This party is traditionally one where the leadership of a province can meet and mingle, so the likely governor-to-be from one province can meet eligible bachelors and bachelorettes.

I'm told the lack of said event when I turned 18 was the closest Thiaghal came to being convinced I was actually dead. This is the kind of party that Mom is determined to host so many years later as I approach 30. Because of grief or fear or who knows what else, my usually smart, down-to-earth mother can't see what a complete waste of time and resources this is. No one will agree to marry me. I probably wouldn't agree to marry me. Come to think of it, I have some concerns about anyone who would. So, on the whole, it looks like we're all setting ourselves up for an evening of people coming and gawking at me, with the evening ending in massive disappointment. At least there's a chocolate fountain. An hour later, I can't take it anymore, and I make my way out to the forest. I wind my way through the paths of the frozen rose garden, across the lawn, and eventually to the edge of the trees where the forest starts. I plunge in.

"Dad?" I say when I reach the clearing with the old oak tree. Dad died after a long illness when I was only 11. The night he died, I had a dream that he appeared in my room. He looked healthy again, steady on his feet with red cheeks, a full face, and a short, dark beard.

"Go to the tree," he commanded. I was suddenly in the forest. I saw Dad walking ahead of me. I followed him to the same clearing, and there was the same large oak tree. "Go to the tree," he said again. As I approached it, I found the old medallion that my dad had always worn tangled in the branches. I heard a voice that sounded as if it came from deep inside the tree.

"Wear it," the voice said, "it has been blessed by your father. When the time comes, it will protect you from evil." Maybe it's silly, but I've worn it every day since. Magic or not, it reminds me of my dad, and I come back here whenever I need to talk to him.

"Well, Dad," I say as I settle against the base of the tree, "I don't know if you can see us from wherever you are, but Mom is trying to fix me up again. It's going to be a disaster. A joke at best, an attempt on my life at worst. On that note, I wanted to say thank you for protecting me last night." I pick up the medallion and look down at it, and remember it burning against my chest. I close my eyes and lean my head back against the sturdy trunk. "I don't mean to complain, but Mom, she. . . I can't ask her yet again to forego this party, especially after last night, but if there's anything you can do . . ."

Suddenly, I freeze and flick my ears forward. I can hear something. Someone is running through the woods. I stand, preparing to fight or flee. *Calm down*, I think. *It's nothing. It's the woods; things run in the woods.* A scream pierces the air, and I jump. My first thought is that Bevin is in trouble again, but it's the wrong scream. A woman, but not Bevin. Bevin and Aydin have no reason to come back through the woods. The scream pierces the air again. Whoever it is, they're in trouble, but I hesitate. It could be a trap with Mark lurking around. A third scream rings out. It's a chance I'll have to take.

I take off running on all fours in the direction of the scream. I follow it to the very edge of the estate grounds where, finally, I find the source. A pack of galley-trots has cornered someone. Whoever it is has been able to climb into a tree, but they're surrounded, and the dogs are leaping and clawing at the trunk of the tree. I take a deep breath and let out a roar. In my younger days, chasing the galley-trot dogs off the estate grounds was a favorite game. I charge at them. One or two try to jump on my back, but they're easy to throw off. Another good snarl, and the whole pack has retreated back into the forest. I take a deep breath and stand back on two feet again.

I turn to face the tree to see who exactly has been trespassing on the estate grounds, then I look up and gasp. My first thought is that she isn't real. She can't be real. Standing in the tree is a girl, or a woman, I suppose. She has dark hair falling in waves to the back of her knees. It's wet from melting snow and has leaves and branches throughout it, making her look a little bit like she's drowned and come back to life. She seems tall; just by looking at her, I can tell that she's closer to my height than Bev and Aydin are. Everything about her is . . . perfect. Rosy lips, soft brown eyes. She's drenched in melting snow, yet everything about her looks warm and soft. I almost can't take it all in.

Returning to the moment at hand, I realize two things. First is that the temperature is below twenty degrees, and this person, whoever she is, is wearing a white sleeveless dress and nothing else. No shoes, no cloak, and no hat. Besides being very beautiful, she is, in reality, probably very close to freezing to death. Second, while I've been processing all this, I realize we've been staring at each other without saying anything for a full two minutes. I clear my throat.

"Um. Hello," I say. She breathes in quickly as if she wants to say something, but before she can, her eyes close and she sways on her feet. "Whoa!" I run forward and catch her before she hits the ground, but she doesn't wake up. With some urgency, I realize that I need to get her inside quickly if she's going to avoid frostbite. I wish I had a cloak to wrap her in. I picked her up with one arm and tried to cover her with the other while walking quickly back towards the house. She stirs and seems to curl in towards my warmth, but still doesn't wake.

I burst through the front doors ten minutes later. The place is still buzzing with the activity of putting up party decorations, and I'm greeted by a blast of warm air as I walk into the room. I can hear chatter as soon as I step inside. At the end of the entry hall, I see Bevin and Aydin, still wearing their cloaks from their trip to town, talking to Mom. As I slam the door shut behind me, the chatter stops, and I feel all the eyes in the entry hall turn to look at me. Bevin and Aydin's expressions of welcome turn to shock.

"This woman needs medical attention," I announce to the silent hall. "Now!" I roar when no one moves. Suddenly, the hall is a flurry of activity again. Mom rushes over and, with Bevin's help, gets the woman out of the entryway and onto the sofa in the sitting room. I vaguely register Maddie running past me to get blankets and Aydin yelling that he's going for a physician as he runs out the door. I follow Mom and Bevin into the library, and Maddie slips in carrying her weight in blankets before Mom slams the doors shut. Maddie and Bevin start piling blankets on the woman as Mom looks on open-mouthed.

"What. . .?" she asks. I explain as best I can the walk through the woods, the screams, and the fall. Mom shakes her head. "I just don't . . . how could she have gotten onto the grounds with the gates around the property? Where are her shoes? How . . ." We all lapse into confused silence and sit watching the mystery woman for several minutes until there's a knock on the front door. The physician, Cilian Alexander, a man who has been our family physician since I was born and looks as though he must be over 100, pokes his head into the room. He's trailed by Aydin, and with his appearance, Mom's shoulders relax. "Alexander," she says. She starts giving an even briefer summary of events than I just gave. Alexander frowns, but he's quick to roll up his sleeves and get to work.

"Well?" asks Mom after Alexander finishes checking over the woman from the woods. Aydin and I have been banished to the other side of the sitting room for privacy, but are obviously still listening. Mads is in the corner with us, and Bevin is sitting next to the mystery woman. This is the closest I've been to Mads in a couple of days. She's been spending so much time in her room since becoming a teenager. Is it my imagination, or are there dark circles under her eyes, too? I wonder if she hasn't been sleeping well since Mark's attack, and I suddenly feel the need to pull her into a hug, to which she rolls her eyes, but accepts.

"She'll recover," says Alexander from across the room. "No idea who she is?" Since this question is addressed to the room at large, Aydin, Maddie, and I come back to join the company in the main part of the sitting room. We all shake our heads 'no.' "How exactly was she found again?" All eyes turned to me on this one. I tell the story mostly truthfully, but I say I was out for a walk, not visiting my dead father's magical oak tree. When I finish, everyone's eyes turn back to Alexander. "Well, she hasn't hit her head. I think the swoon was mostly from shock." He glances over at me.

"She had just been chased into a tree by galley-trots while wearing almost nothing in the dead of winter! I don't think this," I gesture to the still unconscious woman, "is entirely my fault."

"In any case," Alexander continues, "she shouldn't have any problems with memory, so she should be awake soon and filling in the story herself. She'll need warm drinks, broths, and to stay near the fire after she wakes." With that, Alexander gathers up his things and leaves.

"I'll go get some of my winter things for her to wear when she wakes up," says Bevin, jumping up.

"I'll go heat up some soup!" asserts Aydin. He and Bevin hurry out of the room. I look up to see Mom smiling at me.

"What?" She just continues to smile. "Mom," I say.

"Well, sweetie, you can't deny, the timing is very . . . well, it seems like maybe it's fate? Doesn't it?"

"When she saw me, she fainted and fell out of a tree. I can think of better first meetings."

"When she saw you, you had just finished rescuing her from a pack of galley-trots. I can think of worse first meetings. Look at her," she says. She stands and pushes some hair out of the woman's face and tucks it behind her ear. "I wonder what happened." She turns to face me. "I need to continue to oversee the decorations. Will you sit with her until Bevin or Aydin comes back?"

"What if she wakes up? I don't know if I should be the first thing she sees when she wakes," I say. "Mads can sit with us."

"Not a chance," says Maddie, smiling in a way that is somehow more annoying than my mom's smile.

"Just sit with her," says Mom. "Someone will be right back." She stands and strides out of the room, towing Maddie behind her, who now looks completely torn between leaving so that I'll be uncomfortable but not wanting to miss a second of whatever happens next. I lean back in the armchair across from the sleeping woman on the sofa and can't help but feel again like she isn't real. She's just too, impossibly, actually almost comically, beautiful. I stand and pace in front of the fire, looking at her every so often out of the corner of my eye. Just as I'm about to add more logs to the fire, she moves. First, she just turns her head to the side, then she turns under the blankets, stretches her arms. She opens her eyes and . . .

Then she screams. The scream is, if possible, louder than it was in the forest. She throws off her blanket and jumps off the chair, looking frantically around the room. Her eyes finally rest on the window.

"Hey, no!" By the time I reach her, she already has one foot up on the windowsill. I loop one arm around her waist and pull her backwards. She pushes and fights to get out of my grasp. Should I just let her go out the window? It's still winter, and she's still only in a summer dress, so she will very likely freeze to death, but I don't know how many more times I can be kicked in the shin. "Um, Mom!" I call. "Mom!" No answer. I swing her around and set her down on the couch, placing myself between her and the window. For a minute, she just sits looking at me. Suddenly, she leaps up to stand on the sofa.

"Who are you?" she says. "Where am I? Can you . . . can you speak? Are you a person?" I hold my hands up in a gesture that I hope says *'I mean you no harm,'* but I realize too late might just display my claws.

"My name is Tyre," I say. "You are in the governor's estate in the province of Thiaghal in the country of Maradal. And yes," I say, "I can speak." She nods slowly and continues to look around the room.

"What . . . " she says. "How . . . ?"

"We don't really know," I say. "We were hoping you could tell us."

"Right," she says, frowning, and looking down at her hands. "I was in the woods. I was running."

"From the galley-trots?" I say. She looks up quickly and meets my eyes for only a second before continuing.

"I was running, and then I was surrounded by the dogs in that tree. You," she says, looking up at me suddenly, "you helped me." She points a finger at me with such intensity that I have to remind myself that that's not a terrible thing to be accused of. "I don't remember anything after that," she adds.

"Why were you in the woods?" I ask. "In the dead of winter? Without even shoes?" *Trespassing*, I add internally.

"I told you," she says, "I was running." Before I can respond, Bevin bounds back into the room.

"You're awake!" she says. She's closely followed by Aydin and Maddie. The woman looks startled at seeing even more people. "Hello, I'm Bevin!" says Bevin, sitting down next to where the mystery woman is still standing as she extends her hand. The woman takes it, and her expression softens a bit.

"I'm Calla." She eases back down into a sitting position next to Bevin, but I can feel that she's still watching me.

"Aydin," says Aydin, who walks over and shakes her hand as well.

"Madeliza." Maddie waves from across the room, "but everyone calls me Maddie."

"Or Maddie, or Mads, or runt . . . " I add before Maddie punches me in the arm.

"How are you feeling?" asks Bevin. Calla takes a deep breath and shrugs.

"I don't really know, to be perfectly honest," she says.

"Well, here, this will help," says Bevin. She hands her a winter dress and thick socks.

"Oh," says Calla, "thank you." Bevin tows Calla out of the room to get changed.

"So," says Aydin, looking after them, "did she tell you anything? Who is she?"

"I didn't even know her name until she told Bev just now." I kick myself internally for not even thinking to ask her name. "She didn't really tell me how she got out there. She just said she was running."

"From the galley-trots?" asks Aydin.

"No," I say. "I don't think so." A few minutes later, Bev reappears, towing a warmer-looking Calla behind her.

"Welcome back," I offer.

"Thank you." Calla smiles. She opens her mouth but closes it again. After a pause, she says, "Can I . . . I don't mean to be rude, but can I ask something?"

We all look at each other.

"Of course," Bevin finally says.

"Alright," says Calla. As she speaks, her eyes stay on my face. "What's . . . um, what is . . . how?" She gestures in my general direction. I open my mouth to speak, but Bevin gets there first.

"Tell you what?" she says. "I think we all have a lot of questions, so you're going to eat this," she hands Calla the bowl of warm soup that Aydin brought in, "and we're just all going to sit here until no one is confused anymore."

I glance at Calla, and our eyes meet.

"Alright," she says, taking a sip of soup.

4

Calla keeps sipping soup while we all fire questions at her.

"What were you running from in the woods?" I ask.

"Next question," responds Calla, brushing the question off with a wave of her hand. Bevin, Aydin, Maddie, and I all looked at each other.

"Why?" I ask. Calla doesn't say anything and just stares at her feet.

"Next question then," says Bevin, looking pointedly at me.

"Where are you from?" I ask.

"The north," she says. "It was part of Andestine until . . . . recently." She swallows and looks down at her feet again.

"You're from the land Mark's taken," I say.

"Sorry, who?" says Calla.

"No one, sorry. I mean, you're from Umbra, the city overtaken by The Inimical?" Calla jumps and spills some of her soup. "Oh, sorry," I say, handing her a handkerchief. I make eye-contact with Aydin. It's not a good sign that people living close to Mark are this scared of him. "How did you escape the Fog? No one has been able to get in, and as far as I knew, no one had ever been able to leave."

"Yes," she says. "I'm from Umbra. Now my turn for a question. Born or cursed?" She gestures towards me again.

"Cursed," I say.

"Specifics of the curse?"

"Allegedly, I was unkind to someone asking for help. Turned out to be a fairy. She got mad and said something to the effect of 'it's because I'm ugly, isn't it?!' and told me that I would be cursed to be an ugly monster."

"There's no way to change it?" she asks.

"Next question," I say.

"Fair enough," she says.

"How are we doing in here? Oh, you're awake!"

I glance at the living room doors to see Mom enter the room. Calla turns around to examine the newcomer.

"Mom, you knew she was awake when you heard her trying to climb out the window," I say. Calla blushes scarlet.

"I didn't mean to reject your hospitality," she says. "I just didn't recognize anything, and I panicked."

"No, of course; please don't worry," says Mom. "I just wanted to come in and suggest that we all go to bed. She gestures towards Bevin, Aydin, and Maddie. "Big day coming up."

"The party coming up is *for* Tyre," says Aydin, "and Calla almost froze to death today. How are we the ones that need a good night's sleep?"

"You're having a party?" says Calla, turning to look at me.

"You're called 'Calla'?" Mom asks, turning to look at Calla. "Oh, that's lovely."

"My point is . . . " says Aydin.

"Alright, alright," says mom, "All of us then. We all need a good night's sleep. Calla, I'll show you a room you can stay in." I notice that she leaves off the 'for tonight,' no doubt hoping that Calla, whoever she is, will stay forever.

5

I wake the next morning, sure that I have been having a very strange, albeit pleasant, dream. I dreamt that I went to the woods and rescued a beautiful woman from galley-trots, and then she stayed on the estate with us. When I finally drag myself out of bed, instead of going to the sitting room, I make my way towards the breakfast nook off the kitchen. I'm surprised to see the extra staff busy decorating again, and it temporarily confirms that last night may just have been a bizarre dream produced by an overstressed brain. However, when I walk into the breakfast nook, in addition to the usual sights of the bay windows and a large wooden table, I see that it hasn't been a dream at all. In fact, the dream hasn't done it justice. Calla is seated at the square breakfast table, talking with Mom. She looks up when I come in, and again, I'm struck by the feeling that everything about her seems perfectly soft and warm. The light streaming in from the window creates a halo around her hair which now that it's dried falls in fluffy waves around her face and shoulders.

"Hello, dear," says Mom as I walk in. "I was just telling Calla about the party."

"The party?" I say. "Are we still doing that?"

"Yes," says Mom. "Why wouldn't we be doing it?"

"Well . . . " I say, inclining my head towards Calla in what I hope is a subtle gesture.

"Oh, you don't have to change anything on my account," says Calla. "I'm so sorry; I'm inconveniencing you. I can leave." She pushes her chair back as if this has been a casual visit for breakfast, and she's going to go on her way at that very moment.

"No!" Mom and I both reply in unison. Calla looks back and forth between us, and she smiles before slowly sitting back down.

"It's not an inconvenience at all," says Mom. "I think you'll like the party. As long as you're feeling up to it."

I sit down next to Calla as she takes a tentative sip of the hot coffee in front of her. I can't decide how to feel about Calla in this moment. On the one hand, I have no real desire to fall in love with anyone. On the other hand, maybe I can convince Mom that we should cancel the party because clearly, fate has presented another option. Calla wrinkles her nose as steam from the coffee wafts into her face and up towards her hair, where a few wavy strands have fallen forward to hide part of her face. I find myself wondering what it would feel like to reach out and tuck them behind her ear. It then occurs to me that although I'd rather not fall in love, *theoretically,* the *reality* of Calla is . . . interesting. She catches me staring, and the corners of her mouth turn up in a shy smile.

"Do you . . . ?" I say, "Would you like to take a walk?" It would be nice to show her around if she's going to be staying here, but instead of responding right away, she fidgets in her chair.

"Is Bevin coming?" she asks. I know it shouldn't, but it stings. Ever since the curse, I've really only been around the people who love me. No one has been afraid of me unless I've been trying to scare them on purpose, but looking at Calla now, I can see that she's scared. She keeps glancing over her shoulder and leans away from me slightly. I've been around the only people in the world who see me as human for so long, I've forgotten how the rest of the world sees me. It doesn't matter. I have a full day of work that should take priority over a walk with Calla anyway, even if Mom has declared all work canceled.

"Sorry, never mind," I say. "I didn't mean to make you uncomfortable."

"I didn't mean . . . I just . . . " she says, blushing.

"It's alright. I understand." I really do. "You should still stick around for the party next week if you can. Bevin will be there." I smile to reassure her and head to my office. I sit down at the sturdy desk that used to be Dad's and start looking through the mail. I'm surprised there's a fresh stack.

Usually, the Holpies don't deliver the mail until later in the day, but when I look out the window, I see the form of a horse, which I recognize as our usual mail Holpie, trotting away. I'm about to sit down at my desk again when Maddie careens into my field of vision, tearing across the snowy lawn in her nightgown towards the Holpie. She doubles over, catching her breath when she reaches it, and it looks like she's asking a question. The Holpie shakes its head back towards the direction of the house, and Maddie glances towards the window. I can tell the Holpie is annoyed.

Ever since the Kelpies got permanently stuck in horse form, they've somehow been even more standoffish. Maddie is talking fast and gesturing wildly, and if I didn't know better, I'd say she looks panicked. I look down at the stack of mail in my hand, but there's nothing that would make Maddie look panicked. There's a letter from the Maradal Council Health Subdivision titled "*Re: Senzicaria*" and a new stack of budget reports from the past 6 months. As I stare down at them in my hand, Mads bursts in through the office door and lets out a yelp when she barrels straight into me.

"Whoa," I say as she crashes into me. I grab her shoulders before she can ricochet and fall over. "Where's the fire, Mads?"

"Sorry," she says, out of breath. "I didn't see you." Her eyes dart to the stack of mail on the desk.

"Waiting for a letter from someone?" I ask.

"Is there one?" she says. She rapidly recovers from running full force into me and manages to have an attitude. She turns her head to the side and puts her hand on her hip.

"Should I be looking out for one?" I ask, as I smile and shake my head 'no'. Before I can say anything else, Maddie swings her hip-length silver hair around behind her and marches out of the room with more dignity than I would have thought possible for someone whom I just stopped from toppling onto the ground. I look down at the letters in my hand again. It's probably nothing; she's a teenager. But it isn't like Maddie to be secretive. There's probably just another teenager in town that she's got something going on with, but I make a mental note to mention it to Bevin just in case.

I sit down and look back at the mail stack that's caused all the ruckus. After shuffling through it again, I tuck the budget reports into my desk to look at this afternoon and open the letter from the Council Health Subdivision.

Re: Senzicaria

Fellow esteemed members of the Maradal Council of Provinces: does anyone have any knowledge of or additional information about an emerging illness being called Senzicaria? Border provinces nearest Burne and Andestine report news that in the aforementioned countries, people are concerned about a new illness variant with potentially high fatalities— some kind of bleeding sickness with magical origin.

Burne's official position is that it is a hoax predicated on beliefs in folk medicine. Our sources further north tell us that Andestine is less optimistic (although we know Andestine to be more susceptible to folk wisdom, and Burne less so). The purpose of this letter is to solicit information if anyone has it, determine if any members of your province have contracted illness with strange or unknown symptoms or unusual fatalities, and to, of course, alert you to this possible threat.

No formal epidemic threat level is issued at this time. There is no need to worry the citizens as of yet. The nature of this communication is to ask you to actively monitor the health of those in your province and alert the Council Health Subdivision in the capital if you notice concerning trends.

With respect,

Seonaid McClellen

Chief Officer Maradal Council Health Subdivision

I read the letter twice and rub my eyes. I'll need to come up with a plan to monitor health. I suppose I can send a basic survey out with the Holpies, but for some reason, they dislike mass mailings. They seem to prefer personal correspondence. In which case, it would fall on the Thiaghal council to do most of the footwork of going door to door through town to ask questions, and that wouldn't account for the more rural parts of the province. It will just have to go out with the Holpies. Which means I'll need to draft it, get the approval from the council at our next meeting, and then talk to the Holpies. I'm getting my pen and a stack of paper out, my failed attempt to get to know Calla all but forgotten, when there's a knock at the door.

"Tyre?" says a voice from the doorway. I look up to see Calla standing in the doorway, backlit and glowing from the sun, which is odd because there isn't a window in that hallway.

"Hi Calla," I say, trying to cover my surprise and arrange my face into something that resembles friendly. "What's going on? Did you need something?"

"I do, actually. I'm sorry to ask, but I lost something while I was up in the tree. I need to go find it." She hesitates for a minute. "Do you want to come with me?" she asks. "I would go by myself but with the galley-trots around . . . I wouldn't ask unless it was important. I'm sorry."

"Sure," I say, immediately putting down all my work for the day. "Of course. Let's go."

***

"What are we looking for?" I ask as we walk down the stone path that arches through the frozen rose gardens back towards the forest. Calla is wrapped in a borrowed coat from Bevin but seems totally unbothered by the cold, which is unusual since she's from a warmer place.

"Don't laugh," says Calla.

"You lost something funny in the woods while you were being chased by galley-trots?"

"You're already laughing, and I haven't even told you what it is yet."

"No, no. Not laughing, just, you know, clarifying."

"It's a mirror," she says, rolling her eyes.

"A mirror? Calla, we have mirrors in the house. I think we actually have a whole mirror-themed garden if you'd like to see it."

"It's not just any mirror!" she says. I'm happy to see that she's still smiling. She looks calmer than I've seen her so far. She's swinging her arms carelessly at her sides and laughing easily, and she spins in a circle, taking in the sunshine. "This mirror was blessed by a fairy. It has magic." I do my best to keep smiling and look impressed by the mirror. I don't want to scare Calla now that she finally seems to be recovering, but if there is fairy magic just lying around in the forest, we need to get it under cover immediately. We don't need anything to tempt Mark back for another visit.

"You said you lost it when you climbed the tree?" I ask. "That's a long way into the forest. Do you . . . " Calla looks up at me expectantly. "Alright, I know this is a bizarre offer, and feel free to say no, but let me preface by saying that Bevin, Aydin, and I did this all the time as kids, and it's perfectly safe."

"Oh, it definitely sounds like it based on this buildup," says Calla. I do a double-take, pleasantly caught off guard by Calla's sarcasm. "What is it?" she asks. I hesitate and consider dropping the subject altogether. I try to remind myself that everyone here is used to me, and Calla seems to have just warmed to the idea of being in physical proximity to me. I have no idea how she'll feel about touching me.

"Do you want a ride?" I ask. Nothing ventured, nothing gained, I guess. "I can run really fast on all fours. Like I said, it's a long way into the forest."

"You let Bevin and Aydin ride around on your back when you were kids?" she says, biting her lip to keep from laughing. "I'm sure that was quite the spectacle."

"Yes. We're very close. Do you have siblings?" I ask. For just a second, something about her face seems off. Just a flash of something like anger? Sadness? I'm sure I've imagined it. "It's kind of hard to explain without having siblings," I continue.

"Are you sure I won't hurt you if I sit on your back?" she says. "I'm not exactly a kid."

"Totally sure," I say, trying not to look overly thrilled that she's not balking at the idea of touching me.

"Well, alright then," she says. I lean over so she can climb up on my back. Based on appearance alone, I realize that I expected her to be coordinated and graceful; however, her climbing technique makes it immediately clear that that is not the case.

"Oh, and I should tell you," I say, once she finally manages to situate herself, "that when Bev, Aydin, and I did this, the object of the game was for me to throw them off. I'm not sure how far down that reflex is buried."

"I'm getting down."

"Too late," I say, and I take off running towards the line of trees. Calla's screams turn to laughter almost immediately. I feel her lean her head down against the wind and wrap her hands around one of my antlers. After a few minutes, I'm reasonably sure we've reached the right tree.

"I think this is it." I hold still so Calla can climb off my back. Her feet crunch as they land in the snow.

"It should be just here," she says. I stretch to stand up on two feet again and walk over to help her search. As I dig through the snow, something shiny catches my eye, and when I dig it out of the snow, I'm relieved to find a small, silver-handled mirror. It's plain and hardly looks magical, but how many mirrors could there be hiding in the forest?

"Calla!" I call, holding up the mirror to show her.

"You found it!" Before I can process what's happening, she runs over and throws her arms around my neck. "Thank you! You have no idea what this mirror means to me."

"You're welcome," I say, completely caught off guard, but hugging her back. I was right. Touching her is a little bit like touching the sun, and her hair somehow smells like roses. Not like rose perfume, but the actual flower, pollen, and all.

"Sorry," she says, realizing her face is inches from mine. "I'm not always the best with personal space." She lets go and backs up a few paces.

"I mean, I invited you to climb onto my back ten minutes ago, so we can be bad at personal space together," I say. Calla smirks, and I'm immediately terrified that I've been too forward. "Come on," I say. "We should get back. I have a few more things to take care of before I'm roped back into planning for the party." If Calla wonders why I roll my eyes at the thought of the party, she's too polite to ask.

***

"Can I ask you something?" asks Calla as she rides on my back at a slower pace towards the house.

"Sure," I say.

"You said that Bevin and Aydin used to do this when you all were kids, but you also said you weren't born like this. So, when did it happen?"

"Um, when I was eleven, actually," I say.

"You were eleven?" says Calla.

"I was," I say. "Hard year for my mom. Dad died later that year as well."

"I'm so sorry," says Calla. "I . . . That's terrible. I'm . . . I'm really sorry."

"Calla," I say, "are you crying?" How is she suddenly crying?

"Um, sorry, yes. It's nothing. I just feel sad about that story, I guess." I wish I could turn to see her face, but I can't without throwing her off my back.

"It's really alright," I say. "It was a long time ago."

"Right," says Calla, "I know. I'm sorry. You must think I'm so odd." I do think she's odd. I'm also realizing that I like her, beyond just being attracted to her. She's easy-going and open-minded. If this afternoon is anything to go by, she's going to be enjoyable to have around. In the past six hours, she's fallen into step with our house and become more at ease with me than some of the Thiaghal council members who have known me for years. I'm also fascinated by the few moments of sarcasm that have broken through her hyper-polite surface.

"Odd doesn't have to be a bad thing," I say. "I should know. By the way, you never told me what kind of magic does your mirror have?" Calla is quiet for a minute, and I can tell that, for some reason, she's trying to decide whether or not to answer.

"It lets me see my home," she says.

"Your home? Umbra?" I feel her grip tighten on the fur on my back.

"Yes," she says.

"What's it like there now?" I ask, carefully. "I haven't been there since I was a toddler. Definitely not since The Inimical."

"I'd imagine it isn't much different than you remember it," says Calla. "I'm from a small neighborhood in the city. It's really lovely. My family and I lived in a little row of houses all built practically on top of each other, but everyone living there knows each other and helps each other for the most part. I grew up with my grandad, and he makes and sells pottery for a living, and my cousins do some gardening and some apothecary-type work. Oh, look! It's Bevin!" she says suddenly. I feel her let go of my back with one hand and wave to the figure approaching in the distance. Sure enough, I can see Bevin and Aydin coming down the path towards us. I break into a trot to meet them in the garden.

"Hey, heads up!" yells Bevin. "I overheard your mom say to the mail Holpie earlier that she's inviting a few families with potentially eligible daughters to stay on the estate for a few days before the party. I don't know if any are coming, but if they are, they might arrive soon, and maybe the first thing they see shouldn't be a comically beautiful woman riding around on your back."

"Oh, I don't know," said Calla, "it might make some of the suitors jealous. Or competitive. Either way, so much the better. That is the point of all this, isn't it?" she says. "You're trying to find a match for Tyre?" One advantage of having fur is that no one can tell when I'm blushing.

"Well, *we're* not," says Aydin. "But Tyre's mom . . . "

"She's just worried," I say.

"Worried?" says Calla. "Worried about what?" Aydin and I look at each other.

"How much do you know about The Inimical?" asked Bevin. "I know you're from Umbra, so . . . "

"The Inimical is involved in this?" says Calla.

"We're not sure," I say, looking pointedly at Bevin.

"If she's going to be staying with us, we might want to tell her," says Aydin.

"Tell me what?" says Calla.

"Let's all go inside," says Bevin. "We can talk about it there." However, as soon as we get inside, Mom pulls me away for another suit fitting. As I'm walking away, I hear Bevin say something about finding Calla a dress for the party.

***

As it turns out, no one does come to stay at the estate. While, at first, I was worried Mom would take it badly, I'm becoming more worried that she's taking it too well. She's just not acknowledging it, and she's started throwing herself into the party planning with even more purpose. Over the next several days, I start bringing her hot tea every hour to check on her, and taking guest lists out of her hands at night to make sure she's sleeping. I worry she's finally snapped when I think I hear her yelling in the kitchen the day before the party, but when I round the corner to the kitchen, I see it isn't Mom yelling at all, it's Bevin and Maddie.

"You are NOT my mother," yells Maddie. Bevin sits at the kitchen island, clutching a cup of coffee as Maddie paces back and forth in front of her.

"I am your guardian, and my answer is 'no'" says Bevin. I turn to Bevin in surprise. Yes, technically, Bevin has been Maddie's guardian since Bev turned 18, but she's never acted like anything more than a sister. We've always left most of the heavy-duty parenting of Maddie to my mom. Bevin's voice is more controlled than Maddie's, but I can see she's on the verge of tears. Maddie must be thinking the same thing about Bevin being just her sister because she yells,

"Oh, you're my *guardian* now. You know what, fuck you, Bev." She storms out of the room and sees me. "And fuck you too, Tyre!" She slams both palms into my chest and shoves. I have a strong, if fleeting, impulse to shove her right back, but I settle for yelling,

"Maddie! Hey! What did *I* do?" She runs out of the room crying, and Bevin dissolves into tears at the table, burying her face in her hands. For a minute, I consider going after Maddie, but it seems like Bevin needs me more right at this moment. And my chest still kind of hurts.

"Bev, what was that about?" I say, sitting down next to her and putting my hand on her shoulder.

"Tyre, has Maddie ever said anything to you about wanting to go to Clocks?" says Bevin, wiping her face.

"Clocks? As in Clockwork Atheneum, the school with all the mysterious disappearances in Lytwist? Where Dad was a student for a while? No, never. Why?"

"Well," says Bevin, "she suddenly wants to go."

"To *Clocks*?" I say again in disbelief. Bevin shakes her head, clearly as confused as I am. Clockwork Atheneum is the most world-renowned school for combat, medicine, magical studies, creature diplomacy, and international relations. It is very prestigious, very far away, and then there are the rumors about what goes on there . . . "No. No way. Maddie's rarely even left Thiaghal. Why would she want to go to Clocks?"

"That's what I tried asking just now," says Bevin, throwing her hand towards the door. "We were even in Lytwist for a month last year, and she didn't even mention it. Not even a 'hey, this is where Clocks is!' much less ask to go see it, or apply there." She shakes her head, lost in thought. Suddenly, I remember how strange Maddie was acting about the mail this morning. I'm about to hand the information off to Bevin when Calla appears in the doorway.

"Everything alright?" she asks. "I thought I heard yelling?"

"Fine," says Bevin. "Sorry, Calla; I know I was supposed to meet you upstairs ages ago."

"It's no problem," says Calla, sitting down and pouring herself coffee from the carafe on the table. "You're sure you're alright?"

"My sister and I are having . . . a disagreement," says Bevin.

"Your sister is Madeliza, right? Maddie?" asks Calla. Bevin nods again. "She's cute," says Calla. "She seems *very* 15." Bevin's only response is a slightly unhinged laugh. "Want to talk about it?" asks Calla.

"It's alright, Calla. Thanks for asking." She reaches across the table to squeeze Calla's hand and offers her a smile. "Would it be alright if we finalize your dress later?"

"Of course!" says Calla, squeezing her hand back. Bevin gives us both one more half-hearted smile and disappears through the kitchen door. Calla swings her legs around the kitchen stool to face me.

"Hello, Tyre," she says, brightly.

"Hello Calla," I respond, feeling a stupid, involuntary grin creep across my face. I don't exactly know what to make of how Calla looks at me. Sometimes her eyes seem miles away, but sometimes, like now, she makes such intense eye contact, it's practically painful. "What are your plans for the day?"

"Apparently, helping your mom put the finishing touches on the cake order with the caterers for tomorrow," she says, sipping her coffee. I feel a pit in my stomach at the reminder that the party is tomorrow. "You're not the biggest fan of this party, are you?" asks Calla.

"Not the biggest fan, no," I say.

"Can I ask why?" says Calla.

"My mom has been through a lot," I begin, choosing my words carefully. Calla watches me, no doubt remembering our conversation from a few days ago. "Her biggest wish is for me to go back to looking the way I did before the curse."

"That's not something you want?" says Calla.

"Not, really, no," I say, shrugging my shoulders. "The curse is not without its complications, but I was always small for my age. I could never beat Aydin in arm wrestling. Now, I guess I like the power, maybe? Sorry, does that sound bad to say?"

"On the contrary," says Calla, "it sounds refreshing and relatable."

"Yes, that's the title of my forthcoming autobiography," I say. Calla laughs so hard she accidentally spits out her sip of coffee.

"Sorry," she laughs as I hand her a napkin.

"Not that it's not without its drawbacks," I continue, taking Calla's coffee out of her hand and taking a sip. "I'd like to blame my mom, but I can't pretend it's really her fault I hide in this house. I am 29 years old."

"Well, I guess all that ends tomorrow," says Calla, taking her coffee back. "And hey," she says, my heart speeds up as she suddenly stands and steps toward me, closing the gap between us, "it will be alright." She reaches up and puts a hand on my shoulder for a minute. I'm about to reach up and cover her hand with mine when she pulls away.

"Who knows," I say, as Calla pushes her chair in and heads for the kitchen door, I can still feel the space on my shoulder where she put her hand, "after this, there won't be any reason not to go into town anymore, since everyone will know for sure that I exist and I'm a monster. Maybe we can venture out together?" She gives me one more smile before taking her coffee and disappearing out the door.

6

Well, this is it. I'm standing in front of the mirror wearing the first formalwear I've worn since I was 11. Everyone has been thoroughly searched for weapons at the door, so, in theory, no one will be able to assassinate me as I descend the grand staircase in the ballroom, but I'm emotionally prepared just in case.

"Are you ready, dear?" Mom pokes her head into my room. "All the guests have arrived, and the young women are ready to be announced just after you are." Sensing my feelings when I don't respond, Mom comes over to put a hand on my face. "It will be fine. You'll see," she says.

"I know," I say, even though I don't believe it. As I reach over and squeeze her hand, I think, p*lease, if only for my mom's sake, don't let anyone try to assassinate me tonight*. I can smell food and hear the chatter in the ballroom as soon as I leave my room. I'm realizing that, right up until this moment, I thought there was a real chance no one would show up. When no one had come to stay the few days before, there was a part of me that really thought, *well, that's that. No one will come, and I'll be left to pick up the pieces of my mom's dream while attempting to figure out how to protect us from Mark in a real way. I will find a way to protect us all, because it's my responsibility.*

A horrible thought occurred to me as I lay in bed last night. Maddie started this talk about wanting to go to Clocks, a school known for training fierce soldiers, after The Inimical sent someone to attack our home. The thought that's so horrible it makes me feel like I'm going to scream and cry all at once is that maybe Maddie, my *baby* cousin, wants to go to Clocks so she can protect me. I feel my hands and jaw clench as I remember the thought. No more. After tonight's inevitable disaster and ensuring that Mom is alright, I'm leaving to find Mark myself. However, for now, I take a deep breath. I can do this.

"Tyre!" I spin around to see Bevin trotting down the hall towards me. She looks very un-Bevin-like in an electric blue ballgown that highlights her blue eyes and somehow also her many freckles. I gasp as I glance at the woman next to Bevin. Calla is wearing an off-white gown made of some kind of soft, floating material that makes it look like she was walking through the woods and somehow got wrapped in mist.

"Hello," I call out, trying to hide my admittedly obvious double-take at Calla. Bevin rolls her eyes.

"You ready?" says Bevin. I nod, but my throat goes dry.

"You alright?" says Calla, searching my face like she might be able to decode the answer. I try to answer, but I can't move. Now that I can hear the chatter of the crowd in the ballroom, the thought of parading around in front of them is more intimidating than I'd like it to be. Sensing my hesitation, Calla says, "I have an idea." Bevin and I both turn to see her smiling, eyebrows raised. "What you need is a distraction," she says. "You'll walk into the room and people will 'oohh' and 'ahhh'. You need to be followed by something else equally interesting to take some of the pressure off you."

"Sure, that would be great and might work," I say, "but where are we going to get something like that?"

"Well, I don't know if you've noticed," she says as she twirls in a full circle, "but I'm *very* pretty." As she spins, her dress flares out around her, and I'm suddenly struck by the smell of roses again. Bevin laughs out loud, either at Calla's blunt comment or my dazed expression.

"You . . . um, you are," says Bevin.

"I wish I could say that this plan hasn't worked before, but it definitely has," says Calla, tossing her brown waves behind her and squaring her shoulders. "It's not my first time using my looks to run interference."

"Well," I say, cataloging *that* comment to task about later, "I guess anything is worth a shot." I think Calla is mostly using humor to lighten the mood, but the more I think about it, the more I think that she might be right, and this plan might actually help. The sound of Aydin's voice echoes from the ballroom downstairs.

"Come on!" says Bevin. "We'll be late!" The three of us take off running down the hallway. From my room, past Bevin's and Aydin's rooms, but instead of taking the staircase that leads to the entryway, we turn down a secret passage leading to the back of the ballroom. We make it to the back entrance, leading to the grand ballroom staircase, just as Mom is finishing her welcome speech.

"And now," says Aydin, happily playing master of ceremonies for the evening, "I present Governor Tyre Sylvan of Thiaghal."

As I stumble through the doors and onto the entry staircase, the room is silent. The feeling of everyone's eyes in the room on me makes the hair on the back of my neck stand up. I can sense that everyone is holding their breath. Once again, I'm glad my fur can hide when I blush. My face is on fire. I keep my eyes lowered as I walk down the staircase and make my way to the side of the room, trying to disappear into the crowd. Instead of turning back to the staircase, all eyes are staying on me. Aydin's voice begins to introduce all the potential suitors who were brave or unfortunate enough to attend.

"Presenting Calla Helena," he reads. My eyes are still down, but I feel tension in the room break as the room fills with a wave of quiet chatter. The chatter grows until I finally chance a glance up at the staircase to see Calla standing there. Only the threat of pulling attention back to myself stops me from gasping again. I know it's only the chandelier or the candles reflecting off her hair, but, once again, I can't help but feel like she's glowing, literally emanating light, as she walks down the staircase. Where I tried to avoid the crowd as much as possible, she looked right at them. Waving, smiling, pulling them in . . . and away from me. The crowd is enthralled, not only because she's beautiful, I realize, but because she's also one of the first new person to visit Thiaghal in anyone's living memory. She glances over at me once on her way down the stairs and winks.

'Thank you,' I mouth, even though I'm not sure she can see. The brief sense of peace doesn't last forever. As soon as she joins the party, some searing glances find their way back to me. Still, some stay on her, and some return to the stairs to see the newcomers. Her plan accomplished what it was supposed to by giving me a minute to breathe. I need to thank Calla again after the party. After a few minutes, Aydin stopped talking, and music started. Time for dancing. To my intense relief, I see Bev weaving her way towards me through the crowd. She's halfway to me when Mom intercepts her. She tows her away in the opposite direction while shooting me a look that clearly says, 'Dance with potential, future curse-breakers, *not* Bevin'. Bevin looks back over her shoulder and mouths 'Sorry' as mom tows her away.

I sigh and spin around, smacking into a well-dressed middle-aged woman who is dragging a younger woman about my age behind her. "Mr. Sylvan?" she says.

"Oh no, you have me confused with someone else," I say. Typically met by a chorus of courtesy laughter from Bev, Aydin, and Maddie, my dry humor falls flat here, and the few seconds of silence that follow are excruciating. "Sorry," I say. "Just a joke. Yes, that's me, but please call me Tyre." I extend my hand to her, which she ignores. "Nice to meet you," I say, withdrawing my hand.

"I am Annarie Carlon, and this is my niece, Saffron." She shoves the girl, who until now has been mostly hiding behind her aunt, forward. I'm about to say hello when I see that Saffron has tears in her eyes, and she's shaking. Actually shaking. I can see the strands of her hair vibrating with the movement. I think back to last week when I thought that Calla was afraid of me, and I realize how wrong I was. Calla was uncomfortable, still disoriented by her unfamiliar surroundings. This is what fear looks like.

"Excuse me for one minute," I say. "Sorry." As I turn in the opposite direction and start walking, the crowd parts in front of me, and people scurry to get out of my way. When I reach the chocolate fountain, I'm suddenly seized by the desire to send it crashing to the floor. I'm filled with anger at Mom for putting me in this ridiculous situation, at the entire town for coming to gawk at me, and at myself because I know full well that none of my anger is fair. Mom is right, I am, on some level, choosing to stay like this, and I'm angry that this choice allows everyone to think that I deserve to be treated this way. I look back at Annarie Carlon and her niece, and it looks like they are having an argument. They keep throwing me cautious glances until finally I see Ms. Carlon start crossing the room towards me. Desperate for help, I scan the room frantically for Bevin or Aydin. Calla, across the room surrounded by a gaggle of partygoers, catches my eye. She looks up and smiles. I'm trying to think of a way to send a distress signal when . . . "

"Mr. Sylvan." Ms. Carlon has reached me.

"Ms. Carlon. Again, it's Tyre, please. Nice to speak to you again."

"I'd like to apologize for the behavior of my niece," she says.

"No need to-" I begin.

"She's wonderful. Really. She'd make a wonderful wife. She's a good cook. . ." I really have no idea what to do besides try to listen politely as Annarie Carlon lists off all her niece's good qualities. " . . . so you see," she says, "the money and land that would come with the title would greatly benefit our family." I snap back to attention. I missed exactly why my money and land would be so beneficial to their family. I'm about to ask when she attempts to finalize the merger, "I'm sure some kind of agreement could be made." Now I have absolutely no interest in Ms. Carlon or the root of her family's difficulties. I don't want anything other than to be away from this vile woman who is trying to trade her terrified niece for her own comfort and security. Suddenly, I felt two surprisingly strong hands grab my hands.

"Tyre! You promised me a dance. Where have you been?" Calla has somehow appeared right next to me. "You don't mind if I steal him, do you? No. Great!" Without giving Annarie Carlon a chance to voice the rebuttal forming on her face, Calla pulls me away from her and towards the dance floor.

"I think that woman just tried to sell me her niece!" I whisper. "Calla!" I whisper louder when she doesn't respond. She laces her fingers through mine and elbows me in the ribs.

"Smile and wave," she whispers through a plastered smile. "We're the two most stared-at people at this party, and now we're together."

"Calla!" is all I can think to say again as a general disgust for humanity consumes my brain. Thankfully, lost in these thoughts, I almost don't notice that we've reached the dance floor.

"Hey," she says, as she spins to face me, "just get through this dance, and then we can make a swift exit to the balcony. Alright? Just hang in there. Can you do that?"

"Yes," I manage. She tosses her hair over her shoulder and moves me into position for the first dance. The band starts playing a waltz, which helps because I know this dance fairly well. I take Calla's hand with one hand and put my other arm around her waist. Focusing on Calla, I'm suddenly hyperaware of the warmth of her hand in mine, and her body closer to mine than it's been since I carried her back to the house. She is actually a terrible dancer, but it doesn't matter. She radiates warmth that pulls me closer and closer until I almost forget everything else in the room entirely. When the song ends, it's like being doused in cold water.

Ms. Carlon is watching impatiently, and I realize with dread that there are dozens of others at this party waiting to have similar conversations with me. As if reading my mind, Calla moves seamlessly through the final movement of the dance and laces her fingers with mine again, pulling me towards the doors leading to the outdoor balcony, smiling and waving all the while. Only after we're on the balcony with doors closed behind us does she let out a deep breath and drop on the nearest bench. It's hard to contain my amazement at her social maneuvering, and I realize I'm staring at her.

"That was something," I say. She's kicked off her high heels and is massaging one of her feet when she looks up and smiles at me.

"What do you mean?"

"I mean, do you have a lot of experience rescuing monsters from parties? That was like a military operation."

"I have a lot of experience being stared at." She slides her shoes back on and shifts, making room for me as I lower myself next to her on the bench.

"For a different reason, though," I say.

"That doesn't always mean it's better," she says. She laughs as I raise my eyebrows in disbelief.

"Fine, it's better," she says. "It's definitely better, but still . . . not always great." A silence stretches out between us, and even though I want to say something impressive or charming, questions about Calla are all that come to mind, especially about why she freezes up when I ask about Mark. How could I really think of anything else when this entire party is, after all, ultimately all about keeping me safe from Mark? Finally, I can't take the silence anymore.

"Can I . . . ?" I hesitate, knowing the question is abrupt and out of place, especially after she just rescued me, but there's no going back now. "They say no one's ever seen him, you know." I watch Calla closely for a reaction. She frowns and looks up at me. "The Inimical," I clarify. "That's why they call him that. It means just a general sense of intent to do harm. They say he's just a rumor, a ghost, or a shadow, and I've never met someone from Umbra who might know more about him. I'm sorry, I can see it hurts you to talk about this, but have they seen him in Umbra?" Calla's whole body goes rigid as she shakes her head.

"No," she says, "it's like you said, The Inimical is just a shadow."

"Sorry, I shouldn't have asked." The silence washes over us again, less comfortable now than it was before. I need to say something reassuring or maybe apologetic? "Calla," I say, taking a risk and grabbing both her hands, "you know you're safe here? Right? You can stay here for as long as you want to."

"Why would you think I need to be somewhere safe?" she challenges, her eyes darting up to meet mine. At least she doesn't pull her hands away.

"I don't know if you do. I'm just saying, if you do need to be somewhere safe, you are safe here." Calla hesitates and bites her lower lip.

"Tyre, I can't ask you to . . . "

"Hey," I say, standing and pulling her to her feet. "After tonight, I owe you a rescue."

"Thank you," she says. I haven't made a connection with a new person in living memory, and there's suddenly so much I want to tell her. I want to tell her about Maddie going to Clocks to try and save me, and that I know what it's like to be targeted and scared. I want to promise her again to keep her safe, just like I've worked hard to keep everyone in this house safe since I was old enough to know what that meant. I remind myself that if Calla is staying here indefinitely, there will be time. For now, I reach for one of the roses on the balcony trellis to hand her. They're all dead from the cold, but hopefully it's a kind gesture all the same.

"Stop!" she yells, pushing my hand away with her free hand.

"What? What's wrong?" I ask.

"What are you doing?" she says.

"Nothing. I was just . . . I mean, I know they're all dead but—"

"Don't touch the rose bushes, Tyre," says Calla.

"Calla, what? What does that mean?"

"Please, Tyre, I know I don't have the right to ask you for anything else, but please, for me, promise you won't touch the rose bushes. Any rose bushes. Any roses."

"Why?" I'm reminded again, forcefully, that while time is revealing Calla to be pragmatic, and kind as well as open-minded, and fun to be around, she's also very strange.

"Please, just promise," she says. Her grip is like a vise around my wrist. I slowly lower my outstretched hand.

"Alright," I say, moving away from the roses and resting my hands on her shoulders. "Sure, I promise. Come on, it's freezing. Let's get you inside." I put my arm around her shoulders and pull her towards the door. Just when I think I'm figuring out the mystery of Calla, another mystery presents itself. By the time we get back inside, though, the mystery is all but forgotten, because all I can think about is my arms around Calla's warm shoulders and the way she leans against me like it's the most natural thing in the world.

7

Tyre . . . At first, I think it's my dad again. The dream feels so real, which is a quality that only dreams where my dad talks to me tend to have. This time, though, I don't know where I am, and usually when I dream about my dad, I'm in my room. This place is most definitely not my room. It looks like our rose garden. Or some version of it. It must be winter here, too, because all the roses are dead. *Hello, Tyre*. A shiver shoots down my spine as I recognize the voice from our living room the night we were attacked.

"You," I spin around, and there he is, or there *something* is. It looks like the shape that attacked us a few weeks ago. Just a mass of darkness. An oversized cloak wrapped around a shadow.

"Me," it says. Should I be scared? I'm aware that I'm dreaming, but somehow it doesn't feel like a dream. It also doesn't feel like I can wake up.

"I can't touch you here," he says, as if reading my mind. The shape glides towards me, and I manage to hold my ground. The cloak billows around it like it's suspended underwater as it stops just short of me. I still can't see a face, but there are skeletal hands visible at the ends of the sleeves.

"You're The Inimical," I say.

"I don't exactly call myself that."

"And what do you call yourself?"

"That's not something I need you to know," he says. "What I do need you to know is that you have something that I want."

"Antlers?" I say, hoping I sound braver than I feel. It laughs, and it sounds like branches scraping against glass.

"No," he says. "You have something that's mine, but thankfully, I'm willing to make a trade."

I force a laugh. "What could I possibly have that's yours? I'm not sure how familiar you are with Thiaghal, but if something is here, it's been here a good long while. I don't think anything of yours has shown up here recentl-" I pause as a horrible realization washes over me. There is one new thing in Thiaghal. "You want Calla." The shadow stays silent, but it feels like the dark is closing in around me somehow. "You can't have her," I say, as a fierce surge of protectiveness tears through me.

"Like I said, I'm willing to trade," says that shadow. I see a vague outline of what looks like shoulders shrugging.

"I'm not giving you anything." The shadow laughs again.

"I can't come and take her, she's made sure of that, but I *can* hurt her and I *will*, until you give me what I-" I lunge for its throat only to gasp and jerk awake as soon as my hand reaches him. My dad's medallion is warmer than usual against my chest. I sit up in bed trying to catch my breath. I rub my face, trying to decide if what I just saw was real. Looking out the window, I see that dawn is breaking on the horizon. I know that there's no going back to sleep after that. After a few more steadying breaths, I make my way into the kitchen to put on a pot of coffee. I'm expecting to have a few more seconds to myself, so I'm surprised when Maddie is already there.

"Hey, Mads," I say, ruffling the hair on the top of her head and trying to keep my expression as neutral as possible. Between the cold and my fur, I accidentally shock the top of her head.

"Watch out for cracklers," she says. Cracklers are the dragon-like creatures that eat and then breathe electricity. It's why we don't have anything electric in our homes and why we say the traditional "watch out" phrase if we accidentally generate some.

"I'll keep my eyes peeled. Coffee?"

"Already put on a pot," she says, chewing on the end of her pencil and gesturing over to the pot on the gas stove. She has her sketchbook open in front of her, but as I walk past her to get a mug, I see it isn't a sketch she's working on; it's a letter. I'm about to ask about it when she says,

"Tyre, hey, about the other day . . . "

"Oh yes, the other day," I say, sitting down across from her with my coffee. "Want to explain to me this sudden desire to go to Clocks?" She looks down at her sketchbook.

"Do you remember those silly stories I loved when I was 11 or 12? About the Eldrida Hero?"

"Remember?" I say. "Hard to forget. You made us tell you about him all the time."

"Him?" she says. "Like he was a real person? With a real life?"

"Well, yeah, kind of. The Eldrida Hero is a concept that people tell stories about, but there was a specific 'Eldrida Hero' a while back who was a real person, more of a celebrity than a folktale. He was the star student at Clocks for a couple of years, and then he disappeared, probably around the time you were 13. You were so into him that we just kept making up stories about him for another year. That's probably the reason you thought he might just have been a character."

"No, I remember he was a real person, but do you think what they said about him is true?" She's frowning down at her sketchbook. "Wasn't one of the stories about some prophecy? That he was the chosen one who would protect the world from destruction in our darkest hour against a great evil or some shit?"

"Or some shit," I say, "but clearly that was wrong because he burnt out and disappeared long before any big, bad evil could show up." Maddie looks up as Calla enters the kitchen.

"Hey, Calla," I say, standing up to get her a mug. I turn back to look at her when she doesn't say anything, and I realize something isn't right. She's clutching the counter, and she looks pale. "Calla . . . " Then Calla vomits a fountain of blood.

The next few minutes are a flurry of panic and activity. I rush to Calla as Maddie screams, "Aunt Laurel! We need you *now*!" Mom rushes in and helps Calla up, but she can barely stand. I throw her arm over my shoulders and help her walk back to her room.

"I'm fine," she says weakly, "I'm sorry, that was so embarrassing. I think I had too much mulled wine last night."

"Calla, you just vomited blood."

"Red wine," she counters, as vehemently as someone being dragged down a hallway can.

"Well, we're just going to let the physician decide about that," says Mom. "After we get you to lie down somewhere, I'll send a Holpie to get him."

"You don't need to do that, please," says Calla. We've reached her room, and I ease her down onto her bed.

"It's my house, and I can invite the physician here whenever I want," says Mom. She pulls the blankets up over Calla until all that's visible is her head and shoulders. Calla relaxes back onto the pillows and nods, defeated, as Mom sweeps out the door to find a Holpie. She falls back asleep almost the second she closes her eyes. I put my hand under her nose to make sure she's breathing and then go to find Bevin and Aydin. I need to talk to them immediately.

***

"I thought you only ever had dreams like that about your dad?" says Aydin. It took me almost 30 minutes to find them both in this ridiculous house, and then another 30 to catch them up on the events of the morning and my dream from last night. We're talking in the sitting room when I hear Alexander come in and go upstairs.

"Did she say anything when you were talking out on the terrace last night? Anything more about who she is? Where she's from? What The Inimical wants her for?" asks Bevin.

"Not really," I say, shaking my head. "Although there was this one strange moment with the roses," I explain Calla's bizarre reaction to me picking a rose off the trellis.

"I like her well enough," says Aydin when I finish telling the story, "but she's an odd person."

"Yeah, the beauty sort of masks the general strangeness at first," agrees Bevin. "She'll fit in well here." She raises her hot chocolate mug in a symbolic toast and pauses for a minute before speaking again. "So, speaking of odd," she says, "can I ask something? She glows, right? It's not just me seeing that? Not metaphorically. As in, she actually projects light?"

"Yes!" Aydin and I say simultaneously.

"I thought it was just me seeing it!" says Aydin.

"Me too!" I say. "It's subtle. Sometimes I think that it's just the chandelier or the way the sun is hitting her, but sometimes I'm sure!"

"No, you're right," says Bevin, "she definitely glows."

"Why?" I say, dumbfounded.

"I don't know," says Bevin. "Can we ask her?"

“I don’t know if you can just ask a person why they glow,” says Aydin.

“Well, in any case,” I say, “I’m glad it’s not just me. Maybe I’m not as stunned by her as I thought I was.”

“You do like her, though,” says Bevin. “Don’t you? I can tell.”

“Yeah,” I say. “I do.” Bevin smiles and shakes her head.

“What’s up, Bev?” says Aydin.

“I was just thinking,” says Bevin, “if she likes you too, and I think she probably does, that could be it. Curse broken. Isn’t that strange? I just can’t wrap my head around it. Tyre, what do you even look like now? It’s just been this way for so long.”

“Alright, well, there’s a long way between interest and being in love,” I clarify. Come to think of it though, I think we've all just always assumed that by 'love' the fairy meant 'general mutual romantic interest,' or 'true love's kiss.' Unfortunately, she was overly specific. I don’t want to acknowledge it to Bevin and Aydin yet, but I’ve been thinking about Bevin’s point too. Pretty much since Calla appeared at my office door and asked me to go find her mirror with her. As much as I try to convince my mom that I’m indifferent to breaking the curse, not necessarily opposed, I’ve never liked the idea of breaking it. Then I suddenly have a vivid memory of the way that woman, Saffron, looked at me last night.

“It will be good,” I say. “If it happens. I’m not sure it will, but if it does, it will be good.”

“So,” says Bevin, “are you going to tell her?”

“What? That The Inimical has already targeted this estate once and likely will again, so there are many other places she’d be better off hiding since he’s clearly after her?” says Aydin.

“Well, I meant to tell her that he’s interested in her, you know, romantically,” says Bevin, “but that too, I guess.” As I take another long sip of my coffee, it occurs to me that neither of those questions has a simple answer.

"I can't tell her that I'm interested in her," I say.

"Why not?" says Aydin.

"Well, she just vomited blood for one thing," I say, "but as far as telling her that Mark is likely targeting this house and wants her specifically, I think we probably need to have that conversation."

"Do you think she knows?" says Aydin. "I mean, she was running barefoot and half-dressed through the woods when you found her, and we still don't know why. Mark referred to her as 'mine.' It kind of feels like we're not the only ones withholding information."

"Do you think she's like me?" I say.

"How do you mean?" Asks Bevin.

"It's like I'm talking to myself," says Aydin.

"The one thing anyone seems to know about The Inimical is that he's rounding up people cursed or blessed by fairies," I say. "Do you think she's been given some kind of fairy gift and that's why she glows?"

"It would make sense," says Bevin.

"But," says Aydin, "I don't see why we should have to sit here and speculate when someone clearly has the answers."

"Alright, again," I say, "she just vomited blood."

"I know," says Aydin, "but you like her, and I see you starting to get invested in her. We can wait to make sure that Alexander says she's alright, but if she's going to be with you, as your best friend, I want to know the story."

"We have no idea if she's going to be with me." Aydin sips his coffee in what I'm sure he considers to be a dignified silence. I'm about to ask Bevin what she's noticed that makes her think that Calla returns my interest when a small cough comes from the doorway, followed by the appearance of Alexander and Mom.

"How is she?" I ask.

"She'll be fine," he says. "Her pulse is weak, and she has lost some blood, but . . . " He looks lost in thought for a moment. "I can't identify the source of the bleeding. She doesn't have any internal injuries that I can detect. It is possible that most of the vomit was really just red wine, and she hasn't lost quite as much blood as it seems. In any case, she'll need to stay in bed today, rest, and have plenty of fluids, but she should be fine by tomorrow as long as she doesn't overdo it."

"Maddie is sitting with her now," says Mom. "So, she seems to feel up to company if . . . " Mom looks pointedly at me. It suddenly occurs to me that Mom is the only one still living in the glow of Calla and I dancing together and disappearing to the balcony last night, without knowledge of anything else having occurred.

"I'll go see her," I say, "Bevin, Aydin, can you fill Mom in?"

"Definitely," says Bevin.

"I'll just walk the doctor out and be right back," says Mom, throwing me a confused glance.

***

"Hi," I say, knocking on Calla's door a few minutes later. Maddie is perched next to Calla in the bed with her legs curled, showing Calla some of her drawings. Calla laughs at an especially funny caricature of Aydin before looking up and seeing me.

"Tyre!" she says brightly.

"Gross," says Maddie at Calla's obvious delight at seeing me.

"Give us a minute, Mads?" I say.

"I'll come show you the rest later," says Maddie to Calla.

"Sure," says Calla, "definitely." Maddie makes her way out of the room, and I sit down on the armchair next to the bed. Calla watches Maddie until she disappears down the hall.

"Strange question for you," she says, "has Maddie said anything about seeing anyone?"

"What?" I say. "No, I mean not to me at least. Why do you ask?" Calla stares at the place where Maddie disappeared down the hall.

"She was asking me questions. She started off kind of generally asking about relationships, and then she asked if she could ask me something personal. She was asking if I'd ever dated someone older."

"Older?" I ask. My initial thought was that Maddie was trying to do some sloppy match-making and see if Calla is interested in me, but asking about someone older doesn't make sense. Calla mentioned being 31 the other day, so she's actually a year or two older than I am.

"I couldn't get her to tell me anything specific," she says. I frown and tuck this information away, making a note to retrieve it later when I talk to Mom and Bevin.

"There are a couple of older teenagers in town she's close with," I say, "but I'll ask Bevin." Calla keeps her gaze on the doorway where Maddie disappeared, looking worried and pale.

"How are you feeling?" I ask. She shakes herself out of her thoughts.

"Embarrassed," she says, "but fine. I really think I just had too much to drink."

"Calla," I say, "there's something I think you need to know." Almost simultaneously, Calla asks.

"How was the rest of the party after we separated? Oh, sorry," she says, "you go."

"No, it's alright," I say, giving a half smile. "Your question is easier. It was . . . something." After going back into the ballroom that night, someone swooped in to ask Calla to dance, leaving me stranded again. The rest of the night hadn't been as bad as I anticipated. I did have some conversations similar to the one I had had with Ms. Carlon, but I also had a few normal ones and successfully danced with a few people. No one I danced with was anything more than polite, but I counted it as a success that they weren't shaking and crying.

"Meet anyone special?" she asks.

"I think so," I say, looking pointedly at her. *Focus, Tyre.* I came here to explain to Calla that, despite the previous evening's promise of safety, she was possibly in more danger here than she would be elsewhere. As Aydin pointed out, I deserve answers too. I'm not here to flirt.

"Did anyone else try to sell you any members of their family?" she says.

"Not so obviously, but I did talk to a few more people with that intention, yes," I say.

"Uh," says Calla. She wrinkles her nose like she smells something awful. "Sometimes people really disgust me, you know."

"They weren't all like Annarie Carlon. Some of the people seemed to just need help or money and didn't know how to get it. I arranged to have some food and supplies sent to anyone who seemed like they needed it." I don't know what to make of the look Calla is giving me. For a second, I think it's admiration, but then maybe it seems more like sadness.

"Why?" she says.

"I'm the governor. I've got to take care of the people," I say

"That was a really decent thing to do for people who think you're a monster," she says.

"Well, the way I see it, anyone desperate enough to sell a family member to a monster is desperate enough to do anything. Just trying to keep the crime rate down," I say.

"No one else cried upon having to approach you?" she says, raising her eyebrows.

"No, thank goodness," I say. "Although I can't say with confidence that no one was afraid. I think they were all just holding it together a little bit better. You weren't afraid of me when you first met me, were you?"

"I fainted and fell out of a tree, and then I tried to jump out a window," she says.

"You were startled," I say, "but you never looked at me the way some of the girls at that party looked at me."

"You're right," she says, after thinking for a minute. "I was startled. Overwhelmed. Confused. Disoriented. But no, I don't think I was ever really afraid of you, specifically."

"Why not?" I ask.

"I guess I've seen some scary things," she says, "I think it's made me easier to startle, but harder to really scare."

"Are you talking about Mark?" I say.

"Alright, who is Mark?" says Calla. "That's the third time I've heard that name, and no one has explained to me who it is."

"Sorry, that's what Bev, Aydin, and I call The Inimical." Calla laughs so hard I'm worried she's going to throw up again.

"Why do you call it 'Mark'?" she says, wiping a tear from her eye.

"I don't know," I say. "We came up with it in a meeting. Everyone was saying 'The Inimical' this and 'The Inimical' that. It just made it a little less scary to talk about if we gave him an average name."

"So, Mark then?" says Calla.

"Mark," I say, nodding. "Calla, speaking of Mark, there's something I need to tell you." All the amusement drains out of Calla's face.

"What?" she said. "What's wrong?"

While trying not to sound completely disconnected from reality, I explain about the dream. Calla is quiet during the story, but I can see her grip tighten on the sheets until her knuckles turn white. She's gone so pale I worry she's going to be sick again, but there's no going back now. I explain the basic details about the night we were attacked by The Inimical.

"You think it's going to try to come here for you again," she says.

"Yes, but we've beaten him once," I say. "We'll do it again."

"How?" she says suddenly.

"How what?" I ask.

"The Inimical sent someone for you, and you escaped? How? How did you?" I'm startled by the urgency in her voice.

"Calla," I say, taking both her hands in mine, "Calla, look at me. You are safe now. I made you a promise, and I'm telling you this because I want you to know all your options. You can stay here, but I think it's likely that Mark will target this house again, so I want you to know that we can arrange for you to stay somewhere else. Somewhere Mark is less likely to be lurking around." Calla thinks for a small eternity before something in her expression finally shifts.

"The dream was just a dream, Tyre, and I just had too much wine last night. I don't have any reason to think The Inimical has any interest in me."

"Calla . . . " I say.

"I want to stay here," she says. I feel my heart leap in my chest.

"Are you sure?" I say.

"Yes," says Calla. "I want to stay with you. I don't know exactly what's going on, but if Mark is involved, who could keep me safe better than you?" I try to ignore how happy I am about that statement.

"It's settled then," I say. "I'll let you get some rest." As I walk back towards the voices of my family in the living room, I know two things. One, I am rapidly falling for Calla, and two, she's lying to me.

8

"I don't like it," says Mom.

"I know, Mom, but it's the right thing to do." We've assembled in the living room while Calla keeps resting upstairs.

"You're right, it is. It definitely is, but . . ." I'm overcome with another wave of sympathy for Mom. She came downstairs this morning, obviously wanting to gush about what a success the party had been. No one tried to assassinate me, and I disappeared to the balcony with Calla to do who-knows-what for the first third of the night. Before Bevin and Aydin told her about the dream, she was the happiest I've seen her in weeks. "Now, even if you break the curse, you still won't be safe," she says. "Calla seems lovely, and of course, we're going to help her, but wasn't there anyone else at the party you liked?"

"It's more a matter of if there was anyone who liked me, Mom, and the answer is no."

"They don't know you!"

"And also, Aunt Laurel, begging your pardon," interjects Aydin, "but no one is going to meet anyone else as long as Calla's in the room."

"True," says Bevin. "I would have felt bad for all the other women at the party had I not heard that most of them felt a deep sense of relief at not getting any attention from Tyre. Sorry, love you," she says, turning to me.

"She really is very pretty, isn't she?" says Mom. "I wonder if that's how she got The Inimical's attention?"

"She won't actually tell us," says Aydin, pointedly.

"It might not be an easy thing to talk about," says Mom after thinking for a minute. Aydin looks unconvinced.

"We can't just throw her out," says Bevin.

"Agreed," I say. Mom and Aydin look at each other and seem dangerously close to forming a strange alliance on this.

"Mads?" I say. "Tie break?"

"Huh?" she says, looking startled out of a daydream.

"You alright, Maddie?" says Bevin. "You're miles away today."

"I'm fine," says Maddie, coolly tossing her hair in Bevin's direction. "What's the question?"

"Whether Calla stays here," I say. "You're the one who saw her vomit blood, so if anyone gets a vote, you do."

"I like Calla," says Maddie. "She likes my drawings."

"Well, that's that," I say. I try to keep a lightness in my voice, but I'm getting tired of pretending everyone gets a vote here when I am clearly the person most impacted by this decision.

"Tyre," says Mom.

"Actually, I think it's settled," I say. I feel the room tense at the edge in my voice. Mom looks at me for a minute, and I sense she's going to argue. For a minute, I hope she does. It's what she would have done before Bevin and Maddie's parents died, before Dad died, before the curse . . . but after a minute, her shoulders sag, and she just looks tired.

"Keeping her here is the right thing to do," she says. I've gotten exactly what I wanted, and I feel like a monster for it. All I can do is agree and leave the room.

***

During the next week, a routine forms that feels, at the risk of sounding trite, both comfortable and magical. Calla continues to be a very easy person to be around. I feel like every second I'm not with her, I'm looking forward to the next time I get to talk to her. I wake up one morning and realize that I'm looking for Calla every spare second I get, and she seems to be doing the same. She loves books, which I don't particularly like, but we find an old deck of cards buried among the books in the library and realize we both love card games.

Most of our evenings start with playing cards with Bev, Maddie, or Aydin, but we stay up talking long past when everyone else goes to bed. She's happy to chatter about her favorite foods, her family, and her friends in Andestine, but still never approaches the topic of Mark. Towards the end of the week, I look out through my office window and see Bevin and Calla walking arm in arm through the frozen rose garden. Calla looks like she's laughing at something Bevin is saying. I look down at my third piece of mail from the Health Subdivision in as many days, titled "*Re: Senzicaria*." Before I've really decided what I'm doing, I'm walking outside to join them.

"Bev, Calla!" I call, running to catch up with them. They both turn to face me. Bevin smiles, Calla beams.

"Hey!" says Bevin. "We were just talking about you." I don't have time to wonder what that means.

"I want to go into town," I say.

"What?" says Bevin.

"Town," I say, out of breath. I'm not sure what I'm doing, just that I need to do something besides sit in my office indefinitely and read the same piece of mail I've read for the last three days. There's also the concern that if I don't make an appearance soon, everyone will start pretending that I don't exist again.

"I think Calla is supposed to be resting still, but I'm interested in a trip to town. Are you sure?"

"I'm sure."

"Alright," says Bevin, taking a deep breath, "Alright, we're going into town! Let's do this! What do you want to do? I mean the pub obviously, but . . . oh, sorry Calla, we shouldn't be planning this right in front of you when you're not up to going."

"You know, I actually think I'm alright," she says. "It's been over a week. I'm really feeling much better."

"How about this," I suggest, "tomorrow, as long as you still feel well enough. You, me, Bevin, Aydin, and even Maddie if she wants to join. Big trip into town. I'd really like to show it to you."

"Works for me," says Bevin, squeezing Calla's hand.

***

"So first we'll obviously be going to the pub," states Maddie with certainty that evening as she weaves a flower crown into Calla's hair. She's so excited about our big night out, she's even being nice to Bevin again. "Oh! Sometimes there's music in the square. We'll need to see that too!"

"Meeting up with anyone once we get there?" I ask Maddie, raising my eyebrows. "I haven't forgotten about your mystery pen pal."

"What?" says Bevin. "What mystery pen pal?"

"Nothing," says Maddie, "Tyre's just being an ass." Bevin looks worried, but drops it.

"We almost ready?" says Aydin. He walks in holding everyone's coats, cloaks, and hats.

"Done," says Maddie, proudly adding one more flower to Calla's hair.

We walk into town just as evening is setting in. Calla starts off walking up ahead, arms linked with Bevin on one side and Maddie on the other, leaving Aydin and I following behind. Occasionally, peals of giggles and laughter float back to us as we walk.

"You get any answers from our mystery woman?" says Aydin.

"Aydin," I say, then hesitate.

"Tyre," he says, "I know you like her. Sorry if I was hard on her before. I like her too. I just like you more."

"She's, well, she's great, honestly. It sounds so trite to say, but I've never felt like this about anyone. At the same time, she's lying to me," I say. "She's lying to all of us."

"I know," says Aydin, "or at the very least, leaving out some critical details." We both look ahead at the group of girls walking in a little knot ahead of us. Neither of us knows what to say.

***

The six of us are standing practically elbow to elbow outside Holpie's Mane Pub, staring at the door.

"We can't just keep standing here," says Calla.

"It's Tyre's first time, he's nervous," says Aydin. I shoot him a look that I hope kills him.

"I didn't realize there would be quite so many people here," I say. "You guys go ahead, I think I'll just-"

"See, I told you he would do this," says Bevin.

"Execute the plan!" says Maddie. Suddenly, I feel Calla loop her arm through one of mine while Bevin grabs the other, and they both run forward as Maddie gives us all a push from behind. We burst through the door of the pub with Bevin, Maddie, and Calla falling over laughing, making even more of a spectacle of ourselves than we would have just walking in.

"Good to see you, Brogan!" calls Aydin as he waves to the bartender. The bartender raises his hand in a tentative greeting.

"Aydin," says Brogan, giving a curt, quick tilt of his head. Bevin drags us to an open corner table, and I slide into the booth between Calla and Bevin, then Maddie piles in next to Bevin while Aydin gets a round of drinks. I'm aware of Calla's physical presence next to me, and I wonder what she would do if I leaned over and put my arm around her again like I did the night of the party. Despite all the time we've been spending together, we both seem suddenly more self-conscious about touching each other. Before I can think about it for too long, I feel tuck her foot behind my ankle under the table. The casual and intimate physical contact from her makes my heart suddenly race, and when I glance over, she seems totally at ease, like this casual touch is something we do all the time.

Now that we're settled and keeping to ourselves, everyone mostly seems to have stopped staring and is going back to their conversations. People keep glancing over; some of them look nervous, some just curious, and one balding man alone at the bar looks objectively angry. He seems a little familiar, and I think he may be one of the men who work on the pulley system that goes over the mountains to the next province. I'm not sure, but I think I see Calla flick him off out of the corner of my eye when she catches him glaring at me. When I focus on our table again, Aydin is setting down glasses of dark liquor and one glass of mead for Maddie.

"Game?" says Bevin.

"No, never again," says Aydin, who famously loses every drinking game.

"Well, my drink is gone, so if we're playing a game, I need a refill," says Calla, tossing her drink back in one throw.

"Calla, this was for sipping, not shooting," says Aydin. Calla shrugs, unconcerned.

"I've got the next round," I say, smiling and nudging Calla out of the booth with my hip. To avoid the angry-looking bald man, I go to the other end of the bar. Brogan has been the bartender here since my mom and dad met at this pub, so at least he knows me.

"Governor Sylvan," he says, giving me a cold glance of acknowledgement.

"Brogan, seriously?"

"Well, what do you expect," he says, "not coming around. Haven't seen you since you were at my hip height. Thought you were dead."

"You know why I couldn't," I say.

"Same reason you can't now, but here you are." I give him a look, and he holds out the tip jar. I sigh, toss in a handful of coins, and he smiles.

"What can I get you, Tyre?" he says. I order another round, and a double for Calla, who apparently drinks like an aging sailor. I didn't realize how much I'd missed this pub. I used to love it when Mom and Dad would bring me here with Bevin and her parents for dinner. While Brogan is getting the drinks, a man about my age comes and takes a seat at the bar next to me. We nod and acknowledge each other, and then I do a double-take. I'm not saying I know everyone in town, but Thiaghal is small, and most people at least look familiar. This man isn't dressed like most people in Thiaghal. People in Thiaghal tend to wear simple cuts and colors, lined with fur for the cold. This man is outfitted head to toe in well-worn leather. He looks like some kind of vampire hunter. Sure enough, when I chance a glance, he has a knife and a broad sword attached to a belt swung around his hips.

"Meltair," he says, holding out his hand when he sees me look over at him. His name sounds vaguely familiar somehow. I'm put off by the ease with which he introduces himself. He doesn't seem at all put off by me.

"Tyre," I say, holding out my hand and shaking. I probably should have just introduced myself as 'Governor Sylvan,' but it doesn't seem natural. Meltair catches Brogan's eye and orders a drink. Brogan sets it down in front of him before going back to assembling the tray of drinks for my table.

"All for you?" asks Meltair, gesturing to the tray with his head.

"Nah," I shake my head, "ordering for a whole group." I gesture over to the side of the bar where the group is settled, and where it seems Maddie is now arm-wrestling Aydin. Meltair smiles and nods.

"Sounds like fun," he says.

"You're new to Thiaghal?" I say. "It's small, and I thought I knew everyone by sight at least."

He shakes his head. "Just passing through," he says, "meeting with someone." Brogan reappears with the drinks.

"Good talking to you," I say, as I collect the tray and head back to the table. The group cheers as I sit back down.

"Who won arm wrestling?" I ask. After another drink, Bevin is deep into a story about last summer when she and Maddie got lost in Lytwist, and I suddenly feel like someone is watching us. Maybe the dream about the Inimical has made me paranoid, but I scan the pub, just in case. It could be a coincidence, but Meltair's eyes are locked on our table. Looking away, I tell myself again that I'm just being overly vigilant, but I slide closer to Calla and chance wrapping my arm around her shoulders. She reaches up and laces her fingers through mine as she continues chatting to Bevin. When I chance a glance back up, I see Meltair take a long sip of his beer, throw a few coins on the counter, and leave the pub. *See*, I think, *just worried about nothing*. I turn my attention back to the table to realize that the conversation has lulled. Calla is leaning her head against my shoulder, and Maddie stands up and yawns.

"I think I'll head back," she says.

"We'll go with you, Mads," says Bevin.

"Yeah, I'm about ready," says Aydin.

"No need," says Maddie. "I'm good, you guys stay for a bit."

"Maddie, no way are you walking home alone, it's dark," I say.

"It's only 9, I'll be fine," she says.

"Nope, we're out of here," says Aydin. He drains the last of his drink and stands up.

"Fine, well, at least let me go to the bathroom by myself," says Maddie, rolling her eyes. She heads off in the direction of the bathroom. After 20 minutes, she still hasn't come back, and Bevin goes to check on her.

"She isn't there," she says, biting her lip when she comes back.

"She's been acting so strange lately," says Aydin.

"Did I tell you about the letter the other day?" I say. When I finish my story, Bevin looks even more worried.

"I'm sure she's fine," says Aydin. Before Bevin can respond, the front door to the pub opens and Maddie walks in, her cheeks pink from the cold.

"Hey!" she says, as if nothing had happened.

"Hey?" says Bevin. "Where did you disappear to?"

"Just needed some air," she says, "we ready to go?"

Bevin, Aydin, and I look at each other.

"I guess," says Aydin.

"You guys go ahead," I say, "I need to close out at the bar, and I think Calla is asleep on my shoulder. I'm going to wake her up and make sure she's feeling up to walking back." Aydin, Maddie, and a very worried-looking Bevin shuffle out of the bar. As they go, I try to arrange my face to look concerned about Maddie's odd behavior and not gleeful about Calla asleep on my shoulder. I make a mental note to try to pull Maddie aside tomorrow. Lately, she's been more open to talking about things one-on-one. I'm trying to figure out the gentlest way to wake her when I hear Calla stir next to me.

"Where is Bevin?" she says, sitting up and rubbing her blurry eyes, "and everyone else?"

"They went ahead," I say. "You feeling up to walking back? I just need to close out." She yawns and mumbles something in the affirmative.

"I can't believe it's only nine," she says.

"You're doing pretty well considering you vomited blood last week and just drank everyone in this bar under the table." I squeeze her shoulder and slide out of the booth to settle up with Brogan.

The bell on the door jingles as we step out of the pub and into the cold. In the 20 or so minutes since Aydin, Bev, and Maddie left, it's started to snow again, and it's freezing. I put my arm over Calla's shoulders again as we walk. She's already surprisingly warm, but she reaches up and laces her fingers through the hand on her shoulder again. As we start the walk back to the estate, I can smell the smoke from everyone's chimneys as they light fires for the night. We leave town and head into an open expanse of field on the path back to the estate. I pause and offer to let Calla ride the rest of the way on my back, and she accepts.

"So, I have another question for you," I say as we slowly make our way back towards home.

"Why do you always wait until I'm dependent on you for transportation to ask me questions?" she says.

"You've figured out my evil plan," I say.

"Fine, you win," she says, laughing. "You've got me trapped. What do you want to know?"

“Why do you like Bevin so much?”

“Jealous?” she says.

“Should I be?” I ask.

“No, I don’t think so,” she says, laughing again.

“Well, then why?” I ask. “I mean, don’t get me wrong. We all love Bev. Bevin is wonderful and loveable, but you just seemed to take to her so quickly.”

“You’re right,” says Calla. “I loved Bevin right away. I guess it’s because she’s just so . . . .Bevin is just so real. She doesn’t hide anything or pretend to be anything she isn’t. I feel like when I reach out and touch her, I can be sure she’ll feel solid under my fingers. Where I came from, it’s hard to be sure what’s real and what’s an illusion. I miss that certainty.”

“I’m real too,” I say gently, in a way that I hope is comforting.

“Don’t remind me,” says Calla.

“What does that mean?” I ask.

“Never mind,” says Calla. “Sorry. I’m sure that didn’t make any sense.”

“So explain it,” I say. “What does that mean? ‘Don’t remind me?’? Am I such a terrible monster that my being real is horrifying?” It’s the only interpretation I can think of, and it’s a very hurtful one.

“No!” says Calla. “No, that’s not what I meant at all!”

“Well then, what did you mean?”

“You don’t think I know you’re real?” says Calla. “You don’t think I see that you’re the same as Bevin? That you’re honest and kind and make no pretense at being something you’re not? However, unlike you, Bevin is safe to love. She’s solid and real, and I see no reason I would ever hurt her in the future.”

“You’re afraid you’re going to hurt me?” I say.

“Tyre,” says Calla, “I think there is a very real chance I’m going to break your heart.”

"Calla, you're being absurd," I say. "Is this about Mark again?" Calla doesn't say anything. "I can handle The Inimical," I say, "and I can keep you safe. We already escaped from The Inimical once and . . . "

"How?" yells Calla. "Because honestly, I don't believe you. No one escapes from The Inimical. Not ever." I pause. I think about explaining my dad's medallion and how it had worked against the enchanted broom, but I don't want to scare her more than she already is. On my first telling of the story, all I said was that Mark had sent someone, but we managed to fight them off, leaving out the scarier details of golden magic, flowing black cloaks, and enchanted brooms.

"We can drop it," I say. "I'm sorry, I never should have pushed you to talk about this."

"Alright," says Calla, her shoulders sagging. "I'm sorry too. I shouldn't have gotten so worked up." I'm about to respond when I hear a crunch behind us in the snow.

"Did you hear that?" I ask Calla.

"Tyre, if this is a joke, it's a very mean one." I shake my head and listen and hear it again.

"I think we're being followed," I say. "Hold on." I take off running with Calla on my back, but after no more than a few paces, two horses shoot out in front of us, blocking our path. I realize that they must have taken a wide path around us while we were arguing and prepared to block us in. I have to stop suddenly to avoid colliding with them, and Calla is thrown off my back into the snow. She scrambles to her feet as a third man approaches us on horseback. As he gets closer, I recognize the angry bald man from the pub.

"Governor. Mystery girl," he says, inclining his head towards Calla.

"Let us pass, and no harm will come to you," I say. The man laughs. I really don't want to have to tear this man apart in front of Calla, and I can't guarantee that one of the men won't hurt Calla while I deal with the others. Hopefully, this is a simple robbery, but I have a bad feeling. "Let her pass then," I say. "I'm sure she can't be a part of any business you might have with me." In response, one of the two men comes forward and grabs hold of Calla's arm. She doesn't flinch, and I suddenly remember what she said about being easy to startle but difficult to scare. "What do you want?" I say, turning to the bald man.

"Animals," he says, "have no control. They live off instinct. Impulse. Not the kind of creature I want as governor. Not the kind of creature that's fit to be a governor." The man draws a knife from a holster in his belt. I've been holding on to the hope that these were thieves after gold who will leave us alone if they get it. That doesn't seem to be the case. I've encountered this general attitude before, though usually more veiled, from Murchad during our council meetings. A part of me wonders if he's behind riling up some of the townspeople with ideas like the ones this man is spouting. "Certainly, not the kind of creature who deserves a pretty friend like this. What's your name?" he says, approaching Calla.

I growl and step in front of her as she tugs her arm out of the man's grip. Out of the corner of my eye, I see the other man hold up a crossbow and aim it in our general direction. I can get out of this, but I can't think of a way to get Calla out safely. So much for my promises to protect her from Mark when I can't even keep her safe from pub ruffians.

Then Calla laughs.

"What's so funny, girl?" says the bald man.

"Impulse? Lack of control?" says Calla. "Pretty big accusations coming from someone with a gambling problem." The man's eyes widen in surprise.

"How did you . . . ?"

"Doesn't matter," says Calla. "What does matter is that I have a bet for you." The men laugh, but I can see the one who has been talking with us still staring at Calla. He seems to be wrestling with whether or not to ask her what her bet is.

"Well," he says, after a minute of silence. "What is it then?"

Calla smiles and pulls a blank sheet of paper and a pen from a satchel around her shoulder. "My wager is this: if I can write your name on this piece of paper, you let us go. You ride back into town, and you will do your best to be a model citizen for the rest of your days."

"And if I win?" the man laughs.

"Then I'll run away with you, and you can kill the governor," she says, rolling her eyes.

"What's to stop us from doing that anyway?" he says.

"Really?" says Calla. "All of you? Because I look around and I see three men, and I see the governor. I think to myself, sure, he's outnumbered. Eventually, you could succeed, but not *all* of you. Sylvan here will kill at least one of you before you can kill him, and, my balding friend, there is no guarantee that that one will not be you. Now, why take those odds when you can take the ones I'm offering you?" There's a painful moment of silence where I can see the wheels turning in the man's brain.

"Tell me the wager again," he finally says.

"If I write your name on this piece of paper, you will let us go free. If I fail, then I will go with you, and Governor Sylvan here will offer no resistance when you kill him. And," she says, "we both must swear to the fairies that we will honor this bet. I think my friend here is an excellent example of what fairies can do to those who disrespect them." She claps a hand on my shoulder for emphasis.

"I'll take your bet," says the bald man, a sinister smile stretching across his face. Calla smiles back, just as eerily, and nods. I watch as she sits down and slowly writes on the piece of paper. Finally, she stands up, folds it in half, and hands it to the bald man. He begins to laugh.

"What's so funny?" says Calla.

"You," he says. "I don't know what you're up to, but I highly doubt that out of all the names in the world you somehow wrote mine on that scrap of paper. Kill him!" he says, pointing to me. I stand ready to fight. I had had no say in Calla's insane bet, and, ironically, I'm not nearly as superstitious as the rest of Thiaghal when it comes to the fairies. Before the men can attack, Calla speaks again.

"I would open that paper first," says Calla, with a smirk. The man scoffs, but neither of his henchmen attacks me. I watch as he slowly unfolds the paper and reads. His eyes go from amusement to confusion to rage.

"You," he splutters. "You tricked me!" In his anger, his face is turning tomato red. Suddenly, he sways and drops to his knees.

"Now, now," says Calla, "with your blood pressure, I don't know if it's wise to be turning that color."

"How did you know about my blood pressure? What . . . what are you?" He's looking at Calla like she's a ghost . . . or a monster. Calla leans down so that her face is only inches from his.

"I'm clever," she answers. "Now get out of my sight." Glad to finally have something to do, I draw myself up to my full height and stand behind Calla to join her in staring the man down. The man looks back and forth between us and scrambles to his feet and onto his horse. Casting one last terrified glance back at us, he signals to his men, and the three of them ride back towards town.

"Bye!" says Calla. She smiles and waves as the horses disappear into the distance. "Bye! Sorry, what were we talking about before that?" she says, turning towards me.

"No. Wait. What? Calla. What just happened?"

"I outsmarted some ruffians," says Calla, with another smirk. "What was unclear?"

"But you . . . and they . . . and how?"

"Be more specific," she says, rolling her eyes.

"How did you know about the gambling problem?"

"Chips for betting on card games in his belt, bandaged thumb from where it was broken for not paying his debts."

"His blood pressure?"

"Also in the belt. Hibiscus petals. Often used as a remedy for high blood pressure. I was fairly sure they weren't for decoration."

"What was written on the paper?"

Calla laughs. "Now, that one . . . " she says, as she steps into my space, " . . . that answer will cost you."

"Cost me what?" I ask, my brain racing to catch up to what's happening.

"Depends. How badly do you want to know?" She steps even closer to me, and I'm overcome by the scent of roses again. I feel the adrenaline from our almost-fight rushing through my veins, and before I can even think about all the possible consequences of such an action, I lean in and kiss her. She kisses me back and stands on her tiptoes to press her lips into mine. There is a minute where all I can feel is disbelief at having kissed someone like Calla, but before I can float in the joy of that for more than a second, millions of other thoughts flood in, the primary one being the curse. I pull away suddenly and look down at my body. I reach up and feel for my antlers. So far, everything seems to be the same.

"Um," says Calla, "is everything alright?"

"What?" I say. "Yes. Sorry. It didn't work."

"I think I'm offended?" says Calla. She's looking at me like I've lost my mind, and then I remember that Calla doesn't know the exact conditions for breaking the curse.

"No, no," I say, "I need to explain." We stand in the field for another ten minutes as I explain what the fairy said about the curse and how it could be broken. "So, when you appeared out of nowhere . . . " I conclude.

"You thought I was the one," says Calla.

"Is that crazy?" I say.

"No, I get it," says Calla, literally brushing off what should be major information with a wave of her hand. "So why didn't it work?"

"I don't know," I say, "but we'd better get back so we can start figuring it out." Calla nods and climbs back on my back. I stop to let her climb down just outside the front doors. "Calla," I say. Suddenly, I realize once again just how many questions I have about Calla. Why does she glow? What had she written on that paper? Why hadn't she been able to break the curse?

"Hm?" she says. I sigh. It will have to wait. I lean over quickly and kiss her on the cheek. She smiles.

"Shall we?" I say.

The house is quiet when we slip through the front doors, and I wander through the castle with Calla until we find Mom. She's reading in the library off the sitting room, and Bevin is bringing out a pot of tea.

"Tyre!" says Mom as she sees us come in. "Thank goodness; we were starting to get worried."

"It didn't work," I say. Bevin stops serving tea mid-pour.

"What didn't work?" says Mom. I sigh. I hate that the curse has somehow made my personal life everyone's business.

"I kissed Calla," I say, holding up our still interlocked hands. Calla waves with her free hand. "And it didn't break the curse." For a minute, no one says anything, then Mom springs into action.

"You must have done it wrong," she says.

"I don't think you can do it wrong, Mom," I say.

"What? Kissing or curse-breaking?" says Bevin, "Because I have a very definite opinion on one of those two things."

"Both," says Mom. "Alright, let me think . . . " Then Aydin comes in. Calla and I are holding hands, Bevin is beaming, and Mom is pacing with her hands in her hair.

"I've missed something," he says.

"Tyre and Calla kissed," says Bevin.

"But Tyre is still ugly," says Aydin.

"Alright, enough, everyone just shut up," says Mom.

"Mom!" I say.

"Tyre," says Mom, stopping suddenly and pivoting to face me, "you said that you kissed Calla. However, the fairy said that the young lady had to fall in love with you. Maybe Calla needs to kiss you?"

"It's worth a shot," says Aydin.

"I'm not opposed," says Calla. Calla turns to face me, stands on her tiptoes, and quickly kisses me. Still nothing.

"Well, that wasn't a very long kiss," says Mom. "Maybe if . . . "

"Yeah, no, this is getting strange," says Bevin.

"But maybe if-"

"Mom," I say, "face it, the fairy tricked us."

"No!" shouts Mom. "There's only one other thing it could be, and this settles it. You're getting married."

"What?" I say. I feel Calla startle and turn to look at me. "You're kidding, right?" I say.

"I am completely serious," says Mom.

"Mom . . . that's ridiculous."

"Why? That was the point of the party, wasn't it? To find an acceptable wife for the governor? If we had had the party when we were supposed to, you would be married by now. If anything will break the curse, a wedding will. You like Calla, don't you?"

"Yes," I say.

"Well, you're the owner of this estate and governor of Thiaghal, and you're not just going to be casually flirting with half the town. So, either tell Calla goodbye and pick someone else, or start making wedding plans." She storms out of the room. No one says anything until the sound of her footsteps dies away.

"She'll calm down," says Bevin. "Calla? Hey, Calla? You alright?" Calla is standing like a statue next to me.

"I made a mistake," she says. "Sorry. Just excuse me for a minute." She turns and rushes out of the room. I walk over to the sofa in front of the fire and put my head in my hands.

"You're not going to go after her?" asks Bevin.

"I think she needs space. I know I would." Bevin sits down in one of the open armchairs, and Aydin takes the other.

"So," says Bevin, "how did it happen? The kiss?"

"You won't believe this story."

I explain as best I can how Calla had warded off three grown men.

"I have to know," says Aydin, when the story is over, "what was written on the paper?"

"I don't know," I say. "I never got the chance to actually ask her about it. Right when she was about to tell me, we somehow ended up kissing, and then I was just thinking about how the curse hadn't broken. Do you think . . . ?"

"What?" asks Bevin.

"Do you think if I actually asked her to, Calla would marry me?"

"Aw, Tyre," says Bevin. "I like Calla. We all like Calla, but how much do you even know about her?"

"You did just meet her a few weeks ago," says Aydin.

"Well, Mom's not wrong," I say, "In this occupation, a few weeks of courting for political marriages aren't completely unheard of. Do we really even think anyone else will ever even want to kiss me? Much less marry me?"

"Tyre, this isn't the Andestinian monarchy. You're the governor of a tiny town, and giving in to all the bullshit people say about you being unlovable isn't a good reason to marry someone you just met."

"Do you want to marry Calla?" asks Bevin.

"Again, it's like talking to the wall," says Aydin.

"Aydin, I hear you, and I appreciate you, but . . . I don't know. I definitely don't feel completely sure about it, but I would marry her," I say. Aydin throws his hands up.

"Well then," says Aydin, "only one way to find out if she shares that very romantic sentiment."

***

An hour later, I knock on the door to Calla's room, but there's no answer.

"Calla?" I call.

"Come in!" a voice calls from inside. "It's open." I push the door open to find the room empty, but the doors leading to a small balcony are open, and I can see Calla glowing in the distance. I make my way out to the balcony to stand next to her.

"Hi," she says.

"Hi." She's standing in her white sleeveless dress with bare feet, looking very much like she did that day I found her in the woods. She's looking straight ahead out onto the frozen landscape in front of us and won't meet my eyes.

"Calla," I say, "you know you don't actually have to marry me if you don't want to, right? You can still stay here, where it's safe, no matter what." Calla laughs, but I hear her sniffle and look over to see that there are tears on her cheek.

"I know," she says.

"Then what's wrong?" I ask.

"Would it be totally cliché of me to say that it's complicated?" she says. Suddenly, I can't take it anymore, and all the questions come pouring out in a jumble.

"Calla," I say, "who are you? What are you running from? Why didn't the curse break when you kissed me? What was written on that paper? Why do you glow?"

Calla stands gaping at me for a minute.

"I'm not even sure where to start," she says. "I guess, first, my name is Calla Helena. I'm from Umbra, where I live with my grandfather and cousins in a little house in a small neighborhood. That's my story. I don't know why The Inimical would be interested in me, if it even is, and I don't know why the curse didn't break when you kissed me. I'm sorry."

"No, I didn't want you to think it was your fault," I say. "That's not what I meant. I'm sorry."

"What was your last question?" asks Calla. It takes me a moment to think back through my extensive list of questions to figure out which one she means.

"Why do you glow?" I say finally.

"Excuse me?" she says. "Glow? Like, in a metaphorical sense?" Is it possible she doesn't know? Has everyone been too polite to tell her for her entire life?

"No, Calla . . . " I say, "you actually glow. Like, on the way home earlier, I was able to use you as a flashlight."

"What?" says Calla. "I do not!"

"Oh, you do," I say. I look down and see the mirror that Calla and I rescued from the forest sitting face-down on a table next to Calla. "Here," I say, picking it up, "look."

"Tyre, no- don't!" Calla tries to grab my hand, but before I can process what she's saying, I've already picked it up. Inside the mirror, instead of a reflection, there's a scene of a young man asleep in a glowing, golden dome. Whoever he is, he's clearly very unwell. His eyes are closed in sleep that looks anything but peaceful. He's thin and has dark circles under his eyes. Before I can see any more, Calla snatches the mirror from my hands.

"Who was that?" I ask. Calla's eyes are closed as she clutches the mirror to her chest.

"No one," she says.

"Calla!"

"My brother." She wipes a tear from the side of her face. "The Inimical has my brother."

"What?" I say. "Why didn't you tell us?"

"I didn't want to add that to the list of problems you're currently dealing with," she says. "I didn't want to make you feel like you had to be my hero. I can handle my own problems. Especially since you and your mom already fight over what to do about The Inimical. I thought if you knew about my situation, then you might go after The Inimical yourself."

"Of course I will! That's your brother, Calla. We won't leave him there."

"No, Tyre, it's too dangerous," says Calla. "You won't be able to rescue him. You'll have a horrible fight with your only living family member for nothing."

“You forget,” I say, “you’re talking to the only person to have successfully escaped an attempted abduction by The Inimical.” Calla laughs and wipes a final tear from her face.

“Tell you what,” she says, “you tell me how you did that, I’ll tell you what I wrote on that paper this afternoon.”

“Deal,” I say. “Do you see this?” I hold the medal around my neck. “It was a gift from my father. There is an old oak in the forest where my dad told me to go in a dream. I think his spirit kind of waits there in case I need his help.” I watch Calla’s face for any sign that she thinks I’ve lost touch with reality, but, to the contrary, she looks like she’s hanging on every word. “This medal appeared on that tree one day. I was told it would protect me from danger. The night that Mark tried to take me, he used some kind of warm, golden light to make me sleep. The medal burned and woke me up somehow, and I was able to attack Mark’s messenger.” I glance at Calla’s face, expecting her to look skeptical, but all I see is sadness. “What’s wrong?” I ask.

“Your story,” she says, “it just makes me miss my family.” I put my hand on her shoulder. I want to tell her that we’ll go get her brother tomorrow. Preparations can be made in the morning. However, before I can speak, Calla breaks in. “Well, looks like I owe you one secret. A deal’s a deal.” She disappears from the balcony back into her room and reappears holding a paper folded in half, exactly like the one she had given the bald man earlier. When I unfold it, it reads: ‘your name’.

“I don’t get it,” I say.

“My exact words to him were, ‘If I can write your name on this piece of paper, then we go free, and I did. I wrote ‘your name,’” she says with a laugh. Suddenly, I’m amazed by the simplicity of the trick. How had I not seen it?

“Clever,” I say as I hand the paper back to her.

"Thanks," she replies. "Although it's just never as impressive once it's explained." Neither of us speaks for a minute. "Do I really glow?" asked Calla.

"Will you marry me?"

"What?" says Calla.

"Marry me, Calla," I say. "Listen, I'm not totally sure about this either, but just look at the reasons for and against. If you marry me, there's a chance it could break the curse, and if we break the curse, then I'm that much safer going on a quest to bring back your brother. It seems like you're going to be staying here long-term anyway. Please say something."

"You know your mom came in here to talk to me before you did?" she says.

"Oh no. I'm sorry. She means well. I can talk to her."

"No," says Calla, "she was sweet. She said almost the same thing you did. About the rationale for getting married, that is. She's also worried about you, and she thinks this could be your only chance."

"Calla," I say, "I don't want you to feel like you—"

"Yes," says Calla.

"What?" I ask.

"Yes, I'll marry you," says Calla. I watch as a soft smile slowly spreads across her face. "Yes."

"Really?" I say. "And this is because you want to? Not because you feel like you have to?"

Calla laughs and wipes her eyes. "Yes," she says. "Yes, I want to marry you."

I run forward, pick her up, and spin her around. "This is great! This is amazing, well . . . come on," I say, "let's go tell the team."

9

Mom wasn't as thrilled as I expected her to be about the wedding announcement. She smiled and squeezed Calla's hands and did all the right things, but her smile didn't quite reach her eyes. I think it's because she's finally starting to suspect, as am I, that the curse isn't breakable, at least not in the way that we thought. A part of me is glad she's starting to accept it, but I'm also worried about what giving up on breaking the curse will mean for her.

"What about you?" Bevin asks Calla as she, Calla, Aydin, and I gather in the kitchen later that night. It has to be approaching 1 in the morning, but none of us can sleep after the night we've had. Calla and I look at each other and shrug.

"We're happy? I think?" I say.

"It's been a bit of a whirlwind," says Calla.

"You know what I think about this," says Aydin, "but I don't think Aunt Laurel would have let Calla stay here if this wasn't happening, and I don't want her thrown out." He reaches over and squeezes Calla's hand. She looks surprised and squeezes his back.

"Thanks, Aydin," she says. She looks genuinely touched, and her eyes start to fill with tears. I put my hand on the small of her back and feel her lean towards me slightly. Bevin yawns and rests her head in her hands.

"Alright," she says, "I think I'm going to try and get some sleep. If that's even possible."

"Right behind you," says Aydin, as we all clean up and head up to bed.

Calla hesitates outside my door instead of walking on toward her room.

"You alright?" I ask. She glances over her shoulder.

"I'm fine," she says, "just not sleeping well." She stays hovering in the doorway.

"Do you . . . do you want to come in?" I ask, holding my breath.

"Yes!" she says. I've never had a woman in my room before, so logically, I feel like I should be nervous, but now that Calla knows she's welcome in here, her sense of ease is contagious. Although any questions or hopes about what her intentions are in coming here are immediately put to rest when she climbs into my bed, snuggles into the blankets, and closes her eyes. By the time I change clothes and put everything away, her slow breathing tells me she's fast asleep. As I look down at her, I feel a rush of affection that surprises me in its intensity.

The space between us feels electrified when I climb into the bed next to her. I'm not sure what the etiquette is in this situation. A beautiful woman, who is technically my fiancée, I suppose, has just come into my room and climbed into my bed. Everything in me wants to reach out and touch her, but I'm still not sure how she would feel about that. Before I can decide what to do, she seems to sense me in bed next to her and scoots closer to me. I drape my arm over her and finally feel myself falling asleep.

***

"Tyre." This time, I know the voice immediately.

"You," I say. I'm back in the dying rose garden. I try to look around this time to see if I can actually figure out where I am.

"Are you ready to make a trade?" it says.

"You. Can't. Have. Her." I growl.

"Oh, I know," says the shadow. "In fact, I hear congratulations are in order."

I know it's pointless, but I can't stop myself from asking, "How do you know that?"

"Magic, remember? It's one of the few things people know about me. I'm the only human who can use magic."

"So, that at least is true then?" I say.

"Yes," it says, "that at least is true." There's a long silence, and even though I can't see a face, I can feel the shadow watching me. It's clear that the next move is mine.

"If I try to touch you again, will I wake up?" I say.

"No idea," says the shadow, resuming its silent stare. I debate the outcome of just walking away. Maybe if I explore, I can really figure out where I am when I'm in this abandoned place. Ultimately, I decide it's wiser to see what I can learn from The Inimical for now, and I know the question that will move this conversation forward.

"You said you want to make a trade, so what is it that you want?" I ask. As soon as I ask, I feel the medallion start to glow warmer on my chest. I suddenly feel more aware that I'm dreaming, almost like I could wake up if I wanted to, but the shadows get darker too. The air around me feels colder as the shadow floats closer.

"You already know," it says.

"Me," I say, "you want me."

"Yes," it says. "You can come to me in Andestine, or I think I've made it clear what I can do to Calla."

I almost laugh internally. Little does he know, he's about to get his wish as we begin preparing to rescue Calla's brother.

"What do you do with the people you take?" I say.

"Do you think you'd take my deal if you knew?"

"I'm taking your deal either way."

"Really? Well, call me a skeptic, but until you actually show up, I think you'll find Calla's fragile state of well-being remains an excellent insurance policy." I'm about to respond when I hear my name being called somewhere in the distance.

"That's not me," says the shadow when I look back at it, "better go handle whoever has snuck into your room tonight."

"I appreciate your concern," I say flatly. The dream is already fading as the sounds in the waking world get louder.

"I need you alive," the shadow hisses as the last of the dream fades away, and I startle awake.

***

"Tyre," the voice whispers. I stay as still as I can in my bed, trying to figure out as much as I can before this intruder realizes I'm awake. It's a woman, but not a voice I recognize. I keep my eyes shut and listen, trying to sense movement, waiting for the right moment.

"Tyre," the voice says again. The sensation of a hand brushing against my shoulder makes me jump. I swing my arm in the direction of the sounds and hear someone fall backwards, hitting the wall with a thump. As quickly as I can, I light the lamp on my bedside table. When I swing it to face the wall, I see that there, crumpled on the ground, is . . . a fairy. Not just any fairy— *the* fairy. She looks exactly the same as she did when I was 11.

"Tyre," she says again, "Tyre, please—" Suddenly, I know nothing but blind rage as I jump out of bed and grab the fairy by the arm. Her screams echo as I throw open the door to my room and drag her into the hall, throwing her forward onto the ground in front of me.

"How dare you come here!" I yell.

"Please," cries the fairy, "you'll wake the rest of the house."

"Good!" I yell. "Let them all wake up! I'd love for them to hear what I have to say to you!" As the fairy lay crumbled on the ground in front of me, sobbing, I hear the sounds of the rest of the house waking up.

"Tyre!" A voice comes from down the hall, and I see Mom rushing towards me with Bevin and Aydin following. No doubt, Calla and Maddie will appear soon as well. Wait . . . Calla. Was she not next to me when I woke up? Would she have gone back to her room? Why?

"What . . . ?" Mom stops suddenly as she starts to realize what she's seeing. Bevin and Aydin are frozen in terror.

"What do you want here?" I growl.

"Well, it's obvious, isn't it?" says Mom, "She's here to lift the curse!"

"Well?" I say. "Is that it? Are you here to lift the curse?"

"I . . ."

"That's a 'no'," I say. "I ask again, what do you want here?"

She clenches her teeth and smears her hand across her face to wipe away tears. For the first time, I really look at her. Her clothes are torn, her hair filthy and matted, and she has no color, as if she hasn't seen the sun for weeks. Her wings are tucked neatly into her back, but I see a tear on one of them.

"I come to ask, to plead," she says, "for your help." Rage fills me again.

"Why," I say, through clenched teeth, "would we ever help you?"

"I have nowhere else to turn," she says. "Please."

"What exactly," says Bevin, "is it that you think we can help you with?"

"I was kidnapped! Taken by—" Suddenly, the fairy makes a horrible retching sound as if there's something caught in her throat. She starts coughing and then sobbing again. "My kidnapper cursed me so I can't speak," she sobs. "I can't say anything that my kidnapper doesn't want me to."

"The Inimical," I say, instantly, "is that who took you?" The fairy only continues to sob. "I have no wish to help you," I say, "but if I did, what could I do?" The fairy opens her mouth, but no sound comes out. "This is a waste of time," I say. "You can't speak and, as I've said, I have no desire to help you. Get out."

"Wait," says Bevin, "if you were kidnapped, how are you here now? Did you escape?"

"No," whispers the fairy. "My captor is away. I was able to slip through the magic used to bind me and come here, but it drains my strength. Even now, it compels me back. I won't be able to hold it much longer. Please," she says.

"Well," says Mom, "it looks to me like an exchange of information might be arranged. As you can see, your little curse has been playing some tricks with my family. Perhaps if you can tell us why the curse on my son hasn't broken despite him being recently engaged, we might be able to find a way to help you. Why hasn't the curse broken?" Again, the fairy tries to speak, but no sound comes out. She looks desperately back and forth between all the faces in the room.

"You can't tell us how to break the curse?" says Bevin.

"No," whispers the fairy.

"Why?" says Bevin.

"Isn't it obvious?" said Aydin. "The Inimical wants Tyre like this. No magic to drain off him if the curse is broken."

"You're useless to us," I say to the fairy.

"You can't help me now," she says, "but soon, you will need to face my kidnapper. I will help you to do this, and then you will help me by defeating my kidnapper."

"How are you going to do that?" I ask. "I'm sure he's forbidden you from sharing any information that could actually be helpful."

"With a riddle," she says.

"We aren't here to play games and tell riddles."

"Where do shadows come from?" she yells.

"Where do shadows come from? That's the riddle?" I say.

"Yes!"

"I'm done with this."

"It doesn't matter," says the fairy. "I've said what I came to say. I can't stay any longer." Just like that, she starts to fade away.

"Wait!" yelled Mom. "Wait! The wedding, will it break the curse?"

The fairy opens her mouth like she wants to say something, but whatever power holds her stops her. "No," she finally says.

"What? Why?" asks Mom.

"Love cannot live where there is no trust," answers the fairy, as she fades away completely.

We all stand in silence, and my heart races.

"What? What does that mean?" says Bevin, "Love cannot live where there's no trust?"

"I don't know," I say.

"I do," says Mom. We all spin to look at her. "I know that that fairy didn't know what she was talking about when she cursed my little boy, and she doesn't know now. I'm done with waiting for her to solve this problem. Tyre," says Mom, "you're right. You've been right for a long time now. Tomorrow, we begin preparing to take the fight to Mark."

"Woo!" Aydin cheers. I walk over and wrap my mom in a hug so big that it lifts her off her feet.

"Tyre, I can't breathe; put me down," she says. I give her one last squeeze and set her on her feet.

"What's happening?" Calla wanders out of my room and into the hallway, rubbing her eyes. Had she been there all along?

"Well . . ." says Bevin.

"I'll explain in the morning," I say. I walk over and throw my arm around Calla's shoulders as we all make our way back to our rooms.

Once I'm finally tucked back in bed, with Calla's long, even breaths telling me that she's fallen back asleep, I lie down on my pillow and feel something hard pressing into the side of my head. Under the pillow is a note scribbled in a hand I don't recognize on top of a plain brown box. The note reads: *'In case you need it,'* and is signed *'—Briowney 'The Fairy.''* I lift the lid off the box to reveal a thin silver knife and a single long, white candle. As I pick them both up to examine them, I realize there doesn't seem to be anything extraordinary about either of them. Why would the fairy— Briowney, apparently— think that I'll need these? Probably for the same reason, she speaks in riddles and can't lift the curse. She's altogether useless.

***

The next morning, I feel like there's sandpaper in my mouth, and my head feels heavy. It's early, but I can already tell there's no point in trying to go back to sleep. I roll over and try not to wake Calla as I get out of bed and make my way down to the kitchen. Last time I was up this early, Maddie had already put on a pot of coffee. Hoping for a repeat, I'm disheartened to find I'm out of luck and the kitchen is empty. Mom shuffles in a few minutes later.

"Couldn't sleep in either?" she asks, and I shake my head 'no.'

"I was thinking," she says, "it might be a good idea to go through some of your dad's old books from Clocks."

"What for?" I ask, thinking about the pile of his old books already on my desk that I've been using to try to interpret my dreams.

"We'll need to figure out what to bring. What might be helpful against something like The Inimical?"

"We also probably need to find out more about The Inimical himself," I say. I step around her to start making the coffee. "I'll write to provinces on the Andestine border today to ask for more information. I think you need to prepare for the possibility that no one has any more information than what we already know."

"Well, look at you deciding what would be best for me," she laughs. "When did you get so old? When did I get so old?" She looks down at her hands with her fingers spread on the counter.

"You're not so old," I say.

"Well, I hope not," she says, smiling, "with this big journey we have coming." A pit forms in my stomach. A part of me knew this conversation was coming, and here it is.

"Mom," I say, as gently as I can, "you know you're not coming with me, right?"

"I know," she whispers as I pull her into a hug.

"I know Thiaghal will be in good hands while I'm gone," I say.

***

"And then," I say, towing Calla through the garden by hand, "she said, *'love cannot live where there is no trust'*." Calla follows along behind me, tilting her face up and enjoying the first sunny day we've had in a while. I don't blame her; it's warmer in Andestine, and I've wondered how she's been coping with the Thiaghal cold. She frowns when I finish the story.

"So," she says, "what do you think it means? That we haven't known each other long enough to establish real trust?"

"I trust you," I say with a shrug. Calla squeezes my hand. "And if that's it, why couldn't she just say that? It must be more complicated than that." I can practically feel Calla's brain whirring next to me.

"How do you feel about it?" she asks. "About the idea that the curse won't be broken by the wedding?"

"Having second thoughts?" I ask.

"Honestly, no," she says, smiling. "Your mom is right. It's not like you're in a position to be casually attached to anyone. Anyone you're involved with will automatically be serious, Governor Sylvan."

"And we seem to be involved," I say, looking down at our interlocked hands.

"Seems that way," says Calla, smiling up at me as I pull her in to kiss her. I can feel her still smiling in the middle of our kiss. When we finally break apart, many minutes later, I remember that we're supposed to be talking about wedding details.

"How do you feel about having the wedding here?" I ask. Mom has already sprung that she wants to have it in two weeks.

"As opposed to?" says Calla, looking confused.

"In Andestine."

"You'd have the wedding in Andestine?" she says, looking genuinely touched.

"It would be harder," I say, "but if it means a lot to you?"

"It doesn't," she says suddenly, before softening her tone again, "but thank you." I'm suddenly overwhelmed by the feeling again that Calla's life is disappearing into mine. She's only been here two months, and if we get married here, she won't have time to get anything imported from Andestine. She'll wear a dress from Thiaghal and have food from Thiaghal. She seems fine with everything, but can she really be happy?

"Calla," I say, pulling her around to face me, "the second we're married, we'll go get your brother. My mom dug out a bunch of Dad's old books and papers from Clocks. There's got to be something that will help us understand what The Inimical is and how to stop him. Or maybe it? I'm not entirely sure."

"You think I could have a look at those?" she says.

"This? This is what you care about? I've been trying to get you to talk about wedding flower designs for 30 minutes this morning, and this is the first time you've looked interested in something?"

"What can I say," says Calla, "got to keep you on your toes—" The end of her sentence is cut off by a sneeze. When I turn around, I see the ground is flecked with blood.

"Calla!" I yell. She presses her hand to her nose and doubles over, holding her stomach.

"I'm fine," she says, still doubled over.

"You still want to tell me The Inimical has nothing to do with you?" I say. She takes the handkerchief I offer and presses it to her nose. Gradually, the pain in her stomach seems to let up, and she stands up straight again. It's only now that I'm so focused on her that I see she has dark circles under her eyes. I brush one gently with the back of my claw.

"Not sleeping well," she says, "nightmares."

"Come on," I say, wrapping my arm around her shoulders, "let's get you inside."

***

A few days ago, I sent out requests for updated information about The Inimical and information about Senzicaria with the Holpies. The Holpies took the request to the Andestine border and trotted back to the house this morning with a stack of documents. Unfortunately, these documents are all about Senzicaria. Even though the Holpies can't talk, I can tell that they haven't been fond of collecting the health data. I open the massive packet of the latest health data from the province-wide census and adjust my position on the sofa. It all needs to be reviewed before the council meeting this afternoon.

One of the main reasons that I'm working from the library instead of my office and a sofa instead of a desk this afternoon is that Calla is lying on the other end of the couch, reading with her feet on my lap. She seems to have stopped bleeding and isn't doubled over in pain anymore. She's lost in her book with her eyebrows knit together, brushing a piece of her hair back and forth across her lips.

"What are you reading?" I ask.

"Stop procrastinating your work," she says. A few seconds of silence go by. "Fine," she says, in response to my persistent stare. She smiles and holds up her book. "I think it's one of your dad's old textbooks from Clocks."

"Hm. *A Complete History of Andestine Plant Life.* Riveting."

"Oh, so what are you reading that's so fascinating?" she says. I hold up the massive envelope.

"Health data on something called *Senzicaria*," I say.

"Actually, do you mind if I take a look at that?" she says. She sits up and climbs onto my legs while reaching for the file.

"Sure, help yourself, I guess?" I say, handing it over, pressing my free hand into her hip to keep her from falling off the sofa. "Have you heard of Senzicaria?"

"I have. It's a bigger problem in Andestine," she says. Her eyes are already locked on the first page of the report, reading faster than I thought was possible. After a few minutes, her expression relaxes.

"Doesn't seem to have any presence in Thiaghal," she says, easing back on the couch.

"Great news," I say as I pick up her feet and put them back in my lap. "Back to your textbook, leisure reading." She laughs and picks the book up, but doesn't open it again.

"I went there, you know," she says.

"Hm," I say, looking up from the budgets I've picked up. I think I must have heard her wrong for a second. "You went to Clockwork Atheneum?"

"I did," she says, still looking down at her book.

"Hey," says Bevin, knocking on the door.

"Hey," says Calla. "You alright, Bev?" Bevin shakes her head.

"Have either of you seen Maddie today?" she asks. We both shake our heads 'no.'

"I can't find her," she says. "I know it's silly; she might have gone into town or something, but I've looked everywhere, and she's not here. She never really makes her bed, but it doesn't look like it's been slept in. It's exactly the way that it was when we were all getting ready in her room last night." Calla and I glance at each other, then back at Bevin. I don't want to scare Bevin, and while it's true that Maddie could have gone into town or just been holed up drawing somewhere in the house, something doesn't feel right.

"We'll help you look," says Calla, standing up immediately. As we walk through the house to find Aydin, Bevin explains where she's already looked. We find my mom and Aydin, and after another hour of searching, we confirm that Maddie is definitely not anywhere in the house. Later, when the sun starts to go down, Bevin is approaching panic, and Mom isn't doing much better.

"Where would she go for this long?!" says Bevin. "Why wouldn't she tell anyone?"

Calla and Aydin are both sitting shoulder to shoulder on the living room sofa, and Mom is staring into the fire.

I've sent a Holpie to Sheriff Murchad, and we're just waiting for him to make his way up to the house. A blizzard has started, and we all know that that means he won't make it up to the house until there's more light to navigate by tomorrow. There's nothing else to be done, yet no one seems able to face going to bed. This is exactly the type of situation for which Maddie's presence is required. We need her to say something silly and snarky and let the tense air out of the room.

"Where could she be?" whispers Mom to no one in particular.

I carry Bevin up to bed after she falls asleep in the armchair by the fire with tears still streaked down her face. Calla follows soon after. Mom and Aydin are still downstairs staring into the fire, but I can't sit in silence anymore and make my way back to my room.

"Hey," says Calla. I almost jump out of my fur when I open the door and find Calla perched on the bed.

"Calla," I sigh, "you scared me."

"Sorry," she says. "Just wanted to see how you're holding up." I collapse face down onto the bed.

"That well, huh?" says Calla. She flops down next to me on her back. "And you have no idea where she would have gone? There isn't some guy in town? Someone she snuck out to meet up with him and then got snowed in?"

“She’d send a message,” I say. “The Holpies can get through anything, and it’s not like she would have had to hide it. We would have been fine with her meeting up with a guy. A girl. Anyone. She’s just been so secretive lately.” I tell Calla about the letters, Maddie suddenly wanting to go to Clocks, and Maddie asking about the old stories we used to tell about the Eldrida Hero. Calla is a good listener. She nods in all the right places, and the more I talk, the more concerned she looks.

“You never saw one of the letters?” she asks.

“No, and wherever she went, she took her sketchpad with her; it’s the first thing I checked.”

***

I don’t notice myself getting tired, but I must have fallen asleep, because I’m suddenly back in the abandoned rose garden, feeling The Inimical’s gaze on the back of my neck.

“I told you I’d take your deal,” I say, as I turn to face him.

“Not what I’m here to discuss,” he says. “I’m calling a truce.”

“What? Why?”

“I hear you have a missing person,” it says.

“You!” I scream. The thought had been hovering, unwelcome, banished in the back of my mind all day. The Inimical had no reason to take Maddie. I’d taken his deal; it already had some sick control over Calla, and Maddie wasn’t altered by fairy magic. “If you so much as look the wrong way at Maddie,” I yell, as I storm toward the shadow. It disappears and reappears behind me.

“I didn’t take your silver-haired pseudo-sibling,” he says.

“I don’t believe you,” I say.

"I am trying to help you," he yells as the entire garden shakes. I pause. This is the first time that The Inimical has ever shown any emotion besides cool condescension.

"Why?" I say, breathing hard. "Why would you help me?" It stays quiet. "Do you know?" I say. "If you didn't take Maddie, do you know who did?"

"Oh, are you asking for my *help*?" hisses the shadow. I don't grace it with a response. "Maybe," it says after a few minutes, "I have my suspicions. However, if I'm wrong, it will cost you time and resources. I'll share if I find out that I'm right."

"Just tell me!" I roar in frustration.

"No," says the shadow, "but I'll do this for you. I'll leave Calla alone until you can locate the runt of the litter."

"What?" I pause, trying to catch my breath. "Why? I ask again, "Why are you helping? Why do you care about Maddie?"

"I don't hurt kids," says the shadow, its voice almost indifferent. I can see his shoulders shrug underneath the massive cloak.

"Oh, right," I say, letting out what I'm sure is a deranged laugh. "You don't hurt kids; well, that makes perfect sense." Before I can finish the thought, I'm back in my bed with my eyes fluttering open. I press my hand to my forehead. Light is streaming in through the windows, and I can hear Calla's even breathing next to me. I hear a soft knock on the door, and Mom pokes her head in.

"Tyre, the sheriff is here." She pauses when she sees Calla asleep next to me. "Hm," she says, "well, if you weren't getting married before, you certainly are now." I feel an overwhelming sense of relief that Mom is up and joking, because that means this thing with Maddie hasn't broken her. I swing my legs over the side of the bed.

"Cal, Calla, we fell asleep," I say, nudging her shoulder.

"I'm up," she says. She is not.

"I'm heading down to talk to the sheriff," I say. This does finally get her attention.

"Alright. I'm really up; I'm going with you," she says.

Bevin, Aydin, and Mom are already seated in the living room when Calla and I come down a minute later. Sheriff Murchad is sipping coffee in the armchair closest to the fire. He nods to us as we come in and sit down. He breathes out a long sigh as he sets his coffee cup down on the table. "So, my understanding is that we're looking for Miss Madeliza Ruarcc?" he says.

"Yes," says Bevin, "I'm her sister and guardian, Bevin Ruarcc."

"I know who you are, Miss Bevin, don't you worry," he says, smiling kindly at Bevin. He runs his hand through his hair.

"Well, I wasn't able to get up here until this morning," he says, looking out at the still howling storm, "but I was able to make some inquiries in town after I got the message, and I'm happy to report that I do have some news for you." Mom puts down her coffee cup, and every eye in the room is, if possible, even more glued to him. It feels like no one breathes. Even Calla is locked in, with that same laser focus that I've come to associate with textbook reading. The sheriff pulls out an old notebook.

"She was seen around 2 in the morning last night," he says. "Looks like Brogan was shutting down the bar, and he got a look at her. He didn't think much of it, since you all had been in earlier in the evening. He thought you must have stayed in town, gone somewhere else, or maybe she was heading home for the night."

"Alone at 2 in the morning?" I say, an unfair swirl of anger forming in my stomach. If only Brogan had realized something was wrong and said something sooner.

"Well," says Murchad, "that's just it. She wasn't alone. I think Brogan must have assumed she was with one of you all. Once he realized something was wrong, he thought about it and admitted that it might have been a stranger. The more he thought about it, the more he thought he might actually recognize the person she was with from the pub."

"Someone else from the pub?" says Aydin. "There's no one else there that we would have talked to. I mean, we're friendly with some folks from town. Maddie is friends with some of the local teenagers, but there was no one else we knew there that night. Was there? Bevin? Tyre?"

I shake my head.

"No," says Bevin, "no, I would have known if one of her friends had been there. There was no one we knew well."

"Did Brogan give a description?" asks Calla. Murchad looks back at his notes. A man with a cloak on, and he didn't get a good look at his face or hair because of the cloak, but he noticed the clothes didn't look like Thiaghal clothes. They were . . ."

"Worn leather," I say, putting some pieces together.

"That's right," says Murchad, his eyes narrowing in suspicion as he looks at me. "Tyre, what do you know about this?" I had forgotten for a second that Murchad thinks I'm a monster. I resist the urge to snarl at him for the insinuation that I would have any part in hurting Maddie.

"I met him at the bar," I explain, "getting a round of drinks. I noticed his clothes: all worn leather with weapons in his belt. I thought he might be a vampire hunter passing through."

"Did you get his name?" asks Bevin.

"Not his full name, but he said his name was Meltair. He said he was in town because . . . shit, he said he was in town because he was meeting someone." Bevin, Aydin, and Mom look horrified. I'm so focused on them, I don't notice that Calla has gone rigid beside me.

"Say that again," she says.

"What?" I say. "The name? It's— Calla, are you okay?"

"Just need to make sure I heard you right," she says.

“Meltair,” I say. Calla stands up and hurls a coffee cup from the table across the room, where it shatters against the fireplace. Bevin screams.

“Oh, my!” yells Mom.

At the same time, Aydin yells, “Shit! Calla!”

Even Murchad looks startled.

“Meltair,” says Calla, “Delanun Meltair. The headmaster of Clockwork Atheneum.”

I feel like my stomach has dropped out through a hole in the ground.

“Fuck,” says Bevin, putting her head in her hands. “You’re telling me she took off with the headmaster of the death school she’s been obsessed with for the past few weeks?”

“What? Clockwork Atheneum?” says Mom, struggling to catch up. “Everyone, just calm down, and someone explain to me what’s happening.”

“Maddie has been talking about going to Clocks,” I say.

“What?” says Mom. “If she wanted to go to boarding school, we could have . . . Clocks? Why?”

“Because of me!” I yell. “Because she wants to protect me from The Inimical.” All I want to do is throw a coffee cup, sending it crashing into the fireplace the way Calla did.

“Tyre,” says Bevin through her tears, “we don’t know that that’s why. She never said.”

“What else could it be?” I say. “This all started after The Inimical attacked us.”

“I’m sorry she ran off like this,” says Murchad, “I really am.” To his credit, he does look sorry. “But it looks like you know where she is, so . . . ”

“Sheriff Murchad,” says Mom, “you can’t seriously be saying there’s nothing else you can do. A child has been abducted by . . . well, if he’s the headmaster of Clocks, then he's not exactly a teenager, is he?" She looks at Calla.

"Early 30's," says Calla.

Mom looks even more horrified than she had before.

"A teenage Thiaghal girl has been abducted by a 30-year-old man from Lytwist, and you don't think the law should have something to say about that?"

"Maybe it should," he says, "but if she's at Clocks, there's no getting her back. They have their own laws there."

"She's not at Clocks yet," says Bevin, "that's at least a three-day journey, and that's if they were to travel non-stop without sleeping."

"It's true," he says, "but they're ahead of the storm, and no one can travel in this. If this storm is as predicted, Miss Madeliza will have been at Clocks for at least two weeks before you can even think about following her. We all sit in stunned silence as Murchad gathers his things and puts on his coat. He pauses one more time at the door. "I'm sorry," he says, "I really am."

The words land like ice in my stomach. It sounds like what someone would say at a funeral. The sound of the door closing echoes in the silence after he leaves.

"Bevin," says Calla. Bevin's eyes dart up to meet hers. "You searched Maddie's room yesterday, right?"

"Yes," says Bevin, "just to look for tickets or notes, or anything that might show where she had gone."

"Mind if we look again?" asks Calla. Bevin nods. We all follow Calla up to Maddie's room.

"What are you thinking, Calla?" I ask as she opens the door with calm determination.

"Bevin, pull up the floorboards," Calla says. "Aydin, tap the walls for loose stones. Tyre, try to lift and shake all the furniture to see if any secret compartments spring open."

I'm reminded of the night of the party when Calla rescued me from my conversation with Ms. Carlon, and the night she rescued us from the ruffians after the pub. There's something almost militaristic about her focus. Mom watches in shock as Bevin, Aydin, and I tear apart Maddie's room as thoroughly as we can.

"I've got something!" Aydin calls. We look over to see him removing a stone from the wall.

Calla sweeps over to it, and Aydin stands aside to let her pass. She reaches in and finds a huge packet of letters tied together with old ribbon. She sets the pile down on the bed and gently unties it. Then she picks up the first letter and begins to read.

After skimming the first letter, she hands the stack to Bevin with shaking hands and storms out of the room. I hear her slam her hand into the stone wall of the hallway as she leaves. I turn my eyes back to Bevin.

"Well," I say, "what—?" Bevin holds up her hand, quieting my question.

"Shit," she finally whispers.

I've never seen Bevin this angry. She finally holds the stack out to me, and I begin to read.

10

Letter from Delanum Meltair to Maddie Ruarcc, dated six months earlier.

Madeliza,

I was thrilled to hear from you after our chance meeting in Lytwist this summer. It's so rare that we have visitors on the Clockwork Atheneum grounds. Even if you were just lost, it was a delight to meet you, and an honor to escort you to the cafe where you were meeting your sister.

As I said, I'm thrilled to see that you've taken me up on my offer of correspondence. When I met you last month, I had a good feeling about you as soon as I saw you on the Clockwork Atheneum grounds. I hope you don't mind my saying so, but you looked very at home there! I would love to tell you more about Clockwork Atheneum if you ever want to hear about it, but, for now, I look forward to our continued correspondence.

Delanum Meltair

Headmaster, Clockwork Atheneum

Letter from Delanum Meltair to Maddie Ruarcc, dated one week earlier.

Madeliza,

The arrangements have been made. We leave from the Holpie's Mane as soon as you can get away on the night of the next waning gibbous moon. I'll be there to escort you, no matter the time of night. You won't regret this, Maddie. Based on our correspondence, I have every reason to think that the power you hold could be immense. I don't want to get ahead of myself, but you know I feel that it is my sworn duty to find the one who will fulfill the prophecy, the one destined to hold off a great evil. With The Inimical practically at the gates, the timing could not be more urgent. Madeliza, you've shown your maturity throughout our correspondence, and I think you can handle it when I say, there is every chance that you are that person— the one destined to defeat The Inimical. You'll need help, and I am honored to be the one to help you. Congratulations on this momentous decision, Madeliza. I'll see you soon, and I can't wait to show the world what you can do.

Delanum Meltair
Headmaster, Clockwork Atheneum

***

I flip through the rest of the stack and notice that not all the paper has the same texture. Instead of the silky texture of Meltair's stationery, some of the paper has a rough texture similar to the paper in Maddie's sketchbook. I recognize her loopy handwriting in what looks like drafts of letters Maddie has written to Meltair.

~~Hi~~

Hello ~~Mr~~.(?). Meltair (~~Delanun?~~),

~~I can't believe that you wrote to~~

- - -

It's good to hear from you, too! It was great meeting you this summer. Thanks again for helping me out and for telling me about Clockwork Atheneum. ~~*Do you really think*~~ *I've been thinking about what you said, about the work you do, trying to find the person destined to hold back the dark. To be honest, I haven't been able to stop thinking about it.* ~~*And I've been thinking a lot about you too.*~~ *And what you said about how it was a coincidence, my turning up on campus. I've been wondering if there's anything to it. And wondering if maybe it wasn't a coincidence running into you. Tell me about you? What is it like at Clocks? What I mean is, what is it like for you at Clocks? What is it like to be the headmaster of a school like that?*

Madeliza

There are doodles along the sides of the paper. Nothing as simple or as silly as hearts in the margins or an elaborately written "Mrs. Maddie Meltair." Maddie is too smart for that. However, there are places where she's traced over the letters in his name, clearly thinking about what to write. I'm realizing how wrong I've been, and that Maddie's sudden obsession with Clocks has had nothing to do with me at all. With that comes a new wave of realization that we've all been so caught up in me and The Inimical that we've neglected Maddie. We've been treating her like she's an adult, and not a 15-year-old who needed supervision and support. Now she's run off to a dangerous school because of a crush on someone who's probably in charge of recruiting hundreds of students each year. I hand the stack of letters and drafts to my mom and Aydin to let them inevitably come to the same conclusion, and, like Calla only a few minutes earlier, I storm into the hallway.

I don't really have anywhere to go, and end up in my room. It seems as good a place as any to get some space and try to think about what to do. I throw a pillow across the room, and I like the way that it feels so much that

I throw a book, and then everything I can get my hands on is a projectile until even my desk itself goes sailing across the room, landing with a crash that echoes through the house.

"Tyre!" I feel Calla's hands on my shoulders, but I don't care. I reach for the chair that goes with my desk. "Tyre!" she yells again, "Hey!" She pulls me around to face her.

"Let me go!" I try to pull out of her grasp, but she's locked her hands around my wrists.

"Tyre," she commands again. This time, I meet her eyes and struggle to hold back tears.

"We should have watched her," I say. Calla pulls me into a hug, and I sob, not caring who sees or hears. "Kids train to go to Clocks from toddlerhood. She hasn't. Now she's run off to a school with a reputation for danger, in a different country, following after a 30-year-old man we know nothing about. How could I let this happen?!"

"Tyre, it's not your fault."

"It *is* my fault," I yell, stepping back from Calla. "The safety of everyone who lives in this house is my responsibility."

"Tyre!" yells Calla. "We will go get her."

"What?"

"I went to Clocks. I know Meltair. We will go, and we will get her," she says.

"But Calla, your brother—"

"Is stable," she says, "and I have a way to monitor him. The mirror, remember? I've already started writing down everything I remember about Clocks and Meltair, and if we leave as soon as the storm is over—"

Before she can finish the sentence, I push her up against the wall and kiss her. She kisses back with an intensity that I've never felt from anyone before and pulls me towards her with a hand on the back of my neck. When we finally break apart, I pull her into my chest and hold on for dear life.

"Thank you," I whisper into her dark hair. She says nothing, but I feel her tighten her grip around my waist. When she pulls away, her eyes are red, but she quickly wipes them.

"Come on," she says. "It looks like everyone needs a basic introduction to Delanum Meltair."

11

"Delanum Meltair is a self-important, egotistical, fool," says Calla. Aydin raises his hand as if to ask a question, and I reach across and lower it so Calla can keep talking. The stress of the situation has finally caught up with Mom, and she's meeting with the rest of the Thiaghal council in the dining room to discuss temporarily taking back the governorship under the circumstances so we can travel to Lytwist.

"What does he want with Maddie?" says Bevin. "Is he actually interested in her, like, romantically, the way she seems to be in him?"

"No," says Calla, "he's a predator, but not that kind of predator. Meltair is obsessed with the Eldrida Prophecy."

"The Eldrida Prophecy?" says Aydin.

Something pulls at the back of my memory. I feel like I can vaguely remember my dad talking about the Eldrida Prophecy when I was a kid, and then I remember that Maddie asked me about it only a few weeks ago. It's one of those things we told stories about, like the Eldrida Hero or where the Holpies came from.

"My dad would talk about that," I say, "and Maddie reminded me of it just a couple of weeks ago. Almine Eldrida. He was some kind of oracle who had a really excellent success rate for his premonitions coming true. Most of them were about small things, what the weather would be like at sea, for example."

“Since when do you know so much about this?” asks Bevin. “Maddie only ever wanted to hear about the Eldrida Hero. I didn’t even know there was a prophecy.”

“I don’t know,” I say. “I guess this must be from when I was really little, before you and your family moved in with us. I’d forgotten how many stories Dad used to tell from what he learned at Clocks.”

“So?” says Aydin. “I assume the Eldrida Prophecy wasn't about the weather at sea for a year, or how harsh the winter would be?”

“Eldrida,” says Calla, “had a strong premonition of doom. He said there would be an unseen force that would exact an incredible death toll if not contained, and that it could not be totally prevented, but it could be stopped by the right person. He was also a professor at Clocks at the time, and Meltair’s grandfather became obsessed with him and with the idea that, as headmaster of Clockwork Atheneum, it was his responsibility to find the person who would stop the unseen doom and prepare them. To be honest . . . ” she hesitates.

“What is it, Calla?” I ask. “If it could help Maddie, we need to know.”

“To be honest,” she says, “towards the end of his life, it seemed that he was quite mentally ill. He had become obsessed with stopping the Eldrida Prophecy, and with the idea that only he and his family line could. Based on my extensive research, there doesn’t seem to be any evidence for that conclusion other than self-aggrandizement. However, Meltair doesn’t see it that way. His grandfather ingrained it into his father that their family had the great responsibility of finding and training the hero of the Eldrida prophecy and stopping the era of death by an unseen force. Meltair’s father then went on to engrain that into Meltair.”

“Death by unseen force,” I say, as a realization washes over me. “It’s The Inimical. The Eldrida Prophecy is about The Inimical.” Calla frowns and is about to respond when Bevin speaks up.

"But how does any of this help us with Maddie?" she says.

"Meltair recruits young, impressionable people to Clockwork Atheneum in hordes," says Calla. "He seems to think it's a numbers game and that if he just recruits and brutally trains as many people as possible, he'll increase his odds of finding and training the Eldrida Hero. And," she hesitates again, "I don't want to make the situation worse, but the rumors about Clocks are true. In fact, its reputation in Thiaghal is probably tame compared to its reputation in Lytwist."

"What is its reputation in Lytwist?" I ask, tightening my grip on my chair.

"People in Lytwist largely know the truth. That Clocks is prestigious, internationally respected, and, well, dangerous. Kids really do die at Clocks sometimes. The training is brutal, and they can't just leave, even if they want to. In fact, kids die at Clocks somewhat frequently."

My urge to vomit is tempered only by my disbelief. Sure, we all like to joke about Clocks and its dark reputation. But my assumption has always been that everyone jokes about Clocks being so dangerous, and that there are student injuries, or even deaths, maybe *sometimes*, but to call them *frequent* . . .

Bevin looks like she might pass out.

Aydin speaks before I can.

"That can't be true," he says. "There's no way a school that regularly kills kids would be allowed to stay open. There's just no way."

"Thiaghal is small and isolated," says Calla, "so you all don't feel the impact of The Eldrida Prophecy as much. I've actually been surprised at how buffered you are here. Most people are terrified of the Eldrida Prophecy, and Meltair and his family have had years to stir up ongoing hysteria and convince people that 'drastic measures' continue to be necessary."

"Now that The Inimical has actually appeared, people are probably drawn to Meltair even more," I add. Calla flips over an end table and sends it crashing to the ground.

"Shit, Calla, you have to stop doing that," says Aydin.

"Sorry," says Calla. I put my hand on her back and gradually feel her muscles relax as she steps closer to me. "The other thing to know," she says, "is that Meltair's father was not a nice person. Meltair was never good enough for him, but then he was treated like a hero by pretty much everyone else, and it just warped his mind somehow."

"So," I say, "that's who we're up against? We can handle one man with an ego and a tragic childhood."

"I underestimated Meltair once," says Calla, shaking her head. "Yes, he's a ridiculous person, but don't let it make you think he isn't dangerous. I won't make that mistake again."

The rest of the evening is spent elbow deep in Calla's drawings of the layout of Clocks as the storm continues to rage outside. She's holding it together well, but, as the storm goes on, Bevin is unraveling. Calla and I lock eyes when she asks Calla to go over the dormitory layout with her for a 5th time. Calla's arm is already laced through Bevin's, and I take Bevin's other hand.

"Bev," says Aydin, "let's call it a night."

She shakes her head frantically.

"Bevin. Hey, Bevin," says Calla, moving her hand to Bevin's back. Before she can say anything else, a wave of exhaustion overtakes Bevin, and she drops forward towards the table.

"Whoa," says Calla as she reaches forward and catches Bevin's head before it can hit the table. For the second night in a row, I carry Bev to her bed. She sleeps for all of the next day, and half the day after that. For a minute, I think that maybe she'll sleep right through until the evening, but she makes it down to the living room after lunch. Mom has finished making arrangements with the council to take over in my absence and has been dedicating her energy to packing a small travel bag for each of us.

The days pass in a haze of worried planning. Until one night, as we're packing up, Aydin says, "Oh shit. Tyre, Calla . . . your wedding is supposed to be tomorrow."

Calla and I lock eyes, and in the momentary exchange of that glance, I know that we've both decided that our wedding will still be tomorrow. We will get married on the last day of the storm, and the day before we leave to get Maddie and bring her home.

12

As I lay asleep that night, I feel its presence before it says my name this time. It feels different somehow. Before, it felt like The Inimical was standing in front of me. Now, it feels like no matter which way I turn, he's standing right next to me, practically touching me.

"What do you want?" I say, trying to ignore the prickling sensation all over my body. I close my eyes, as if that will make this all stop and go away.

The Inimical doesn't say anything for a long while. I feel it getting closer, if that's even possible, like the darkness is licking at my skin. I'm so tired from late nights of frantically planning Maddie's rescue that for a second, the darkness almost feels good. This darkness has a magnetic quality, and I feel some part of me reaching back as it stretches out towards me. I feel a warmth in my chest that I know is my dad's medallion, and when I open my eyes, I'm in my room again, but I'm not in my bed. I'm standing beside the bed, looking down at myself, and I see Calla asleep next to me with one hand knotted in my fur. She's taking up more than her fair share of blankets, as usual. I can even still feel the strange, pulling darkness that I'm coming to recognize as The Inimical, but when someone speaks, it's my dad's voice.

"Dad?" I say, hearing him but still not seeing him.

"Tyre," he says, "listen, bring the knife. Bring the knife with you to Clocks."

"Dad? Where are you? Why?"

When I turn around, I'm in the old rose garden again. The change is so fast I feel nauseous.

"Get out of my head!" I roar, furious at being robbed of the few hazy moments with my dad.

The darkness forms its usual shape of something or someone in a billowing, black cloak, with its face hidden.

"Something has changed," it says. A shiver runs down my spine. What does that mean? Something has changed with Maddie? It's going to start attacking Calla again?

"What does that mean?" I stop myself just short of begging him not to start hurting Calla again.

"Something will happen tomorrow, and it will make you think that you need to come to me right away instead of retrieving Madeliza. I promise that you don't."

"What?" I say. "What does that mean?"

"Do you trust me?" he says. I actually have no response to that. The question exists in an alternative universe so absurd that I can't fathom it being asked in this one. "Fine, have I ever lied to you?" says the shadow, sensing my astonishment.

"I have no way of knowing that," I say.

"Has anything happened to Calla since I said I'd leave her be?" I don't have an answer to that either, so I stay silent.

"I'm trying to tell you," says the shadow, "that while I *am* dangerous to you, I don't have any grand evil plan for the world. Certainly, nothing that gets put in place tomorrow. You're going to think that you need to change course and try to stop me tomorrow, and you shouldn't. Stick with Maddie."

"What's going to happen tomorrow?" I ask.

"If I tell you, you'll try to stop it. Can't have that."

I flutter my eyes awake a second later with Calla's long hair spread across my face. I breathe in the smell of roses for a second before pushing her hair back to her side of the bed and wrapping my arms around her waist. I curl my body around hers as my heart rate slows, and I eventually fall back asleep.

***

When we wake the next morning, Calla and I both tiptoe out of my room and find the cake Mom ordered the second Calla agreed to marry me. We cut slices and eat them with our hands, barefoot and still in our pajamas. For a second, I forget about Maddie, Meltair, and The Inimical, and there's only Calla laughing at me because I have frosting on my nose. She leans her head against my chest and snuggles into me after we finish our last bites of cake. I snuggle my face into the top of her head and breathe in her rose shampoo, and I know that I'll associate this smell with her for as long as I live.

Weddings in Thiaghal are small and beautiful, kind of like Thiaghal itself. Usually, it would be a small ceremony and then a huge party, but today it's just a small ceremony. Mom canceled all of the party arrangements when Maddie went missing, but it doesn't matter. No one can sleep, so we gather at dawn on the terrace that overlooks the rose garden just as the sun is coming up. The storm has finally broken, and the world is silent and covered in snow. Calla and I say the simple Thiaghal vows in a ceremony officiated by my mom, and attended only by Bevin and Aydin. In the midst of everything, when I say "I do," it somehow feels the way I think it's supposed to feel.

I pull Calla to me and kiss her to end the ceremony. I wait for a second, but nothing happens, and really, I don't think anyone expected it to. I remain the same as I've been since I was 11. Something in my mom finally seems to break in the silence after the ceremony, and she starts crying as she walks inside. In that moment, I know she's accepted it. There's no breaking the curse, and I worry it's forever changed something in her.

As Calla and I look at each other, I know we're thinking the same thing. We'll rescue Maddie, and then her brother, and then we're going to stop The Inimical. Maybe we'll stop the entire Eldrida Prophecy while we're at it. Bevin and Aydin both return our smiles, and we all stand shoulder to shoulder for a minute, looking out at the Thiaghal snow. Calla is slumped against me, and something about her in this moment feels more fragile than normal. When I really look at her, I see she still has dark circles under her eyes, and it makes me wonder how much she's really been sleeping. I loop my arm around her waist, and she leans to put even more of her weight on me. By the time we go inside, I feel like I'm practically carrying her.

Maybe it's the wedding or the quiet of the snow, but for the next hour, as we're getting the last of our things packed, some of the heaviness of the last few days falls away, and we chat about nothing in particular, just as we did the night we all went to the pub. *The night Maddie disappeared*. I push the thought away and replace it with the thought that Maddie will be fine, and that she only needs to hold on at Clocks until we can reach her.

At noon, we're finally packed when the sound of the doorbell clangs through the house. Bev, Aydin, Calla, Mom, and I all look at each other. For just a second, I think that it's Maddie, that she broke away from Meltair on the road, and that she's just been sheltering somewhere through the storm waiting to come home. Of course, it isn't; it's Sheriff Murchad. He's climbing off a Holpie when I open the door, and my stomach drops. The Holpies only let people ride them if there's an emergency.

"He's moved," says Sheriff Murchad as soon as I open the door.

"What?" I say. "What do you mean? Who's moved?" I stand aside to let him come in. He walks into the living room looking like he's seen a ghost. He drops into the same fireside armchair he sat in a few days ago when he told us about Maddie, and we gather around him. Mom gets him a hot cup of tea, which he drinks in one gulp, and then asks for whiskey. Once he's taken a sip, he says:

"The Inimical, he's moved." The dream from last night rushes back to me.

"Moved where?" I say. "Just shifted or expanded?"

"Expanded," he says. "The Fog has expanded 50 or so miles in all directions. They've tested it, and it's still true that where the Fog has overtaken, no one can get in or out. He's got even more hostages."

"That's even closer to the Maradal border," I say. Murchad goes pale again as he nods. The voice from my dream echoes in my head. *Stick with Maddie*. Am I really going to trust The Inimical? Just because it asked me nicely to pretty please not stop it from absorbing all of Andestine and starting in on Maradal? But . . . Maddie.

"The grand council is having an emergency session at the Andestine border," says Murchad. I look at Calla.

"Your call," she says, her expression unreadable. Bevin looks terrified; Aydin looks angry. Mom is miles away. Everything is unraveling, and the choice is being left to me: protect Maddie or protect Maradal? I feel Calla lace her fingers through mine before stepping in front of me toward Mom.

"Can you do it?" she says, looking at my mom. Mom startles and looks back at her. "Can you represent Thiaghal at the grand council? Because if not, Tyre will stay. We can do that. We can pivot. But understand that Clocks is nearly impenetrable, and we can't get in without someone with Tyre's abilities and residual fairy magic. So, if you cannot do this, if you cannot fight The Inimical with Tyre gone under these circumstances, no one will judge you. However," she glances at me, "that means Tyre will stay, and the reality is that means Maddie does not come home. So. Can you do this?" Calla's words have the intended effect on my mom, who seems to shake herself out of a stupor. She stands up on shaky feet.

"I can do it," she says. "I can hold off The Inimical until you get home with Maddie." She meets my eyes and nods.

"Good," says Calla. She turns to me, Bevin, and Aydin. "We need to leave." She pulls herself to her full height, tosses her hair back, squares her shoulders, and walks out of the room.

Sheriff Murchad stares after her, trying to process what's happened, until my mom says, "Sheriff, if you'll wait in the grand dining room, I'll be in shortly to discuss alerting the rest of the Thiaghal council and plans for the grand council at the Andestine border. I need to see my children off on their journey first."

***

"We'll be back in a couple of weeks," I say as I squeeze Mom's hand at the front door. Bevin and Aydin have each added their packs to a horse and are already seated. I'm too big for horses, and I'm built to walk long distances, so I'm planning to carry Calla and our packs on my back.

We travel most of the day until we reach the base of the first of the Eagach Mountains, and we wait for the pulley. Maradal has an elaborate open-air pulley-car system that carries passengers and goods over the many mountains in the Eagach range that make up a huge portion of Maradal. It looks like we've gotten to the base of the westernmost pulley as the sun is going down and as it's opening for its first run after the storm. There are a few other people waiting for seats in the pulley car, but it mostly looks like hired hands transporting goods that are too large to be mailed with the Holpies.

In the terror of realizing Maddie was gone and the magnitude of marrying Calla, I haven't had time to really think about what's happening. Now, as I feel the wary and even angry eyes of the other people waiting for the pulley, I realize I'm leaving home, *really* leaving home, for the first time in almost 20 years. I suddenly feel very much like I did at the party a few weeks ago, a nauseating combination of angry and self-conscious.

Aydin notices people staring and glares back at them, then moves to block their line of sight to me as best he can. Calla and I meet each other's eyes as she's sitting on the ground with Bevin, who's somehow fallen asleep with her head on Calla's shoulder. Calla glances in the direction of a woman who is giving me a particularly disgusted stare, rolls her eyes, and gives me a wry smile. I give a half smile back and turn back to talk to Aydin until the pulley car arrives.

Our first stop is a small inn at the base of the west mountain called the Lir Haven Inn. Bevin is still drowsy, and I'm beginning to worry she's coming down with something, so while Calla helps Bevin get settled on a sofa in the entryway, Aydin and I check in. Well, Aydin checks in, since the teenager checking people in at the front desk is too scared to talk to me.

Bevin is in a sound sleep when we make our way up to our rooms. We paid for two, but we all file into one. I think we're all feeling hesitant to separate unless absolutely necessary. Aydin lies down and falls asleep next to Bevin in seconds, leaving Calla and I alone in the dark in the second bed, our legs wrapped together under the blankets. I can see her outline in the moonlight streaming through the window. I sense her gently tilting her head up to meet my eyes, and see her tilt her head toward the door. She slides out of the blanket and heads for the door, and I silently slip out of bed and follow her out into the hallway, closing the door behind us.

"Drink?" she says, after the door clicks shut.

"Drink," I agree. We make our way back down into the pub. With Bevin and Aydin asleep upstairs, I'd forgotten that it was relatively early. There are people from Lir Haven pouring in, greeting friends. With a surprising pang, I find that I miss Brogan behind the bar. Calla and I settle into a quiet table in the corner where it's easier for me to go unnoticed. Calla goes to the bar and comes back with two tumblers of something. I don't care enough to ask what.

"Should have brought the bottle," I say, raising my glass and clinking it with hers. She laughs and takes a long drink from her glass.

"So," I say, "you said you underestimated Meltair once before?" She puts down her glass and grimaces.

"We were at Clocks together," she says. I sit quietly, waiting for her to continue. I think I've been patient with Calla's hesitation to confide in others, but I've decided to stop letting her wiggle out of some of these conversations. "Hm," she says, sipping her drink again after I don't break the silence, "well, look who's decided I'm not made of glass."

"Excuse me?" I say.

"You," she says, "you usually let me off the hook at the first sign of discomfort."

"Well, sorry for being considerate, I guess." I bristle with the unfairness of the statement and the implication that I've been treating her like she's weak, when I've just been trying to be kind. Calla screws her eyes shut and shakes her head.

"Sorry," she says, "you're right, that was an unkind thing for me to say."

"It's alright," I say, thrown off by her sudden vulnerability, "sorry if I made you feel weak."

"You didn't," she says, leaning her chin on her hand. "You never do. Honestly, Tyre, you've shown me more kindness than I've seen in a long time. For years of my life, in my immediate surroundings, kindness has been in short supply. The passive implication that I'm weak, however, has been plentiful. It's hard to unsee."

"Tell me all about it," I say. "Neither of us can sleep, and the next round is on me."

"I have no money with me, and you're the governor of a neighboring province; all the rounds are on you," she says.

"Stop deflecting," I say. I'm smiling, but I mean it.

"Huh, I like this new Tyre," she says. I keep a straight face and continue to wait for her to share, but I'm realizing explicitly for the first time just how good Calla is at deflecting. She tucks a piece of hair behind her ear and settles in.

"You said your dad went to Clocks, right?" she says. "It's not a deflection, I'm explaining," she says when I don't answer.

"He did. Before I was born, and then very briefly when I was small. He didn't graduate, as far as I know," I say.

"How much did he tell you about it?" she asks.

"Almost nothing," I say. "Just anything that he learned there that was a story a kid might like. The Eldrida Hero, The Holpies, things like that."

"I love the Holpies," says Calla, "Do you really think they're Kelpies that got stuck as horses?"

"Calla."

"I'm not deflecting, I'm conversing!" she says. I poke her in the center of her forehead.

"Fine," she says, smiling. "Alright, so he told you bedtime stories, but you don't know much about what Clocks is actually like?"

"Sounds about right," I agree.

"Clocks is physically dangerous," she continues, "but to be honest, a lot of the danger of Clocks is psychological. You remember I said that between Meltair's father and his admiring public, he was psychologically warped? Clocks has a little bit of that effect on everyone in different ways. The faculty there, at a school that harms kids, you want to believe they're all evil, right? Like caricatures wearing dark cloaks and lurking in the shadows . . ."

I shiver internally as the image of The Inimical that lurks in my dreams appears in my mind.

" . . . but the reality is that they're just people. They've got kids of their own who they love and protect, yet they harm kids on a regular basis. The kind of mental cartwheels they have to do to compartmentalize that . . . It changes them. It changes everyone who goes there. The culture is that the kids who die deserve to die, because the alternative feels too catastrophic to everyone's sense of self. Everyone at Clocks distorts reality in this miasmic, unspoken agreement. If you die, it was your fault for not being good enough, smart enough, strong enough, or fast enough. In a world like that, any act of kindness is best interpreted as a threat, or at least a commentary on how you won't be missed."

"Alright," I say, "I'm with you so far. That sounds horrible. What does this have to do with Meltair?"

"He's been faculty for a while," says Calla, "and now obviously headmaster, but Meltair and I were students together. Things between students at Clocks tend to go one of two ways: an intense trauma-based bond, or an intense competition sugar-coated in pleasantries."

"Which were you and Meltair?" I ask.

"Meltair was only ever the second with anyone," says Calla. "His history with his grandfather and his dad never gave him any chance at the former; he was too brainwashed into thinking that he had to 'win' at Clocks at any cost. He had a soft spot for me because I refused to compete with him. With anyone, really. I much preferred to keep to myself."

"So, no trauma bonds, and no rivals?" I ask.

"None to speak of," says Calla.

"Calla," I ask, "how did you end up at Clocks?"

"My family didn't have much growing up. In places like the greater Umbra area in Andestine that aren't as remote or hard to get to as most places in Maradal, Clocks offers families a stipend to send their kids to Clocks if those kids seem especially talented."

"They're buying kids?" I say.

"Pretty much," says Calla. "If he knew then what I know now, there's no way my grandfather would ever have allowed me to go to Clocks, but that talk about how prestigious Clocks was got him pretty good. We also had my little brother to think about. Granted, I didn't know the little idiot was going to follow me into Clocks not two years later."

"How much younger is your brother?" I ask.

"Six years," says Calla, "so 25 now."

"How old were you when you went to Clocks?" I ask.

"14," she says, "which was pretty brutal considering there are kids who have been there since they were seven." I'm struck by a wave of respect for Calla.

"I'm not sure I could have done that," I say. "I feel like I would have been wiped out the first week."

"You would have made it," she says. I can't tell if she really thinks that or she's just being nice, but I'm getting the strangest feeling that being nice isn't actually in Calla's nature; or, if it ever was, it's something that's buried at Clockwork Atheneum.

"So," I say, "Meltair. You underestimated him once?"

"Like I said," she continues, "Meltair and I had a kind of truce. I was no threat to him, and I think the sheer relief of that made me feel like an ally to him. We would sit and study together, eat together sometimes, and even team up for group projects. There was a surface-level, cordial sort of agreement between us that eventually felt like friendship, even though it wasn't. Meltair and I were in the same year, but he graduated early and took on a job as faculty. About that time, Meltair made a mistake, and it had a terrible cost. I tried to talk to him, tried to get him to put it right, or even acknowledge it, but Tyre, he can't. I don't even think it's a choice anymore. In order to survive, his brain has built up this blind spot around his own perfection. In his own mind, he's infallible, because the alternative is too terrifying. When I begged him to help me undo what he had done, he told me that I was confused, that I didn't understand the situation, and everyone I tried to go to for help believed the great Delanum Meltair."

"What was it?" I ask. "The mistake?"

"I'll tell you," she says, "but not yet. Not until I see you meet Meltair and not fall under his spell."

"What? What does that even mean?" I ask.

"Meltair is charming and smart. Not as smart as I am, but still reasonably intelligent, and I won't be tricked again," says Calla. "There were people whom I thought I could trust back then, at least as much as you can trust anyone at Clocks, and all of them believed Meltair. You're in charge of distracting Meltair once we get to Clocks, so you'll get to spend some time with him. You remain uncorrupted, we'll talk."

"Calla, if we're going to be a team, you have to trust me, not put me through a bizarre series of tests while we're trying to rescue my little cousin from a death school."

"I know," she says, sighing, "I want to."

"You will," I say, as I reach over and squeeze her hand.

"Oh, you're so certain?" she says, raising her eyebrows.

"Yes," I say, "because you can." She squeezes my hand back.

"Tyre?" she says.

"Yes?"

"Do you trust me?" she asks. She looks afraid of the answer. I think for a long time before responding.

"I love you," I say, "and I want to trust you."

She looks shocked, but whether at my declaration of love or lack of trust, I can't tell. She gapes at me for a minute before saying, "I love you too." I realize with a sudden shock that despite our wedding this is the first time Calla and I have actually said 'I love you' out loud. I just felt it and said it without giving much thought to any of the implications. I startle and glance down at my hands. Still claws.

"Ladies and gentlemen!" a voice calls from the bar, distracting me. Calla and I both spin our heads towards the sound. A man with a lute is standing on the bar, and this must be a regular occurrence because most of the pub starts cheering.

"Ugh," says Calla, "I didn't realize this was a pub with live entertainment."

"You know you're kind of grumpier than I thought you'd be when we first met," I say. Calla smirks and rolls her eyes. She pulls her chair around so she's sitting next to me, facing the bar, and takes another sip of her drink.

"What will we be hearing tonight?" calls the bard, walking back and forth on the bar. People call out different songs and stories. He strums up a tune about a lovelorn traveler, which gets a laugh but doesn't stick. People keep calling out for their favorite songs and stories.

"The tale of the Eldrida Hero!" Someone calls.

"Ah!" says the Bard. "No such thing! You all know why there's no such thing, don't you?" A cacophony of responses from the audience echoes through the pub. "Well, I'll tell you why there's no such thing . . . " He strums a chord on his lute to quiet the crowd and starts to tell the story. "Once, not so long ago, there was a talented student at the old Clockwork Atheneum. He fought Wyverns, vampires, and banshees. He quested for magical items and protected the weak and downtrodden. So impressive was he that people started to call him the Eldrida Hero. People started to think that he was the one the prophecy foretold who would stop the great darkness that kills unseen!" Cheers fill the pub.

"But, my friends," says the bard, "his fame was to be short-lived. He embarked on a final quest. All that is known, all that is whispered, is that he set off into Andestine, and then . . . " The bard makes a 'poof' motion with his hands, " . . . was never seen again. Then, The Inimical rose up . . ." I feel my stomach clench, and wonder how the grand council at the Andestine border is going. " . . . and the Eldrida Hero was nowhere to be found. He was only the chosen one for a time, only the hero of a single, short age."

A hush falls over the pub as the bard whispers the last part. Just as everyone is silent, he yells, "So, let's raise a glass to Atreo Ballesteros! Now, who wants to hear a tale from before he disappeared? The tale of when he slew the Wyvern!" The pub erupts in raucous applause again. I'm almost excited to hear the story of The Eldrida Hero and Eastern Wyvern, and I'm wondering how similar it will be to the story my dad used to tell. Clearly, since Lir Haven is on the main throughway of Maradal, they have new and different information. I'd never heard a story that referred to the hero by name before, *Atreo Ballesteros*. I'm settling in to listen when I notice Calla shaking next to me.

"Calla," I say, "what's wrong?" She bolts from the pub. "Calla, whoa, Calla!" I stand up too quickly, knocking my chair over and causing a scene as I scramble to follow her out of the pub. "Sorry, sorry," I mutter to horrified onlookers. Thank goodness Calla glows; I can see her light bobbing in the distance, tearing into a field across from Lir Haven Inn. I don't have much of a choice but to go after her, although I hope against hope that no one thinks I'm attacking her and resolves to address the situation with a crossbow.

When I finally reach her, Calla is collapsed in the middle of the field sobbing.

"Calla, you're alright." I drop down next to her and wrap my arms around her. My first thought is that it's Mark and he's hurting her again, but this seems different. There's no blood, for one thing, and I can't remember the last time I heard someone cry like this. Calla certainly hasn't ever before. Perhaps Mom, or Bevin when Bevin's parents died, but if they did, then they hid it from me. Probably the last time I heard a cry like this was my own sobs when Dad died. I hold Calla for what feels like forever, until it feels like she finally starts to catch her breath. "Calla," I say. I'm hoping the look on my face asks all the questions, because I'm not sure I can find the words.

"It was the name," she says, "I wasn't expecting to hear the name."

"The name?" I say, my brain racing to catch up. "The name from the story? Atreo?" She closes her eyes and nods.

"He was the mistake," she says. "Meltair sent Atreo on a stupid, unnecessary quest. I know kids die all the time at Clocks, but Atreo . . . he was good. He was the best, and the deaths at Clocks, well, the deaths have a rationale. There's a training goal, or some kind of quest for a needed item. This was just . . . this quest was about Meltair's ego, and the consequences were horrible."

"He got Atreo killed," I say. Calla buries her face in her hands. When she looks up, her sadness has transformed into something else.

“Come on,” she says. I may not know Calla as well as many husbands know their wives, but I remember the look on Calla’s face before she took down the pub ruffians in Thiaghal.

“Calla, Calla . . . ” I say, following after her as she strides back towards the pub, “What’s the plan here, Calla?” When we re-enter the crowded pub, the bard is clearly on a break, sipping a pint at the bar. Every so often, people come to pat him on the shoulder and place a tip in the jar next to him on the counter.

“You,” says Calla, striding up to him. He does a spit take on registering Calla and I. Thinking about it, I realize that we look bizarre. Me looking like me, and Calla looking like Calla, but covered in dirt from where she collapsed on the ground. “Where did you get the name?”

“Excuse me?” he says. He stands up from his barstool and tries to back away as Calla steps towards him.

“Calla,” I say, registering the glances from the rest of the pub as the crowd becomes more and more concerned. “Please do not kill this man.” The bard’s eyes flick back and forth between Calla and I.

“Atreo Ballesteros,” she says. “Who told you that name?” A look of recognition crosses his face.

“You must be Calla,” he says. He swallows and continues, “Meltair left a message in case you stopped here. He says he saw you at the pub in Thiaghal. He says, ‘don’t follow me’, he says . . . ”

Unfortunately, I’ll never know what else Meltair said because Calla lunges at the bard.

“Calla, no!” I say. I catch her around her middle and swing her back away from the bard as people in the pub start screaming. I feel Calla clawing at my arm and kicking my shins as the bartender yells at us to get out.

“We’re going! We’re going!” I drag Calla up the stairs back towards our room.

***

"Alright, alright!" says Calla as I swing her over the threshold to the spare room so we don't wake Bevin and Aydin. "Put me down, I'm fine!" I set her down, and she paces the length of the room, eventually swatting at a vase and knocking it off the table.

"Cal, let's just try to calm down," I say.

"Curse Meltair!" she yells. "Curse him and his entire family line!"

"Alright, so, cursing a man's entire bloodline is the opposite of calming down. Calla!" I raise my voice so she hears me over the sound of herself shoving over an end table. "Hey, Calla!" I walk over and brace my hands on each of her shoulders and push her back against the wall, rescuing another innocent vase in the process. She stops and looks up at me, breathing hard. I can't interpret the look she's giving me, and I'm about to ask her what's wrong when she crashes her mouth into mine.

I'm momentarily knocked off balance by the surprise, but I recover and press my mouth back into hers. I'm not totally sure what's happening, but I'm also not questioning it. She keeps kissing me fiercely, running her hands along my body underneath my shirt until she eventually pulls it up and over my head. I slide my hands underneath her dress, along the sides of her thighs to her hips. I've barely registered the feeling of her skin under my hands before she pulls her dress over her head and pushes me backward.

***

"Well," I say, lying against Calla later and running my claws down the length of her bare arms and back. "I guess it's good to know that that also doesn't break the curse."

***

We both tiptoe as quietly as we can back into the room with Bevin and Aydin a few minutes later. "What's happening?" says Bevin, sitting up and rubbing her eyes.

"Calla attacked a bard," I say.

"Great," says Aydin, rolling over and putting a pillow over his head.

"Sorry," says Calla, realizing that despite our best efforts, we've woken Bevin and Aydin up.

"It's alright," says Bevin, looking around and registering the situation. "Let's get you cleaned up." I glance at Calla and realize she's had no choice but to put back on the dress that still has mud on it. Bevin gets out of bed and walks towards Calla.

"No, Bev, I'm sorry. I've got it," says Calla.

"Hey, no one take this the wrong way, but everyone shut up," says Aydin from under the pillow. I flop down onto the bed next to Aydin as Bevin pulls Calla towards the bathroom.

"Aydin," I say. He grunts from under the pillow, which I assume means he's listening. I give him the full details of what happened at the bar. I consider giving him the details of what happened in the other bedroom, but decide it might not be the time or place. He begrudgingly takes the pillow off his head.

"So, she has serious issues with this Meltair guy then?" he says.

"Seems that way."

"And that's who has Maddie?" he says. I swallow and nod.

"Atreo, huh?" says Aydin. "She say how he died?"

"No," I say, "just that Meltair sent him on a quest that got him killed."

***

The rest of our journey is much less uneventful. Bevin seems more herself by the time we arrive in Lytwist. I hate to admit it under the circumstances, but the second we arrive, I like Lytwist. I haven't been out of Thiaghal in years, much less Maradal, and the city is amazing. To my relief, I'm somehow less noticeable here. There's so much movement, and so many different kinds of people, that it's easier to blend in. For the first time since leaving Thiaghal, I feel like I can breathe. As we enter the city, Calla throws the cloak of her hood up.

"Meltair knows me," she says. "No reason to let him know we're coming if we can help it. He's got plenty of eyes around the city."

She doesn't seem scared, just cautious, but she inches closer to me as we walk. Ever since Lir Haven, I almost, the operative word being *almost,* need Calla to touch me less. Ever since sleeping together in Lir Haven, and once or twice after, it seems like she's always resting a hand on me, linking her pinky finger with mine, or resting her feet on mine while we sit. She wasn't kidding when she said that she's not really great with personal space. I lace my fingers through hers when she inches closer to me and see her shoulders relax a little bit.

Calla clearly knows the city and leads us through a winding network of streets until we reach a tall hotel made of white brick. A very competent woman with her hair in a tight bun checks us in and shows us to our rooms.

Bevin runs down to the dining room and brings us up hot coffee, tea, and something to eat, and we settle in to go over the plan one last time.

"The campus of Clocks," Calla reminds us, "is essentially one giant enchanted item."

"I was still out of it for this part of the conversation a few days ago," says Bevin. "What does that mean? I thought humans couldn't use magic?"

"One can," I say.

"But Mark isn't involved in this," says Aydin.

"Correct; no human is actually using magic to enchant Clocks," says Calla. "Meltair's grandfather basically paid an army of fairies to enchant the entire campus of Clocks after the Eldrida Prophecy. So, no, humans can't use magic, but the campus itself can. It has a sort of sentience. If it doesn't want you there, you won't be there. Unfortunately, what the campus wants and what the headmaster wants are usually aligned. So, while Meltair won't necessarily order the campus to expel us, if he doesn't want us there, the campus may act on its own. Tyre," she says, looking at me, "this is where you come in."

"You're hoping that because I'm covered in residual fairy magic, Clocks will think I'm just part of the campus."

"I don't think, I know," she says. "You're not the only one cursed or blessed by fairies, and students have exploited that weakness before for everything from smuggling sweets to exam answers."

"And you," says Bevin, turning to Calla, "are hoping you'll be able to get in because Clocks will recognize you, since you used to be a student."

"We," says Aydin, swinging his arm around Bevin's shoulders, "probably won't be able to get in, but we're going to try by carrying the knife and the candle that Briowney gave Tyre, and hoping it's enough fairy magic to disguise us."

"Excellent," says Calla. "Now, once we're inside?"

"Meltair will immediately realize there's been a change on the Clocks campus because of surveillance built into the enchantment, and that is where I come in. I head straight to his office. Act like I've come to talk to him man to man about taking Maddie home and keep him distracted," I say.

"While I," says Calla, "find Maddie and pull her out."

"Now, wait, why can't Maddie just leave again?" says Bevin, pressing both her hands to her temples. "Wouldn't it be easier to get her a message and let her know we're here to help her get back to Thiaghal?"

"The students are essentially prisoners," says Calla. "They sign an 'education contract' agreeing not to leave until their petition to withdraw is granted— which it never is, unless they're kicked out or they graduate. The rationale used to justify this is to discourage them from quitting, and, of course, the faculty act like guards. They patrol, and if they see her trying to leave, she'll be dragged back to her dorm and probably face some harsh consequences. Like Murchad said back in Thiaghal, Clocks is a small country with its own laws, and Burne is supportive of it, so we won't have any help from Lytwist police." Bevin nods. She looks pale again, but steady.

"So, we're going in through a weak spot in the magic?" says Aydin.

"Correct," says Calla, "the one most often used for smuggling things in and out of campus. It's an irrigation passageway that lets out into a river."

"Has anyone, you know, ever successfully done this?" asks Bevin. "Smuggled a human being out of Clocks?"

"There were always rumors," says Calla, "but I don't know for sure."

It feels impossible that no one hears how loudly my heart is pounding as we make our way towards the city center and Clocks campus. I see the archways that mark the entrance in the distance and students in what must be their uniforms, dark brown leather trousers and simple white shirts, making their way across the grounds. People are just bustling by on the street outside, not knowing or not caring that children are dying feet from them.

"They hide it well," Calla whispers next to me, as if reading my thoughts. "It's all pretty grounds and rolling lawns on the outside. It's easy to convince yourself that's all it is if you really want to."

We're not foolish enough to walk right in through the front gates, nor could we if what Calla says about the enchanted grounds is true. We make a sharp right and make a wide circle around the perimeter of campus into a large park in the eastern part of Lytwist.

"This is it," says Calla when we reach a tunnel opening deep in the park woods with a river flowing out of it. "We may run into students smuggling things. Ignore them, and they'll ignore you. Remember, once we get Maddie off the Clocks campus, we're safe. Meltair can follow us wherever he wants, but he has no real power outside of Clocks, and he won't follow us. He'll just keep recruiting other vulnerable kids." The words land like a brick and make me think that once we're done with The Inimical we might want to turn our attention to Delanum Meltair. We follow the passageway for about ten minutes until we reach a ladder.

"Up we go," says Calla. Calla goes first, then Aydin, Bevin, and me. The ladder leads to an open drain in a kind of long groove at the bottom of a hill. I can't see anything over the hill, but as we walk and crest the top, I can barely make out the arches we just saw in the distance to the west, and what I assume are academic buildings in the distance in another direction. As Calla predicted, there are students around, but not many, and they keep their heads down and hurry on their way.

"Meltair knows we're here, so—" says Calla, but before she can finish, there's a disgusting sound somewhere between a squelch and pop, and Aydin disappears. There's only about a second to watch Bevin look shocked before the sound repeats, and she's gone too.

"Rats," says Calla, "not enough magic. The campus expelled them. I guess that means you and I are safe."

"You're sure they're alright?" Calla had said they'd be fine if they were expelled when we confirmed the plan the night before, but the horrible squelching sound was more off-putting than I'd like to admit.

"They're alright," she says. "They're just back in the tunnel at the last point before the Clocks campus. So, like I said, Meltair knows we're here. You go to Meltair; I'll get Maddie. Meet you at the mouth of the river where we came in. Just get me as much time as you can."

"You got it," I say.

13

Excerpt from the journal of Delanum Meltair, made the previous day:

I know the fairy-cursed small town governor and his family are in town. If I know Calla, and I think I do, all of them or some of them will find a way to turn up here tomorrow. "Tyre Sylvan, I take it?" I'll offer him my hand, although I know he won't take it. It doesn't matter. It's the offer that is important. In the grand scheme of things, Madeliza Ruarcc is a small thing, but she sets a precedent.

The reputation of Clocks is everything, absolutely everything, when it comes to saving the world. If word spreads that nervous guardians can come and collect their kids, it breaks the spell that keeps Clocks running. Not a literal spell, of course, although there is that too. What I mean is that Clocks' reputation for being strong, being impenetrable, and, most importantly, being necessary, is the only thing that allows people to tolerate the lengths we go to here to achieve our goals. The goal, of course, is to save the world by stopping the Eldrida prophecy.

If people think that kids can just leave Clocks on a whim and that nervous caregivers can just come and collect them as if this were a fancy boarding school, it cracks the armor of just how necessary Clocks and our mission are. Earlier tonight, I took a second to just stare into the fire and allow myself to feel tired. I can practically hear my dad's voice telling me that allowing myself to feel tired is a useless indulgence. Sometimes I do it for just a second, before doing what I always do: stepping up to do the right thing. I need to make Tyre Sylvan understand the truth that I've made all of Lytwist, even all of Burne, understand that what we do at Clocks is for the greater good.

***

I follow the map Calla gave me of the grounds until I reach Norwood Hall, where I know the faculty offices are. I'm amazed at how little the students, and even the other faculty in their flowing robes, pay attention to me. Clearly, unusual things aren't out of place at Clocks. Only one student even seems to see me, and it's a short little teenager with a mop of white hair and gray eyes that look unfocused. The teenager looks in my direction right as I'm approaching Norwood Hall, and we lock eyes with each other. The teenager slowly begins to raise a finger to point at me, and it's all feeling a little too creepy, so I duck into the Norwood Hall foyer and out of sight.

"Name?" says the woman sitting at the reception desk. She doesn't even look up from the paper in her hand.

"Tyre Sylvan," I say, deciding on honesty.

"And you're here to see?"

"Delanum Meltair. He's expecting me."

She nods and puts her pen down with a sharp click.

"I'll need to escort you to the Headmaster's office," she says, looking annoyed about it. We wind through a series of halls with doors marked with faculty names. The entire building is old stonework, and there's a rich red carpet lining all the floors. There are very few windows, but sconces with flickering flames accent the walls every few feet. It feels, in some ways, very similar to the library at the manor back in Thiaghal, and I hate myself for thinking it feels cozy. Meltair's office door is at the very end of the hall, behind a large mahogany door. The woman knocks twice on the door, and a voice calls from within, "Enter." The woman gives me one curt nod and turns to walk back down the hallway. I take a deep breath and open the door. Inside is an office with a huge mahogany desk and a roaring fire. The plush red carpet from the hallway doesn't continue, but there is a large red rug with swirling patterns spread on the middle part of the stone floor.

"Tyre Sylvan, I take it?" The man I met at the bar weeks ago stands up, wearing very similar clothes to the night that we met, well-worn leather with weapons in the belt. I really look at him and take him in now. He looks to be about 30-something. Dark hair, fit with broad shoulders. He's tall, although not as tall as me, and looking closer, I notice he has a strong jaw. The rest of his features, however, are boyish, which he's tried to disguise with a short stubble. He walks towards me and extends his hand. Immediately, I feel anger surge inside me. He comes to my town and kidnaps my little cousin, and he thinks I'm going to shake his hand like this is a garden party?

"We've met," I growl, staring down at his outstretched hand.

"We have," he says. He seems maddeningly unfazed.

"On the night you kidnapped my cousin," I say, just in case he can't place the memory.

"I would never kidnap anyone," he says. "I encouraged Madeliza to talk with her guardian- although she told me that Bevin Ruarcc, not you."

"I am responsible for the well-being of everyone in my household," I say.

"As am I," says Meltair. "Madeliza made it clear that if she were to talk with you, she was worried she wouldn't be allowed to go."

"She wouldn't have been," I say. Meltair nods as if he's just made an excellent point.

"And you think she should be allowed to make the decision?" I say.

"I didn't say that," he says. "I think it's more complicated than that."

“It’s not.”

“Mr. Sylvan,” he says, walking over to a cart by the fire and pouring two amber colored drinks. “Can I ask you to sit?” Sitting, sipping a drink with this man is the last thing I want to do, but unfortunately, I can’t ignore the amount of time it will buy Calla to sit sipping drinks and having a long chat. I slowly walk over, take the drink, and sink into one of the armchairs by the fire. He does the same.

“I’d like to explain,” he says. “Tyre, may I call you Tyre?” My only response is to take a long sip of my drink.

“Tyre,” he says again, “you’re the first parent or guardian I’ve actually gotten to talk with like this, although I’m sure there are a lot who have wanted to.” He forces a laugh and stares into the fire. He seems younger suddenly, more like a peer and less like the brooding headmaster of Clockwork Atheneum. “Enchanted campus, you know?” he says.

“I’ve been told.” Something about his presentation in that moment softens me the slightest bit. I hate to say it, but so far he isn’t exactly the monster I had been picturing. He seems pompous, but there’s a tiredness I wasn’t expecting, and it unsettles me that he’s a peer. I’m suddenly acutely aware that in another lifetime, he could have been drinking with Bevin, Aydin, and I on a Friday evening. He isn’t exactly posturing and monologuing like the villain that I’d built him to be in my head. I remind myself sternly that he took Maddie from her home, and he’s willfully leading a school that’s harming kids.

“Right,” he says, looking suddenly angry, “you’ve been told by Calla? I saw you with her at the bar in Thiaghal when I made the trip to escort Madeliza. It was a shock. I haven’t seen Calla in years.”

“Yes, by Calla,” I say. “She’s not the biggest fan of yours either, by the way.” He adjusts his expression.

"I don't have a problem with Calla," he says, taking a long sip of his drink. "Not anymore anyway. We've had some disagreements. Had our differences, I guess."

"Your kidnapping of my cousin being one of them?"

"I don't see it that way," he says.

"Please tell me how else one could see it?" I stand and pour myself another generous helping of his alcohol. It comes out more genuine than I want it to. I mean it to land as a ridiculous question, but there's a genuine curiosity in it that I didn't intend. He sighs and runs a hand through his hair.

"I'm assuming you know about the Eldrida prophecy?" he says.

"You think that justifies kidnapping-?" I start, but he holds up his hand.

"Just let me get this out," he says. If I didn't know better, I'd say he looked sad. "People are terrified of the Eldrida Prophecy, and I'm the only person they look to for help. I'm the only one who can help them. My dad died years ago now. I didn't ask for that responsibility. Do you have any idea what that's like? An entire country looking to you? Believing you have their fate, and the fate of everything they know, in your hands? I don't know about you, but that isn't a responsibility I take lightly. I can't take it lightly." I do relate to what he's saying. It's not totally different than how I felt growing up after my dad died. The crushing weight of the responsibility for all of the people that you love. What would it be like if that were an entire country of people? Or if I really believed it was the entire world?

"That doesn't explain why you took my cousin," I say.

"I didn't exactly 'take' her," he says. "I offered her a place at Clockwork Atheneum. I encouraged her to talk it over with you, her aunt, and her sister. She was determined to get here on her own. So, seeing that she was going to make the journey no matter what, I offered to help her."

I sit quietly, thinking it over. There's some merit to that. No one has ever really been able to tell Maddie anything.

"Let me ask you," says Meltair, "what would you do in my position? A man, placed as the headmaster of a school. Tasked with stopping the destruction of the world by an entirely unknown force, with unknown power and resources. Tasked with doing so by finding a champion. A hero of incredible ability. How would you go about that besides finding and interviewing capable students?"

"I see what you're saying," I say slowly, "but what you're doing isn't exactly 'finding and interviewing.'"

"Look, I'll own that. I'll own that I sometimes help students, older students, come to Clocks of their own free will against their guardians' wishes. However, if the worst anyone can say about me in my quest to save the world is that I disregarded a few permission forms for students who would be able to choose to come to Clocks of their own free will within a few years anyway, then I'll take that blame."

"Students die at Clocks," I say, in one last attempt to remember why we hate this man. "You kill your students."

"Why would I set out to kill the very people who I think could be the key to saving the world?" he says. "I train my students. Harshly sometimes, yes. They're training to excel in dangerous conditions, so we need to practice in dangerous conditions. We make the training as safe as we can, but ultimately, what our students are training to do is not safe. Risks have to be taken to prepare them. Every risk we take at Clocks is calculated and necessary."

"That's not necessarily true from what I've been told," I say as the memory of Calla sobbing in Lir Haven flashes across my mind.

"Did Calla tell you that?" says Meltair. "Atreo, right? Atreo Ballesteros?"

I narrow my eyes and give a curt nod.

"Yeah, well, Calla isn't actually in a position to be objective on that, is she?" he says. I don't know what to say to that. Why wouldn't Calla be in a position to be objective about Atreo? Meltair looks confused.

"How well do you actually know Calla?" he says. I hold up my claw to show my wedding band.

"We were married just last week in Thiaghal," I say. With some satisfaction, I can see that, of everything I've said to Meltair, this is the first thing that's actually shaken him. He only takes a second to regain his composure, but it's still surprisingly satisfying to see him rattled.

"Wow. Well, congratulations. Calla . . . married. Wow," he shakes his head like he's trying to clear it. "In any case," he continues, "you should probably know then, Atreo was her brother."

***

I don't remember much of the walk back to the weak point in the Clocks campus besides hoping that Calla had enough time to get Maddie, but I'm disappointed when I see her alone by the entrance to the irrigation drain.

"Where's Maddie?" I say.

"Tyre," she says. I can tell right away that something is wrong. She has tears in her eyes, and her face is red.

"She's not . . . ?" I start. I feel like ice water has just flooded my entire body.

"She's alive, as far as I know," says Calla, "but he moved her. He knew we were coming, or knew when we got here, and made sure she was well supervised in the Speckled Tower. It's the most guarded building on the campus. I couldn't get to her, I'm sorry." She looks it, but I don't care. I'm confused, and for some reason irrationally angry at her.

"Point me towards the Speckled Tower," I say, turning back towards campus.

"Tyre," she says, grabbing my arm and pulling me back. "You can't. We will regroup and come up with a new plan for tomorrow, but you can't go after her. You'll get killed or get her killed."

"Why," I yell, "should I believe anything you say?" There's a part of me that knows being this angry at Calla over a seemingly innocuous omission of information doesn't make sense, but I don't understand *why*. Why would Calla leave out the piece of information that Atreo is her brother? Why can she not be straightforward about anything?

"Whoa," she says, "what is going on?"

"Atreo?" I say. "Anything you might have left out of the story about Atreo?" Recognition crosses her face.

"Meltair told you," she says. "Tyre, you have to understand, he's—"

"Did you really think he wouldn't?" I ask.

"Honestly," says Calla, "yes, I was hoping it just wouldn't come up."

"You know what, it doesn't even matter, because I don't care that Meltair told me," I say, "I care that you didn't!" A few students in the distance look our way.

"This isn't the place for this conversation," she says. She turns and disappears down the ladder into the drain, and I follow.

"Calla," I say. I grab her arm and spin her towards me as soon as we make our way into the tunnel. It's dark, but there's just enough light from the drain opening in the distance that I can see her face.

"Tyre," she says, "Meltair is—"

"I don't care about Meltair," I say. "I care about you! You should have told me Atreo is your brother. *Why*? Why wouldn't you tell me something like that?"

"Because it's hard to talk about," she says.

“Not good enough,” I say. “Not anymore. I haven’t pushed for information because I care about you, and I can tell it’s hard to talk about—”

“Oh, is that what you’ve been doing?” she says, “And is that why?”

“Yes,” I say, confused by the sudden turn in the conversation, “why else would I?”

“Tyre,” says Calla, “you are one of the nicest people I’ve ever met, but you are so delighted just to be seen with me that you let me do whatever I want. I’m not walking all over you on purpose . . . It’s complicated . . . but sometimes I don’t know how you’re fine with the fact that I just appeared out of nowhere and refuse to answer so many of your questions.”

“Oh, it's because I’m just so delighted to be seen with you?” I know I shouldn’t yell. I should do those breathing exercises that mom taught me as a kid, but I can’t remember ever being angry with someone like this. “You think that you’re so incredibly beautiful and I’m so incredibly pathetic and monstrous that I’m letting you say and do whatever you want because I’m just so grateful to be in your presence?”

“That’s not what I—”

“Because let me tell you what it really is, Calla Helena, or as I’ve recently learned, Calla Ballesteros, I’m fine with it because I can’t remember the last time I was allowed to be *not* fine with anything!” She opens her mouth like she’s going to talk again, but I cut her off. “Dad dies but Mom is falling apart so I have to be fine with it; I get changed into whatever all of this is and Mom is still falling apart so I have to be fine with it; Bevin’s parents die but Bevin is falling apart and Maddie is an infant so I have to be fine with it; I need to take over as governor of Thiaghal despite the fact that I haven’t left my house in years so I need to do my stupid breathing exercises and just be fine with it!” I yell. “So yes, Calla Ballesteros, when something good finally dropped into my lap instead of something horrible, I’ve tried to just be fine with it!”

Neither of us says anything for a long while. We just stand staring at each other, looking at the ground, and breathing hard. Finally, Calla speaks.

"Sylvan," she says. "You said, 'or as I've recently learned Calla Ballesteros' and yes, while my name when you met me was Calla Ballesteros, I believe it's Calla Sylvan now." She tosses her hair back over her shoulder like this is a very important point, and I let out a breath I've been holding.

"I guess so," I say. I'm not ready to stop being angry. This conversation is far, far from over, but we need to move on. "Come on. You can do the work of explaining this entire mess to Bevin and Aydin."

14

Bevin and even Aydin are being much kinder about the Atreo situation than I had hoped, which, of course, makes me feel bad for hoping that my friends would be unkind to my wife. Bevin, Aydin, and I are up late talking, tucked into a corner of the hotel tavern. Bevin is holding up as well as can be expected, and Aydin looks lost in thought.

"It's not like we didn't know Calla was hiding things," he says, shrugging, "and it's not like this is something she did to someone. This is something that was done to her and her little brother."

"Why would she hide something like that?" I say. Suddenly, I feel crazy for being so upset. No one says anything for a while until Bevin finally speaks.

"Calla doesn't seem to have a lot of practice in sharing what she thinks," says Bevin, "or maybe more so what she feels? Think about it. From what we've learned about Clocks since Maddie left, personal connections were probably a huge vulnerability."

"I guess," I say.

"I'm not saying you have to be alright with her lying and keeping secrets-" says Bevin.

"In fact, you shouldn't be," Aydin adds.

"I'm just saying, I could see being that way if I'd lived her life instead of mine. It's not like she really knows us that well. You two have had this whirlwind romance, and we've all had this forced proximity in the name of curse-breaking."

"Which didn't even work," I say, staring down into my pint.

"Sure, but you didn't want it to," says Aydin.

"No, I didn't. Does that make me . . . ?" I hesitate, not sure how to finish the sentence.

"A monster?" says Aydin, smirking.

"Yeah," I say, managing to crack a smile.

"Nah," he says. "Just odd."

"As we've already established," says Bevin, "Calla is also deeply odd. So, I wouldn't give up on her just yet. With you know, the caveat, that we'll support whatever you want to do." Her comment startles me into realizing that in this entire conversation, I haven't even considered splitting up with Calla. It just never occurred to me as a possibility. Now that it has, despite how angry I am, I'm surprised to find that I still don't want to consider it.

"I'm not splitting up with Calla," I say. "I'm angry at her, but she's . . . " I pause searching for the word.

"Part of the team now?" suggests Bevin. She covers my hand with her hand, and Aydin stacks his on top with a smack.

"Yeah," I say.

"Now," says Aydin. "Explain to us again why we don't hate Meltair?"

"I hate Meltair," says Bevin. I shake my head and take a long drink from my pint.

"It's not that we don't hate him, it's more that, I guess, I don't know if I hate him. The way he explained things, when you think about it from his perspective, he really believes this Eldrida Prophecy stuff. He truly thinks that if he doesn't find and train the Eldrida Hero, the world will be plunged into destruction by an unseen force. In his mind, he's just getting a head start on training people who are coming to Clocks of their own free will, but wouldn't be able to do so without a guardian's permission for another three years. It's not great, but is it really evil?" Aydin looks like he's considering, and Bevin sits chewing on her lip. "Plus," I add, "we don't actually know for sure what goes on at Clocks. Would Lytwist and even all of Burne really be sanctioning it if it's as bad as Calla says? I mean, I'm sure they take risks, and I'm sure there are accidents, but. . ." My voice trails off.

"What was he like? When you met him?" says Aydin.

"Fine." I say, "Normal. Honestly, he seems like someone we would enjoy spending time with. He also seemed tired."

"So, what does that mean about Maddie?" says Bevin. "I'm her guardian, and I'm not leaving her here. Not without at least talking to her first."

"No way," I say. "Meltair could be the coolest, leather-wearing heart-throb this side of the Eagach mountains. No way do we leave Maddie anywhere with anyone without seeing her, making sure she's alright, and having a long talk."

"Agreed," says Aydin.

***

I leave Bevin and Aydin playing cards downstairs in the tavern and wander back up to our room, where Calla is curled on a sofa staring out the window into the city. It's lit up with candles in most of the windows of most of the city buildings, and for a second, the glow of hundreds of tiny lights takes my breath away.

"I've actually never really seen Lytwist like this for as long as I've lived here," says Calla. "The view is so different from the dorms on the Clocks campus. It's beautiful." I sit down next to her on the sofa, and she pivots to face me. She's framed by the city lights pouring in from the window, which would have made her glow even if she didn't already do it on her own. Before I can say anything, she speaks.

"Tyre," she says, "I'm sorry. I can't give you all the answers and information you deserve. I can't explain right now, but what I said about you and what I implied about your character was wrong. I was wrong, and I'm sorry." I'm sorry too, but I'm not ready to say it yet.

"Tell me about Atreo," I say.

"You already know," she says, "you've seen him, actually."

"Your brother? The one I've seen? But he isn't dead?" Suddenly, all the pieces click into place. "The Inimical," I say, "whatever mission Meltair sent your brother Atreo on, put him in the path of The Inimical."

"More or less," says Calla.

"I'm sorry I yelled at you," I say, finally ready to say it, "and I'm sorry that . . . I don't know, Calla. I know it sounds ridiculous because we've only been together for a few months, but I really love you. And sometimes it makes me forget that we don't actually know each other that well. If there are parts of yourself that you're not ready to share with me, then I can try harder to understand that, but just tell me in the future. Just warn me when there's more to a story, even if you're not ready to share it. I can try to respect that." She screws her eyes shut, and I see tears roll down her face. I feel guilty for the shot of irritation that courses through my body, but I honestly don't understand why she's crying when I feel like I'm asking for the bare minimum.

"Sure," she says. "I can do that."

"Calla," I say, reaching out and taking her hand, "why are you crying?"

"I love you too," she says, "but that's a story I'm not ready to share." I sit caught in the trap of my own good intentions and let out a long breath.

"Can we talk about Meltair?" I say as a pivot.

"Meltair?" says Calla, wiping the tears off her face. "What about him?"

"Remind me again, why do we hate him exactly?" I can feel a frisson through the air as the energy changes in the room.

"He got to you, didn't he?" she says. Even though Calla's voice stays pleasant, I can feel something simmering under the surface.

"What do you mean?" I ask.

"Charming Meltair," she says, no longer able to hide that her tone is dripping with hatred, "with an answer for everything."

"Better than you with an answer for nothing," I say. I regret it the second I say it, but it's too late.

Calla stares at me like she's been slapped.

"Calla," I say. I watch every movement of her face, trying to figure out exactly what she's feeling.

"Tyre," she says, "I'm not going to pretend I'm being fair to you, but please don't be fooled into thinking that Meltair is your ally. Meltair has one ally, and that is Delanum Meltair. If he was charming to you, then that means exactly one thing: it benefits him."

"He wasn't charming," I say, "he was exhausted, and from the way he sees it, what he's doing benefits everyone."

"Why, because of the Eldrida Prophecy?" says Calla. "Tyre, his entire justification for putting the lives of hundreds of children in danger is the word of one single man that has been transcribed and distorted across three generations of egomaniacs."

"Clocks just can't be as bad as you say it is, it just-"

"Are you forgetting that I literally went to Clocks?" says Calla. "This is one of the things about my life that I actually have shared, and you don't believe me. Gee, I wonder why it's so hard for me to open up."

"Well, maybe if you opened up more, it would be easier to believe you," I snap back. I'm not off to a great start with the whole 'respecting stories she's not ready to share' thing.

"Tyre," she says, standing and starting to pace, "I'm going to give you the benefit of the doubt and say that this is because you're a good person, and because you're a good person, you can't imagine that people can be so terrible as to convince themselves to forget about what's happening at Clocks. However, I promise you that people can be that bad. You would be surprised what people can convince themselves to forget." I'm opening my mouth to respond when Calla flops back down on the couch next to me.

"How about for now," she says, "we just focus on getting Maddie? We still agree about that at least."

"Calla, it's not that I don't believe you," I say. "It's not that simple."

"It's hard to believe something you'd really rather not believe," she says, shrugging. She's acting indifferent, but I don't think she is. I think she's very hurt. I suddenly want to reach out and hug her, but it feels dissonant since I'm both still a little mad at her and I'm the one who seems to be causing her current pain. I settle for reaching out and cupping her face in my hand. I move my thumb so it brushes against her cheek.

"I agree," I say, "let's focus on getting Maddie." She half smiles and reaches up to press her face into my hand.

"Agreed," she says.

***

It's been weeks since I was pulled into the dying rose garden in my sleep. It seems hazier this time somehow. I see The Inimical before I hear him. He's just a collection of shadows in the far corner that slowly solidifies to look like a vaguely human shape, still shrouded in shadows and a huge cloak that hides his face. For the first time, I actually get to watch him move, and he does so with more effort than I imagined. I find myself wondering if he's injured or older than I thought. He still hasn't acknowledged me. Is it possible he doesn't know I'm here? I thought this place only existed when The Inimical used his magic to suddenly summon me from my dreams. I had fallen asleep with my mind full of Calla, Meltair, Maddie, and, most of all, of Atreo Ballesteros, still as death, encased in a glowing dome somewhere in the depths of The Inimical's domain like a trophy. Is it possible that I've forced my way into The Inimical's mind for once and not the other way around?

"Hm," says the shadow suddenly, "how did you get in here?"

"What do you want with Atreo?" I say. I'm not even sure how to process the admission that I'm right and I've somehow invaded his mind.

"Your obsession with Calla and her brother bores me," he says. "Calla and Atreo are not your concern. You should be focusing on Madeliza, who, last I checked, is your concern. You should also focus on holding up your end of our deal, that is, if you even still care about Calla. I hear she hasn't exactly been the model wife in terms of openness and honesty lately."

"I would say my marriage is high on the list of things that aren't your concern," I say.

"Well then, let's add a clause to our agreement that says we each mind our own business, until you turn yourself over to me in Umbra," he says.

"Calla is my wife," I say, "anything that concerns her is my business."

"Then you're going to be very disappointed with the lack of information you'll get from me about her," he says, "now get out of my head."

I wake with a start. I gulp down a glass of water and rub my temples. I don't know what to make of this new information that I can use the connection between The Inimical and myself in reverse. I try to go back to sleep, but it's useless, so I stare out the window and wait for the sun to rise.

***

"Alright, so we're clear on the plan?" says Calla. We're back on the Clocks campus at the entrance in the irrigation drain.

"I'm going to go back to Meltair's office and say that I totally bought into his explanation of why Maddie left," I say.

"Which you have," says Calla. I ignore her jab and keep talking.

"I'll tell him I'd love his opinion-"

"Expertise," says Calla. "You have to say you'd love his expertise. If you say that he won't be able to resist."

"Fine. I'll tell him I'd love his expertise on the nature of a magical item," I pull my dad's medallion out from under my shirt and hold it up. I'm not a huge fan of this part of the plan, to be honest. I don't like advertising that my father left me a magical protection medallion, much less showing it off to strangers. Calla had, however, made the excellent point that Meltair will be suspicious that we're back for round two, and stroking his ego by asking for his expertise might be our only viable option to keep him distracted.

"Exactly," she says. "I'm going to head straight for the Speckled Tower this time, so . . ." Calla doesn't get to finish reviewing her part of the plan. A horn sounds in the distance and echoes across the campus. It's so loud I have to resist the impulse to cover my ears. Calla's expression changes to one of terror.

"Shit," she says, "Tyre, we have to go."

"No way!" I say, "I'm not leaving without Maddie for a second day in a row!"

"No," she says, "not leave. We need to go. We need to go that way, towards the Copper Beeches."

"What? Why?" I say, scrambling to pull information about the Copper Beeches from my memory. It's a grove of trees that surrounds an arena of sorts on the school grounds.

"The Arena," she says, "we need to go there now."

"Why?"

"Tyre," she yells, "please just trust me! Now!"

"Climb on," I say. I throw Calla on my back and take off running on all fours at a full sprint in the direction Calla pointed until I see the grove of beech trees and the arena looming over them in the distance. I let her off as we approach, and we sprint towards the doors. I can hear a crowd gathered inside. I tug on the doors, but they don't open.

"Let me try," she says.

"Calla, if I can't open them, I doubt you can," I say. Apparently, I've spoken too soon because the doors fly open with one pull for Calla.

"Benefits of having gone here," she says. We tear into the stadium, but we don't run into anyone.

"They're all inside," says Calla, thinking the same thing. Sure enough, we turn a corner and the main arena and spectator stands come into view. We press ourselves next to the wall by one of the openings to the stadium and peer around. It looks like the stands are filled with all of the Clocks faculty and many of the students. There are other students clustered into groups of threes on the field in the center of the arena. I'm scanning the students on the field when I see her: Maddie.

A knot unties somewhere in the center of my chest just seeing her. She's alive, and whole, and right there. We're going to be able to talk to her in just a few minutes. I point to where Maddie is standing, and Calla nods, but she's gone pale. She points across the field to the opposite entryway from the one we're standing on. At first, I don't know what I'm looking at. While the entryway we're standing in is open, the one across the way is barred, and there's some kind of creature behind it. It's huge, and blue, and it seems to be throwing off blue sparks.

"Crackler," whispers Calla. I feel my entire body go cold. A crackler? What is a crackler doing here? At a school? Cracklers are essentially dragons, but while dragons are dangerous and unpredictable, they're also reasonable and intelligent. You can have a conversation with a dragon. Cracklers are all the danger of dragons, but with animal brains, and instead of fire, they carry electricity. Then I notice that all the eyes of the students in the field are locked on the crackler, and they all look terrified.

"Calla," I ask, "what is going on?" Deep down, I already know.

"Looks like the training exercise of the day is fighting the crackler," says Calla. I'm trying to remain calm and think of a plan when the bars fly open, and the crackler is out and sprinting straight for the students on the field.

"Maddie!" I yell. Before I can think or plan, I'm sprinting onto the field toward her. Everything is chaos. I can hear screaming all around me as the crackler runs, slinks, and flies at students. It's leaving the crowd alone for now, probably some sort of fairy magic protecting the stands. I can hear the crowd yelling, but can't separate the voices from the shrieks of the students on the field. I watch the crackler sink its teeth into the top half of a blond boy, and the bottom half of his body falls to the ground. I know I should be horrified, but my focus on reaching Maddie in time is all-consuming. I dodge a rogue shot of electricity by sliding forward on the ground and scramble to my feet to keep running to the last place I saw Maddie, but I've lost her in the chaos.

"Tyre, down!" yells Calla, slamming into me and somehow managing to tackle me to the earth. We barely miss an arrow that goes flying past.

"Why are the students shooting this way?" I yell. "We're nowhere near the crackler!"

"They think *you're* part of the challenge!" yells Calla.

Right. Of course they do. Because I'm a monster.

"Maddie!" I yell, spinning in the chaos as three more students rush at me. Calla drops to the ground and swipes her feet out from under one of them with her leg, and he manages to topple into the other two. "Maddie!" I call again, panicking.

"Tyre, there!" screams Calla. I see Maddie across the field, but at precisely the same time, so does the crackler.

"No!" I yell. I sprint towards her, but the crackler gets there first. It slashes towards her and two other students with its tail. The other two students are knocked sideways into the wall, but Maddie manages to jump out of the way. For a second, I'm relieved, but it's short-lived. Maddie is left on the ground in close range when the crackler turns around and lunges towards her with its mouth open. She doesn't have any weapons, but she manages to grab a piece of metal piping that the crackler knocked loose from the arena wall and holds it out in front of her as the crackler locks down with its jaw. Maddie shrieks as she tries to hold the crackler at bay, and electricity swirls around them.

"NO!" I yell. I'm finally in range and, without thinking about the complete stupidity of such an action, I try to tackle the crackler. My dad's medallion sears white hot against my chest as I collide with the crackler. While the impact doesn't faze it at all, it does seem to recoil from the burn of the medallion. As it screeches and pulls away, there's a round burn on its side. For a second, I think it's going to go for us again, but it seems to decide that other students are easier prey and slinks off.

"Maddie, Maddie, hey, I'm right here!" I run and slide to where she's lying on the field.

"Tyre?" she sobs.

"Yeah, it's me, it's me, I'm here." I don't even care that she's still giving off sparks of blue electricity; I crush her into a hug, and she clings on to me in a way she hasn't since she was a toddler. "Come on," I say, "we're going to get you out of here." Seeing me seems to have shaken something loose in Maddie, and she's crying harder and starting to hyperventilate.

She won't let me pull away from her, and she just keeps saying, "No, Tyre, please help, please help, don't leave, please don't, I can't." I can tell I'm not going to be able to get her to stand up, so I stand and pull her with me, gripping her torso with one arm and slinging her legs over the other. She clings to me so hard I'm sure she's leaving bruises. Suddenly, I'm 14 again and holding her for the very first time, looking down at this tiny, breakable human and knowing that it's my job to protect her. Clockwork Atheneum will pay for this.

"Tyre, we've got more company!" yells Calla. I realize with a shock that Calla has been holding off all the students who think I'm part of this sick challenge. I look towards where she's pointing and see that Meltair has stepped onto the field. A rogue blast of electricity hits him, but it doesn't seem to impact him at all. We lock eyes across the field, and he comes towards us.

"Fairy cursed armor," yells Calla. "He's got decent protection, even from a crackler. We need to go." I nod, and we take off running with Maddie. Suddenly, Maddie shrieks,

"No! My team! My team, Tyre! I can't leave without my team!"

"Who?" I yell.

"Her team," says Calla. "The other two kids that trained with her. There's usually a pretty heavy trauma bond there."

"Maddie, we have to go! I'm sorry!" I say. Maddie starts flailing in my arms so violently, I'm worried she's going to injure herself.

"There!" she screams. "They're right there!" She points to the two kids she was standing with earlier, who were knocked into the wall by the crackler's tail. The smaller of the two is huddled, trying to protect the head of the larger one, who seems to have been knocked unconscious. I growl in frustration.

"I can get to them," I say. I try to put Maddie down, but she shrieks and clings to me again. "Maddie, if you want me to get your friends, I need you to go to Calla!" She lets me hand her off to Calla, who can't carry her but manages to stay upright with Maddie clinging to her neck. I sprint up to Maddie's teammates, and suddenly recognize one as the eerie white-haired kid who pointed at me outside Meltair's office.

"I'm—" I start to say, thinking I'm going to have to explain I'm not an enemy, but to my surprise, the little white-haired one says,

"I know who you are! Can you carry him?" The other teenager is still unconscious next to us. As quickly as I can, I sling the unconscious teen over my shoulder.

"Sylvan!" Meltair has reached us. I turn in time to see him pulling out a sword from his belt.

"Meltair!" I yell. "You don't have to do this!" Maybe I can make him see that he's a victim of Clocks too, maybe much like my dad was. Then again, maybe while we're all being attacked by a crackler and he's coming toward me with a sword isn't the best time to have this conversation. I don't feel the medallion glowing, so it looks like Dad isn't coming to the rescue this time. Suddenly, a memory of his voice echoes through my mind, 'Bring the knife with you to Clocks.' A fairy knife against fairy armor seems worth a shot.

Before Meltair can raise his sword, I take two quick steps towards him and make a wild slash with my knife. To my intense relief, it cuts through the armor over his torso and draws blood. It isn't deep, but the sheer shock of something penetrating his armor is enough to make him step back and lose his grip on his sword. I take off running with the unconscious teen over my shoulder and hope the other one is following. Calla and Maddie are huddled in the entryway where we came in. Maddie is still emitting occasional electric sparks, which seem to be electrocuting Calla, but she keeps moving, dragging Maddie with her.

We run and run and don't stop running until we're out of the tunnel, and then Maddie is crashing into Bevin's arms at the tunnel entrance. Maddie and Bevin are holding each other and sobbing as Aydin sprints over and throws his arms around me, and Calla collapses on the ground trying to catch her breath.

"What happened?" says Aydin, finally taking stock of the situation. "Who are these people?" He looks at the large, muscly teen slung over my shoulder, and the small, white-haired one with faraway eyes who is blinking at everyone way too calmly.

"I'll explain on the walk back," I say.

***

We make our way back to the hotel as quickly as we can, gather our things, and settle our packs on the horses. There aren't enough horses to carry all of us, so we give them to the teenagers.

"I thought you said Meltair doesn't have any real power outside of Clocks?" says Bevin as Calla rushes us all to pack and then hurries us through the streets of Lytwist.

"He didn't when we were just leaving with Maddie," she says. "You're her legal guardian, but, unfortunately, we've just taken off with two other teenagers, and I'm fairly certain a report of kidnapping is being made to the Lytwist police as we speak. We need to get out of Burne as quickly as possible. Ideally tonight."

"Shit," says Aydin, rubbing his hand across his face. Thankfully, we do make it out of Burne, which at least puts us out of danger of immediate arrest. It leaves us facing the two-day trek through most of Maradal back to Thiaghal with three traumatized teenagers in tow. Calla gets the older teen to drink some water, and he wakes up as we're scrambling to pack. His name is Hugo, and the small teen with the white hair and gray eyes is named Pax.

As we make our way through Maradal back towards Lir Haven it's clear Maddie is in bad shape. She won't walk unless she's physically anchored to one of us, preferably Bevin, whose hand she has locked in hers in an unbreakable grip. The other two, Pax and Hugo, stick close to Maddie and each other but don't say much. Pax is expressionless, and Hugo seems wary. He keeps shooting glares at all of us, especially me. We walk for the most part in tense silence until suddenly Calla yells,

"Bevin!" Calla sprints over and wrenches Maddie's hand out of Bevin's just as an electric current shoots through Maddie's body. Maddie doesn't seem to feel the electricity, but Calla doubles over as she tries to cling to Maddie. Even though she doesn't seem hurt by the current, Maddie panics when her hand is wrenched out of Bevin's, and she's shrieking, flailing, and clawing at Calla, trying to get back to Bevin. As soon as the current stops, Calla lets go of Maddie and drops to the ground. Pax and Hugo immediately run to Maddie and help her up and back to Bevin.

"Calla!" I yell and run over to where she's collapsed to the ground on her back.

"Mmmmmm," she groans, screwing her eyes shut. "That is not pleasant."

"You alright?" I say, dropping down next to her and helping her to a sitting position.

"Yeah, I will be," she says, "just a little stunned." I get Calla back on her feet, and we keep moving. The teens are orbiting Bevin like moons. They seem to have decided she's the most trustworthy one in our little cabal. Occasionally, she glances at me with confused eyes and shrugs. I give her what I hope is an encouraging smile.

"How long is she going to keep doing that?" I ask Calla as quietly as I can, gesturing to Maddie whose hair ends are still smoking from the last blast of electricity that shot through her body. Calla shakes her head.

"Not many people go up against a crackler and live to tell the tale," she says. "I'm watching her like a hawk because she could seriously injure anyone she's touching when it happens, besides you or me. For us, it's just unpleasant, but as far as what this is, what effect it will have on her, and how long it will last? That's all kind of a giant question mark." I fight the urge to bury my face in my hands and let out a sob. I feel Calla lace her fingers through mine and squeeze.

"Why you?" I say. "Me, I understand because of the fairy magic, I guess, but why can you get shocked?"

"That's one of those things," she says.

"One of those things?" I say.

"One of those stories I'm not ready to tell," she says.

We make it the rest of the way to Lir Haven without incident and get checked into two rooms. At first, we were going to split with Bevin, Calla, Maddie, and Pax in one room, and Hugo, Aydin, and I in the other, but the teens won't separate, and Maddie is still latched on to Bevin. So, once again, despite having paid for two rooms, we all end up in one with Maddie and Bevin in one bed, Hugo and Pax in the other, and Aydin, Calla, and I shoulder to shoulder on the floor. I can't imagine that any of us will be able to sleep, but we're so exhausted that we all pass out until Pax wakes up screaming at three in the morning. This sends Maddie into a panic and Hugo into a rage. While Calla tries to settle Pax, Aydin and I dodge punches from Hugo, and Bevin tries to get Maddie to breathe with her. Finally, we get all three teens back to sleep, but all the adults lie awake shoulder to shoulder on the ground waiting for the sun to come up.

When Maddie, Hugo, and Pax wake the next morning, the sleep seems to have done them all a world of good. Maddie almost seems like her old self again, if still shaken, but she's at least able to be more than a foot from Bevin without going into fight or flight mode as we set out on the road for the day.

"Hey runt," I say, making my way over to where she and Pax are walking and gently putting my arm around her shoulders.

"Hey," she says. She wraps her arms around my side and nuzzles her face into my fur like she used to when she was a little kid.

"I'm so glad you're alright," I say. I don't mean to, but I start crying, and my voice catches.

"Tyre, I'm so sorry," says Maddie, her eyes also filling with tears.

"Mads, hey, it's okay, we don't need to talk about anything right now. You are safe, that's the most important thing."

"You could have died," she says, "you and Calla. I am so, so, so sorry."

"I know, Mads," I say, "You're safe. That is all that matters." She nods and wipes her eyes, just in time, too, because I see a tiny spark shoot out of her hair. Maybe the electric pulses are related to her emotions.

"Oh, Tyre," she says, her voice brightening a little bit, "I'm being rude. This is my friend Pax. Pax, this is my cousin, Tyre Sylvan."

"Hello," says Pax. "I'm Pax." I know it probably makes me a bad person, but Pax makes me anxious. This person just seems too calm, too vacant, yet somehow also too focused, and has a stare that makes me feel translucent. It's like Pax is looking right at me, but also at a million other things right behind me.

"Tyre," I say, holding out my hand.

"I know," says Pax, "I had a vision about you a few days before I saw you on the Clocks campus."

"Pax is an oracle," Maddie explains. *Great*, I think to myself. "Actually, related to the most famous oracle of all time— Almine Eldrida." I feel my stomach sink.

"How closely related?" I say.

"Not sure," says Pax. "Closely enough that we've got the same name. My full name is Pax Eldrida."

"Great to meet you, Pax," I say, trying to sound calmer than I feel. "Excuse me for a second, I just need to go check in with my wife about something."

"The vampire?" says Pax. I look at Maddie for an explanation, but she's as confused as I am.

"Tyre isn't a vampire," she says. "He was cursed by fairy magic when he was 11."

"Huh?" says Pax. "What did I say?"

"Never mind," says Maddie, giving Pax a gentle smile. "This happens sometimes," she says quietly to me. "Pax gets confused between things from visions of the future and things that have actually happened. It's hard to keep everything straight, so sometimes what Pax says doesn't make any sense." I nod and leave Bevin to keep an eye on Maddie and Pax while I walk up further to where Aydin and Calla are trying to keep Hugo occupied by seeing who can kick rocks the farthest as they walk.

"Cal, can I grab you for a second?" I say. She drops back as Aydin and Hugo walk ahead.

"What's up?" she says.

"We may have a problem," I say, glancing back at Maddie, Bevin, and Pax.

"A bigger problem than the kidnapping?" she says.

"Related," I say. "Pax's full name is 'Pax Eldrida.' Any chance Meltair will just let us take off with an Eldrida descendant just because we've reached the safety of Maradal?"

"Nope," says Calla, glancing back at Pax. "No chance at all."

15

The rest of the journey home is thankfully uneventful, but exhausting. Mom called Alexander to look everyone over the second we arrived and explained what had happened. With the exception of bumps and bruises, we all received a clean bill of physical health, except for Maddie and her electric sparks, which he could not make any sense of.

"The teenagers are all sleeping in one bed again," says Calla a few weeks later. She comes downstairs into the kitchen, rubbing sleep out of her eyes. She's the third one up, besides me and Mom. Mom shrugs as Calla drops down into the chair next to her. We've given up on trying to keep the teenagers from all sleeping in one bed.

Bevin was the first to discover this quirk the night after we returned. After much crying and hugging of Maddie, Mom sprang into action, getting the guest rooms set up with fresh linens and towels. But the next morning, when Bevin went to check on Maddie, she discovered Maddie, Hugo, and Pax all curled like puppies in Maddie's bed. We'd discouraged it for a few days, but even two weeks later, it's almost impossible to deter. It seems to be the only way to avoid one of them waking up screaming.

"They're going to have a hard time separating when Hugo's parents finally get here," Calla sighs as she pours cream into her coffee.

"Maybe they won't have to," says Mom. "I've told Hugo's parents that they can stay as long as they like. We may just have more guests for a while."

I had thought that my mom would be the first one to insist on contacting parents, but, surprisingly, Calla had beaten her to it. Almost as soon as we were through the doors on arriving home, she was taking names and contact information from Pax and Hugo and sending for a Holpie.

Hugo, it turns out, is from a particularly rural part of Maradal, two hours outside Lir Haven. His parents, like Calla's grandfather, had been offered a stipend for his attendance at Clockwork Atheneum and didn't know the truth about the severity of what went on at Clocks any more than we had. They had already written back to express their relief that Hugo was back in Maradal and would have been here already to pick him up if it wasn't for another snow squall.

Pax's parents are more of a mystery. They live in an expensive and stylish part of Lytwist and sent a message back simply asking us to send a bill for any of Pax's expenses and that they hoped Pax was having a good time. Pax shrugged when reading their response, but I noticed Maddie's hand reach for Pax's, and Hugo moved closer to them both as if preparing to somehow shield Pax from emotional pain.

"I'm just glad the kidnapping thing is settled," I say.

"Don't count on it," says Calla. "Meltair might not be able to claim kidnapping now that both sets of parents have given permission for the kids to be here, but he's not letting go of Pax without a fight."

***

The fight, as it turned out, arrived later that afternoon.

"Tyre!" I hear Aydin call from the main foyer.

"We're in here!" I yell. The teenagers are all sitting on the rug, and Maddie is sketching in front of the fire. Little blue sparks are shooting out of her as she draws, so Hugo and Pax aren't actually touching her, but their proximity suggests they would all be on top of each other if they could be. I actually feel like I've been making some progress with Hugo now that his parents have let us know he likes sports. I've been taking him out to teach him some archery each day.

All the teenagers tense up at Aydin's yell, but Hugo's shoulders practically rise to his ears. "What's up?" I call back to Aydin, trying to make my voice light and casual. Aydin appears in the doorway a few seconds later, looking pale and practically shaking with rage. I can feel the teenagers' anxious eyes all locked on me, so, as casually as I can, I reach out and take the paper in Aydin's hand.

"This came in your daily briefing for the council meeting," he says.

An Update From the Desk of Delanum Meltair, Headmaster of Clockworks Atheneum

Residents of Lytwist and likely, most of Burne, will already know that one week ago, the grounds of Clockwork Atheneum were attacked by a monster made from cursed fairy magic. I have had suspicions about something of this nature brewing for some time, but did not wish to make an announcement until I was absolutely certain. We have all known for some time that individuals made into monsters by fairy magic have been taken by the dark force known as The Inimical. I know that we have all feared that these individuals have been harmed or even killed.

I, for some time, have had a different fear, which was finally confirmed yesterday when one of these creatures attacked Clockwork Atheneum. I think we all suspect that The Inimical is the unseen force foretold by the Eldrida Prophecy. This attack, and subsequent abduction of three students, confirms that, far from being his victims, the fairy magic monsters are his foot soldiers.

The Inimical has now amassed an army of these monsters, and his first act of war outside of Andestine has been to send one of them to kidnap none other than Almine Eldrida's descendant, Pax Eldrida, as well as two other students, Madeliza Ruarcc and her boyfriend, Hugo O'Reed.

While we still do not know the extent of The Inimical's power, he seems to have sources inside Clockwork Atheneum, as only those in the closest circles could know that, mere days prior to this kidnapping, Pax Eldrida made a prophecy declaring that Madeliza Ruarcc, affectionately known as Maddie, is the Eldrida Hero destined to stop The Inimical's path of destruction. We are desperately searching for Pax, Maddie, and Hugo, and urge citizens to help return them to their rightful place at Clockwork Atheneum. The fate of the world may depend on it. Please, I urge you, if you encounter any monsters cursed by fairy magic, exercise extreme caution.

I step out of the room as calmly as I can and pull Aydin with me. "Who has seen this?" I say.

"The entire Thiagal council, and the Maradal grand council, but Meltair has put it in newspapers too. This is just the official briefing," says Aydin. I can hardly think, my head is pounding so hard with rage.

***

"As if people cursed by fairy magic weren't already targets!" I rant to Calla in our room that night. "You remember what happened that night on the road home from the pub. He's put people in danger just to serve his own warped agenda."

"Aren't you the last one?" says Calla.

"We think so, but it's not like people advertise when this happens. There could be others we don't know about."

"Well, I am sorry your budding friendship had to end this way," says Calla.

"Could you not be a jerk right now, please?" I snap.

"Sorry, sorry," she says. "I guess, I just . . . this is what Meltair does. He twists and turns and warps the truth so it serves him. He may actually believe some version of this at this point." Calla gives the official announcement a look like she's smelled something awful. I put my head in my hands.

"But why?" I yell. "He knows where Maddie is! He knows exactly who took her! Why would he say this?"

"Because," says Calla, "Meltair has no real power. He's not Lytwist police, or a local sheriff. He's a school headmaster, and he just happens to be a famous one. The only thing he can really do is influence public opinion. If he wants Pax back, he needs to create enough public outcry that it makes the people with actual power take notice."

"Oh, and don't forget Maddie," I say, "who's supposedly the 'Eldrida Hero' now."

"We need to find out what Pax actually predicted," she says.

"What makes you think Pax predicted anything at all?" I say. "Meltair could have just made that up, too."

"Still," she says, looking unconvinced, "if Pax made a real prophecy and it involves Maddie, we need to know about it. Especially given her current condition." I feel a pit in my stomach. Instead of getting gradually better, Maddie seems to be having more and more attacks of electricity.

"We can talk to Pax tomorrow," I say. "Oh, and Calla?"

"Hm?" she says. I flop down on the bed next to her, and she turns and nuzzles her head into my arm. An idea has taken hold in my mind, and even though I can't quite see how it could be true, I also can't quite ignore it.

"I think it's Meltair," I say.

"You think what is Meltair?" she says, propping herself up with one elbow on the bed and one arm draped across my chest.

"The Inimical," I say. "I know it sounds impossible," I add quickly, seeing Calla's look of skepticism, "but who benefits from The Inimical more than Meltair? Think about it; the more powerful The Inimical gets, the more people get scared, the more powerful Meltair gets. Who knows more about magic than someone who's lived and breathed at the magical Clockwork Atheneum their entire life?"

I watch Calla as she considers. Sensing an opening, I keep going. "And", I say, "remember the night The Inimical came for me here? The thing in the cloak that came to 'collect me' was just a broom. What if there's no "Inimical" at all? What if Meltair has figured out how to harness fairy magic to enchant objects, and he's essentially got a giant marionette holding all of the greater Umbra area hostage?"

"Alright, let's say you're right," says Calla, smoothing a piece of fur behind one of my ears, "if Meltair can use fairy magic at will, why did he let us take off with Pax Eldrida and the Eldrida Hero and, apparently, her boyfriend? We should ask Maddie about that, by the way."

"I don't know," I admit, "but no human has ever been able to use magic at will before. Maybe there are limits or rules, or he's just not great at it yet?"

"Yet good enough at it to trap a major city?" says Calla.

I shrug.

"I'm not saying you're wrong," says Calla, "and good on you for not underestimating Meltair. He's definitely dangerous enough to be The Inimical. I just can't make the timeline add up."

I eventually have to give in and acknowledge that she has a point. I don't have additional information or evidence to share, but I start to fall asleep still feeling sure that I'm right.

"Calla?" I say as she snuggles into my side.

"Hm?" she says.

"If he is The Inimical, maybe we can help him. Maybe we can talk with him and get him to stop."

This gets Calla to pop her head up off my chest and look at me.

"What?" she says. "Why?"

"From what you've told me, he's as much a victim of Clocks as anyone." Calla's face is stone still as I stare at her, trying to discern what she's thinking in the dark.

"You'd want to help The Inimical?" says Calla. "After all this?"

"If he could be helped," I say. Calla lies back on my chest and is quiet for so long that I think she's fallen asleep.

"Well, I know Meltair," she says, "and some people can't. Some people can't be helped."

***

"Hello there, my little foot soldier," says a now familiar voice from behind me. I'm in the dead rose garden again.

"Hello, Meltair," I say, turning around to face the shadow.

"I'm not Meltair," says the shadow.

"That's exactly what Meltair would say," I joke, sounding braver than I feel. There's something especially ominous about the darkness in this place tonight. I feel like it's reaching for me somehow, and I can't quite track where the dark ends and I begin.

"On the contrary," says the shadow, "I've never known Meltair to refrain from taking credit for anything, much less something he's actually done.

You think he'd be able to harness fairy magic without posting it to the morning news?"

"You seem to know a lot about Delanum Meltair," I say.

"What I know," says the shadow, "is that it's time for you to make good on our deal. I've given you weeks to get the kid settled back home with her family. It's time to head north."

I feel like I've been doused in cold water, because he's right. I've known for a long time now that it's time to go and get Calla's brother. Calla has been patient and not mentioned it, but the night before, I'd found her huddled in our bed, curled around the mirror, watching Atreo's troubled sleep. I haven't been able to bring myself to leave Maddie just yet. Not after we came so close to losing her.

"There won't ever be a right time," says the shadow. Its voice sounds almost compassionate, and the dissonance of that makes my skin crawl.

"What if I don't?" I say out of sheer spite, knowing full well we're going north anyway to rescue Calla's brother.

"Then I'll torture Calla," says The Inimical, "you know I can do it."

"You know," I say, a sudden realization washing over me, "I'm beginning to think that Calla can take care of herself." As I say it, I'm realizing it's true. Our romp through Lytwist has altered the way I see Calla. I don't want her hurt, and if I can, I'll do anything to prevent it, but there's suddenly something about her that doesn't feel helpless. "You know what," I add, "whatever you have going on with Calla, you may think you have the upper hand, but I assure you, whatever power you think you have over her, you're underestimating her."

The darkness around the shadow shakes like it's laughing, and the breeze scrapes through the dead trees. "Tyre Sylvan," says the shadow, "you are full of surprises. Fine. I'll sweeten the deal. Be here in two days' time, and I'll give you a cure to send back for the little lightning bug."

"You're bluffing," I say, feeling my heart start to race, "you can't know that you can fix whatever is wrong with Maddie."

"Maybe," says the shadow, "but according to you, I *am* the headmaster of Clockwork Atheneum. If anyone knows, I do."

"This isn't a joke!" I yell. "Maddie is sick! You know what, the more I talk to you, the more I think you're not a mysterious shadow at all. You're just a man. If you're not Meltair, and I still think you might be, then I will figure out who you are."

"You want to guess my name, Tyre Sylvan?" says the shadow, an unexpected sadness creeping into the eerie voice again. "I can promise that you won't be able to guess it."

"Oh, and why is that?" I say, "What makes you so sure?"

"Because if you do," says the shadow as the garden starts to fade from around me, "then this has all been for nothing."

16

"Hey, runt," I say, making my way into the library where Maddie is, before I realize she's napping. She has dark circles under her eyes that remind me of Calla's. The morning light is streaming in through the library window down onto her face, and I see little sparks whizzing around her hair. I wait for them to stop before I pull a chair up next to the window seat where she's napping and shake her shoulder. As gentle as I try to be, she still jerks awake. "It's just me," I say, putting my hand on her shoulder and easing her back onto her pillows. She lets out a breath and slumps backwards.

"Sorry," she says, "I'm not sleeping that well at night right now."

"Why, because you and the other teenagers sleep in a giant pile?" Maddie blushes, but I see more of the Maddie I know when she takes a huffy tone and says,

"Pax and Hugo are the only reason I get any sleep at all. And how do you even know that?" She crosses her arms and squints at me.

"To be honest," I say, "we're all watching you like hawks, Mads." The fight goes out of her, and she sags against her pillows again.

"I know," she says. "I really messed up. I'm so sorry."

"That's not what I meant. I mean, you did," I joke, "but I just meant that we all love you and we just want to make sure you're safe."

"I know," she says, her small smile coming back.

"Mads," I say, "can I ask you something?"

"If it's about whether I'm dating Hugo, then the answer is, it's complicated."

"You know it's not, but I would like to talk about that."

"Later," says Maddie, waving her hand, "I'll fill you in after you tell me what your question is."

"This prophecy that Pax made about you being the Eldrida Hero? Is there any truth to that?"

"I think," says Maddie slowly, "you need to ask Pax about that." She sounds calm, but she's gone pale. "Hugo as well, actually. He's Pax's scribe."

"Pax's what?" I ask.

"Scribe," says Maddie. "The way Pax explains it is that sometimes people go into a state a bit like a trance when they have a vision or make a prophecy. Usually, when it's just snippets or glimpses, Pax can hold on to it, but for something long, like a true story-form prophecy, someone needs to be there at all times to take notes so it isn't lost. For Pax, that person is Hugo."

"Do you know what the prophecy says?" I ask. Maddie hesitates and chews her bottom lip for a minute before responding.

"Hugo recited it to me once before he and Pax gave the official written version to Professor Hatt, which he had to do," she says, seeing the look on my face. "As a scribe, he was required to turn over any of Pax's prophecies to one of the Professors, or he would be in serious trouble if anyone found out." At the mention of 'serious trouble,' I see her hand tighten on her blanket until her knuckles turn white.

"I understand," I say. "Do you remember what it said?"

"Not very well," says Maddie, " but Hugo probably does. I'm having trouble remembering a lot of Clocks right now. It all feels a little . . . Her gaze wanders off into the distance, and I see sparks form on the tops of her shoulders.

"Maddie." Without thinking, I reach out and take her hand, and she practically jumps out of her skin. "Sorry, sorry," I say.

"It's alright," she says, shaking her head as the sparks fade. "Anyways, Hugo will know. He'll remember the entire prophecy."

I start my quest to find Pax and Hugo in the kitchen, but find Bevin instead. She looks better rested than Maddie and Calla, but not by much.

"Hey, stranger," she says, brightening when she sees me.

"Hey, yourself." I know I should keep up my search for Hugo and Pax, but Bevin isn't kidding when she says 'stranger.' In all the chaos, I feel like I haven't been able to sit and properly talk to her or Aydin in days, maybe even weeks now. I drop onto a stool across the table from her and pop a cookie from a plate on the table in my mouth. "How are you holding up?" I ask between bites. She rubs her hand across her face so hard it looks like she's trying to remove her freckles.

"Um, I'm holding up," she says. I reach out to squeeze her hand and then hesitate, having a flashback to startling Maddie.

"Ah, I see you've also made the mistake of trying to comfort Maddie," she says, watching my hesitation.

"I was just talking to her over in the library," I say.

"Did she tell you about this love triangle that's going on with her, Hugo, and Pax?" says Bevin, smirking.

"No!" I say. As much as I want to know about this love triangle, there's another question I need to get Bevin's thoughts on first. I explain my theory about Meltair being The Inimical. Bevin frowns, following along as I present my case. She chews on her bottom lip, thinking it over.

"It's possible," she says. "It's definitely possible."

"But?" I say.

She looks even more thoughtful.

"I don't know, Tyre," she says. "There's something totally horrible and wrong and offensive that I've been wondering about."

"Wow, what a lead-up!" I say.

Bevin doesn't laugh.

"Bev," I say, "How long have we known each other? You can tell me anything."

"I just don't want you to be mad," she whispers.

"I won't be," I say, wondering what could possibly make Bevin this hesitant.

"It's something I've been thinking about since you first told us about talking to The Inimical in your dreams, and how the only other person you talk to in your dreams is your dad."

Suddenly, I understand what she's getting at.

"You think The Inimical is my dad?" I ask, louder than I mean to.

"You said you wouldn't get mad!" she says. "I'm sorry, it's just, it's been bothering me and . . ."

"Bevin," I say, keeping my voice as calm as I can. I look at Bevin's exhausted face and worried eyes and find myself calming down. "Bevin," I say again, "my dad is dead, not haunting a city in Andestine."

"Yeah, you're right, of course. I feel so ridiculous for thinking it. It's all this stress." Bevin genuinely looks like she's about to cry.

"Bev," I say, "you and me, we're good. Always." I put my hand on her shoulder, and she reaches up and squeezes my hand. "Now," I say, changing the subject, "tell me about this love triangle. All Maddie told me about her relationship with Hugo is that it's complicated." Bevin laughs. It's a forced laugh, but she does brighten a little bit as she leans in, in a conspiratorial way.

"Well, apparently—" she says, but she stops mid-sentence and looks up at something over my shoulder.

"Pax, sweetheart? You, alright?" she says.

I turn around and see that Pax has wandered into the kitchen and waves when Bevin and I look up. Bevin smiles and waves back. Pax continues to smile and blink at us.

"Um, Pax, honey," Bevin tries again, "you need something?"

"Tyre has a question for me," says Pax.

Bevin looks at me and raises her eyebrows.

"I actually do have a question for Pax," I say, answering Bevin's unasked question. "But Pax," I say, turning around fully, "Maddie says we need Hugo to answer it. It's about the prophecy you made naming Maddie as the Eldrida Hero."

"I did not name Maddie as the Eldrida Hero," says Pax, looking offended, "I don't even know if I believe in the 'Eldrida Hero,' but I did make a prophecy about Maddie."

"Do you remember it enough to share it with us?" asks Bevin.

"Not the whole thing," says Pax. "Tyre is right. We need Hugo for that."

Pax, Bevin, and I spread the word, and by that night, the entire team assembled in the sitting room for a formal reading of prophecy: the team being me, Mom, Bevin, Aydin, Calla, Maddie, Hugo, Pax, then Ronan and Molly O'Reed, parents to Hugo O'Reed. Hugo's parents arrived midafternoon and have not let Hugo out of their sight since. At first, I had tried to keep this small instead of making an entire production of it, but Hugo refused to read the prophecy without Maddie and Pax present, and it snowballed from there. Hugo stands in front of the fireplace, facing the room and looking as nervous as I've seen him in the last few days. There's something familiar about this kind of nervousness.

"As you all know," he starts. With a pang, I realize that he reminds me of me when my dad died, playing at being a grown man without any clue what that might mean. A wave of sympathy washes over me, and I give him an encouraging smile. He takes a deep breath and goes on. "I am Pax's scribe." He gives Pax an affectionate smile, and Maddie reaches out to squeeze Pax's hand. "As such, I am responsible for recording any prophecies Pax makes. I would like to share the prophecy made by Pax last week that is referenced in the recent slanderous publications by Meltair." The room goes even more still and quiet as Hugo takes out a small leather notebook and starts to read:

Where do shadows come from?

Why are teacups full of blood?

Why are all the roses dying?

Why can this battle be stopped but not won?

These questions will have answers.

And when they all do, Hugo O'Reed will kill The Inimical under the light of the watching moon.

No one speaks for a moment as we all process the words. Maddie is the first one to speak up, her eyes full of tears. "Hugo," she whispers, "you can't change it just by changing the words."

"Why not?" Hugo practically yells back. I see he's crying too, and I'm beginning to realize something is wrong. The prophecy we've just heard doesn't mention Maddie at all. "It's not fair. You are NOT the Eldrida Hero. It's too dangerous, I can't lose you. I can do it instead. I can take your place!"

"Hugo," Maddie whispers again, starting to cry in earnest now. Pax is tearing up as well.

"Son," Mr. O'Reed's low voice echoes from one of the far armchairs, "right now, you just need to tell us what you've really heard. Everything else, we sort out after that." His father's voice seems to steady him and, for a second, I have a pang of ridiculous jealousy. Hugo takes a shuddering breath and repeats the last line of the prophecy again.

"Madeliza Ruarcc will kill The Inimical," he whispers, "under the light of the watching moon."

"So you see," says Pax, wiping away tears, "I didn't say that Maddie is the Eldrida Hero at all. That makes an assumption that the Eldrida prophecy is about The Inimical, which we don't know for sure!"

"Right," says Aydin, "however, you did just predict that Maddie is destined to kill The Inimical. Which is, you know . . ." Aydin's voice trails off.

"Not great," Calla fills in when Aydin's voice dies out.

"I don't want to kill anyone," Maddie whispers so quietly that, if it weren't for the room's attention locked on her, no one would have heard it. Then she says louder, "I don't want to kill anyone at all!" She runs sobbing from the room. Before anyone can go after her, Pax's tear-filled voice fills the room.

"This always happens! This isn't my fault! I didn't ask to be like this!" Then Pax runs crying from the room as well.

A dumbfounded silence surrounds us for a moment, and then we break into action at once. Bevin goes after Maddie, Mom runs after Pax, and I can hear Hugo's parents asking Aydin if there's a place where they can have a little more privacy to calm Hugo down, who is now also sobbing. Aydin shuffles them out of the sitting room towards the library, leaving Calla and I alone in the sitting room. We both open our mouths to speak, but neither of us knows where to start. She crosses the room towards me and searches my eyes like she's trying to read my mind. I lean down and kiss her forehead, and we stand side by side looking into the fire until there are only embers left.

17

"Alright, good," says Calla, as Maddie kicks her foot towards her. "Now just remember, if someone is trying to kick you, you actually want to step closer to shorten their range and then go in like this," Calla goes on to demonstrate another throw, but Maddie snaps at her.

"Yeah, I learned all this at Clocks!" she says.

"Alright, alright," says Calla, holding her hands up in a 'calm down' gesture. She's being incredibly patient with Maddie, all things considered. We're outside with mats spread out on the frozen ground in the gardens. I feel bad about how irritable Maddie has been, considering that it took some serious convincing to get Calla to agree to continue the training Maddie started at Clocks. Once it was clear that Maddie was now implicated in a prophecy that seemed to inevitably involve some kind of combat, it seemed unwise not to continue her training, and the only one who really knows anything about fighting in this house beyond basic self-defense is Calla.

When I first approached her about it, she was surprisingly hesitant, considering how much she loves Maddie, but I couldn't really blame her. Lately, Maddie's general tearfulness and jumpiness seem to have given way to outbursts of irritability and generally just being an asshole. I also wonder if Calla's hesitation has to do with Atreo. She still hasn't brought it up, but I know she's anxious to go get him. It's well past The Inimical's deadline, and there's a part of me that wonders if she's vomiting blood again as well and just hiding it from me. I watch as she and Maddie start sparring again. As terrible a dancer as Calla is, she's a surprisingly good fighter, and it's mesmerizing to watch the way she moves and twirls. At least, until Maddie falls on her rear end and screams at Calla to knock it off.

"Sorry, Mads," says Calla. She offers Maddie her hand, and I hold my breath. Thankfully, Maddie takes it.

"I'm sorry," says Maddie, all the fight going out of her. "I've been such a nightmare lately." She wipes her hand across her face.

"You're traumatized," says Calla. "It happens."

"So are Pax and Hugo, and they're not like this," she says. "Well," she considers, "Pax isn't."

"No," says Calla, "Pax is just a million miles away for most of the day. Very psychologically healthy." That at least gets Maddie to crack a smile as Calla pulls her to her feet.

"This is silly," says Maddie, "I'm going to die."

"You're not going to die, Runt," I say, walking over.

"Why would you think you're going to die?" says Calla.

"Because, apparently, I'm destined to fight The Inimical?" she says. "And I can't even fight my brother's strange wife?" This gets a belly laugh from Calla.

"Mads, the prophecy says very clearly you're going to kill The Inimical, not fight it, so I wouldn't worry too much about dying," says Calla.

Maddie shakes her head.

"I can't kill someone," she whispers, "so if I ever cross paths with The Inimical, I'm done." She sits down on the ground and curls her arms around her knees.

"You'd be surprised what you can do," says Calla, sitting down next to her and pushing some of her hair out of her face. I sit down on her other side. It might have been well-intentioned, but apparently, that was not the right thing to say because suddenly Maddie is bawling huge, heaving sobs like I haven't seen since Calla was crying outside of the pub in Lir Haven.

"I. Want. Out." She sobs.

"Maddie," I say.

"NO!" She shrieks. "All the stories and the songs and legends. They all make it sound like, I don't know, an adventure, or fun, or glamorous. I was wrong. I was so wrong. I want out. I want it to end. I don't want to do this. I don't." At this point, she's crying too hard to really be understood anymore.

Calla puts an arm around her, and she sobs into Calla's shoulder while Calla looks at me with worried eyes. I feel another pang of guilt for not leaving to rescue Atreo, but how can I leave with Maddie in this state? As if to confirm my point, a bolt of electricity pulses through Maddie's body, and Calla screws her eyes shut in pain but doesn't let her go.

"There will never be a right time." The Inimical's voice from my dream floats back to me, along with, *"I'll give you a cure for the little lightning bug."*

***

"Tyre," Aydin's voice echoes as we walk inside, "we have a problem."

"Ahhh!" I yell, "Of course we do!"

"Emergency council meeting," he says.

"The Inimical?" I ask.

"Not this time," says Aydin. He turns, and I follow without a word. Instead of going up the stairs, we head straight down the hall that leads to the ballroom and turn again down another short flight of stairs that opens into the stone council room.

Mom is already here, as is Sheriff Murchad. Aydin and I make four, so we must be waiting for the two other council members. We don't speak to each other as we settle into our seats around the large stone table. I can't help but feel as though Sheriff Murchad is staring at me just a little harder than usual. Mrs. Colwan, the keeper of the small Thiaghal library and historical archive, arrives as councilor number five, and Mr. Shea, who runs the bank and serves as treasurer, makes six.

The only counselor I can say I've ever outright failed to get along with is Murchad. The rest have always been polite to me; I think mostly out of loyalty to my parents. Today, there's a definite tension in the air, and I have the sinking feeling that Meltair's letter is at the root of this meeting. Although surely Aydin would have warned me if I was walking into an ambush? I glance at him sitting next to me and try to catch his eyes, but he's glaring at Murchad. Once everyone is seated, I ceremonially stand, then sit again and pull my chair to the table to signal that the meeting has started.

"I recognize and respect the tradition that we would usually present our business in order of Governor first, followed by seniority on the council," I open, making sure to acknowledge the ever-important insistence on sameness and tradition in Thiaghal. However, I am told this is an emergency meeting, thus emergency rules apply. I invite the councilor who called the meeting to speak." I look around the room, curious to know who has called this meeting. To my surprise, Colwan stands and clears her throat.

"I would like to discuss the growing threat of Senzicaria," she says.

I do a double-take and let out a sigh of relief. When Aydin said this meeting wasn't about The Inimical himself, I thought the only thing it could be about was Meltair's letter and my supposed allegiance to The Inimical.

"Senzicaria?" I ask. "The illness in Andestine?"

"I've been in close correspondence with the health council there," says Colwan, "partly because my sister lives in Andestine, in Delante de Bosque. I'm not quite sure why we're ignoring the threat," she says, casting a nasty look at Shea, "but if I could present some information, I'm certain we won't ignore the threat any further."

"Of course you can," I start to say when Shea lets out a snort. "Do you have something to say, Shea?" I ask, feeling my temper flare at his rudeness. I'm pleased to see he's startled at my tone, even though he tries to hide it by taking off his glasses and cleaning them in a way I'm sure he feels is nonchalant.

"Senzicaria isn't real," he says, shrugging. "It's a silly, fictional illness, made up by impoverished people in an ailing country to try to gain access to emergency aid from neighboring countries for necessities like food and clean water. Sad state of affairs, but hardly worth our time when there are much more serious threats." Colwan is still staring daggers at Shea.

"That's nothing but prejudiced nonsense," she hisses through gritted teeth. "Andestine is at least as well-off as Maradal, and has more great cities, to be certain. A fine thing for you to judge from your position of managing the banking of the great metropolis of Thiaghal."

Shea goes immediately red. Before he can say anything, I stand and hold up my hand.

"Please," I say, "continue, Mrs. Colwan."

"To understand Senzicaria," she says, "you need to understand the Claret Garden."

Shea scoffs again.

"Shea," I say, "make another sound and you will be removed."

"But," he splutters, "the Claret Garden is an Andestinian fairytale! A bedtime story for children! A nonsensical waste of our time!"

"As was the tale of the Eldrida Hero in Thiaghal until very recently," says Mom seriously, "and we see how that's turning out. If our keeper of records has received information that this threat is serious enough to call an emergency meeting, and this garden is a part of it, we will hear it."

I feel Aydin nodding next to me. Colwan offers my mother a tight smile and continues.

"As it stands," she says, "he's not entirely wrong. It is a legend, and the absolute truth of it all has likely been lost. However, if I may . . ." She pulls out a frail-looking book of stories and begins to read. I dart my eyes to Shea, daring him to scoff again. He manages to stay quiet, but his lips are pressed into such a tight line I worry they're going to disappear.

Colwan begins:

Many, many years ago, in the land of the fairies, there was a king who loved his queen very, very much. This queen loved nothing more than flowers of all kinds: oleander, narcissus, snapdragons, rhododendrons, and above all, roses. Her dearest love was planting and cultivating her wonderful gardens.

After the birth of her first child, her husband wished to give her a gift. He planted a garden of enchanted roses that smelled sweeter than any other roses, were redder than any other roses, and as long as they remained tethered to their roots, never faded even in the coldest months. The queen loved this garden and spent many a very happy day there with her young daughter.

However, as often happens in these stories, things did not remain happy forever. Anyone who knows the nature of fairies knows that— like vampires, and cracklers, and banshees— they are hungry things. While vampires crave blood, and cracklers crave electricity, fairies crave the use of their magic on other beings. It won't do to alter fairyland, for if they do not use their magic to affect other creatures, they go slowly mad. Some take on human godchildren and grant them gifts, others appoint themselves as arbiters of justice, punishing creatures they perceive as doing wrong.

I avoid everyone's eye contact at this point in the story.

Unfortunately, the claret garden, like other magical entities, turned out to be a hungry thing. Eventually, it filled the plot appointed for it and kept growing. Anyone who tried to trim it began to feel sick and strange. The legend goes that they would begin to feel feverish and experience chills and nausea. Then, the fever would worsen, and they would bleed from their pores, from their eyes, their noses, and their mouths. Everywhere their blood touched, claret roses grew. Once the bleeding began, they lived for three weeks, no more and no less. Inevitably, they all died, with more claret roses springing from their graves. Eventually, the garden was magically contained in fairyland, and no one's blood has since grown a claret rose."

"So," concluded Colwan, "that is the fabled origin of Senzicaria. The bleeding fever that allows the claret roses to spread."

"Clearly," says Shea, "this is just an early explanation for a terrible illness. Even if there was such a garden, why would it suddenly be impacting people now?"

"I don't know," says Colwan, "I just know that there are increasing reports in Andestine about these symptoms followed by a three-week bleeding and fever, and invariably, death. No medicine has been able to touch it. Everyone who contracts it dies."

"And are these mythical claret roses growing out of the blood of the affected?" spits Shea.

"Unclear," says Colwan, cooly, "we can't expect everything from legend to be exactly true. It's been passed down for centuries after all."

"So fairytale or not," I say, "what I'm hearing is that there is a growing threat of an epidemic coming to Maradal from Andestine, and it's an epidemic that has no known cure. What else do we know? How long can someone have it without showing signs? How is it spread? How many in Andestine are affected, and how close to our borders? The last communication I received on this was weeks ago, and that made it sound like a possibility of a threat and not a full-blown emerging epidemic with no cure. If this is true, why is this information coming from an emergency council meeting called by our record keeper, and not through usual channels?" I expect Colwan to answer, so I'm surprised when Mom speaks.

"Because," she says, "most people outside of Andestine are of the opinion that Mr. Shea so loudly shared earlier. That Senzicaria is a folktale, and that the reports from Andestine are from impoverished city neighborhoods that want additional resources from other countries. The Andestine monarchy generally supports what Mrs. Colwan said about increasing rates of a bleeding fever, but they're not saying it's resulted in death in all cases."

"Could they be trying to prevent public panic?" says Aydin.

"Perhaps," says Mom. "All of Burne has taken an official firm position that, based on the data from the Andestine monarchy, there is no immediate threat of epidemic. Maradal has generally been following their lead, although the counties that border Andestine have been understandably more concerned."

"Why is this the first I'm hearing of how serious this could be?" I ask.

"The first time the potential seriousness of it was made clear at all was in the meeting at the Andestine border to discuss The Inimical's movements. The representatives from Andestine made overtures that they'd like to arrange a meeting to discuss it, some calling it rising rates of a bleeding fever, and some outright calling it Senzicaria, like we've seen in earlier correspondence. Of course, the focus of that meeting was on The Inimical's movements."

"Which is what we should all be focused on," says Murchad, "not fairytale illnesses from a dying country."

"You're parroting the rhetoric of a filthy smear campaign," hisses Colwan. "Andestine is not dying. Just because they have a monarchy does not mean that they're backwards and inept."

"Again," says Aydin, "fine judgment coming from us. We only have one pub in the entire town, and it doubles as a post office."

"A smear campaign perpetrated by whom?" says Shea, "For what purpose? Honestly, this talk of conspiracy is for children. Andestine is having an outbreak of illness, and it's very sad, but for us to be dedicating our resources to it when The Inimical remains at the gates is utterly preposterous."

"This is just as immediate a threat!" yells Colwan. "My sister says—"

"Yes, that's another thing," says Shea. "I think we may want to discuss your conduct in using your capacity as a city councilor to call an emergency meeting based not on official correspondence, but on the fretting of a nervous family member."

Colwan turns bright red, and before she responds, I hold my hand up to call the meeting to silence.

"If this is a possible threat, I think we should take precautions at a minimum," I say. "Distribute information. Complete another survey to check for illness. It's the least we can do. Then we can obviously consider quarantine measures if we need to."

"You'd like that, wouldn't you?" says Murchad, glowering as he leans back in his chair.

"Excuse me?" Aydin says before I can.

"You'd like everyone chasing around after Senzicaria while your pal The Inimical extends his shadow all the way to Thiaghal, wouldn't you?"

"How dare you!" yells Mom, standing up and knocking her chair backwards.

"I think," I say, surprised at my own calm, "that you need to leave."

"You can't remove me from this council without a majority vote," he says, "and I won't go unless I'm removed."

"Then shall we vote on it?" I say. "All in favor of the immediate removal of Sheriff Murchad from the Thiaghal city council?" I raise my hand along with Aydin, Mom, and Colwan. Shea sits, continuing to look around the room with an unreadable expression as Murchad scowls and stands from his chair.

"You'll regret this, monster," he whispers as he passes me on his way out of the room.

"Well," says Shea, as the sound of his footsteps disappears down the hall, "wasn't that dramatic."

"All in favor of implementing level one epidemic precautions throughout Thiaghal until further notice, while we continue to monitor the threat of Senzicaria?" I say. Again, Shea is the only one who doesn't vote in favor. I approve the motion, end the meeting, and leave the room without another word. I feel Aydin walking close behind silently. I'm not sure where I'm going, but I end up on the ballroom terrace where Calla and I were married. I take long breaths of cool air with Aydin still my silent shadow.

"You don't have to do that, you know," I say, after a few more long, deep breaths with Aydin continuing to hover behind me. "I'm fine."

"I know," says Aydin. We stand together in silence for a few more minutes.

"Can I ask you something?" I say to Aydin. I make my way to the bench where Calla and I sat the night of the party, and my eyes trail along the dead rose bushes clinging to the trellis.

"Anything," he says.

"How would you prioritize it?" I ask.

"Be more specific," he says, coming to sit next to me.

"Obviously," I begin, "getting Maddie home was the priority, but now . . . Is the new priority helping Maddie get well and figuring out how to stop her electric spells? Is it rescuing Calla's brother? Is it dealing with the threat from The Inimical? Is it finding a way to bring down Clockwork Atheneum? Is it trying to convince the town *yet again* that I'm not a monster now that Meltair is stirring up everyone's mistrust? Is it figuring out what is actually going on in Andestine with Senzicaria?" I put my head in my hands and rub the base of my antlers, trying to stave off a headache. Aydin sighs and leans back against the wall. We sit side by side, looking out at the snowy landscape.

"You know, when we were in our early 20's, and you were preparing to take over from Laurel? She was worried we weren't taking your new role seriously enough, and we just kept saying . . . "

"Nothing ever happens in Thiaghal." I smile, remembering much younger, almost ten years younger now, versions of Aydin and I.

"I don't know what it is that you should do," says Aydin, "but whatever it is, you won't be alone. Laurel can take over as proxy governor again, and Bevin and I can keep looking for something that will help Maddie. It seems like the only thing that no one else can really do is . . . "

"Deal with The Inimical," I say, "and rescue Atreo."

***

A few hours later, I find Calla napping in the library, curled in a sun puddle cast by the last rays of the day on the window seat. She stretches and uncurls when I touch her shoulder.

"Hey," she says. As soon as she looks at me, everything I had been trying not to feel since the council meeting rushes to the surface. I sit down on the edge of the window seat and pull her into a tight hug, burying my face in her hair and breathing in the smell of roses. "What's wrong?" she asks when I finally pull away. I tell her about the council meeting, and it's totally dark by the time I finish the story. She cups my face in her hand and presses her forehead to mine.

"Are you alright?" she asks.

"No," I say. "Calla, I'm not. I can't stay in this small town with these hateful, small-minded people for the rest of my life. I cannot spend the rest of my life lobbying the greater Maradal council to divert funds to us for a second post office that isn't also a pub."

I don't know where all this is coming from, but once I start talking, I can't stop. I had meant to tell Calla that we're leaving tomorrow to rescue Atreo, not that I want to leave my entire life and all my responsibilities behind. Yet, the more I talk, the more I hear my heart pounding out the one word that I'm realizing has lurked in the back of my mind since I saw Calla glowing, dripping, and freezing in that tree in the forest: *freedom*. My resignation to prioritize rescuing Atreo has broken something loose, and the idea of leaving, really leaving, Maradal for an extended period of time has unleashed thoughts that I had dismissed and buried.

"Tyre," she whispers, as a tear frees itself from her eye and slides down her cheek. I pull her into a kiss. She presses her lips back into mine and pulls me to her so tightly that I feel her fingertips leaving bruises on my shoulder blades. I pull back and press my forehead into hers.

"Tomorrow," I say between breaths, "tomorrow we leave to rescue Atreo."

"Tyre," she says, shaking her head.

"It's time," I say, holding up my hand. Aydin and Bevin will look after Maddie. Mom will look after Thiaghal. You are the only person who can help Atreo, and my job as your husband is to help you."

"No, Tyre," she says, crying harder, "it's, it's not that. I have to tell you something. I need your help." She's shaking.

"Of course," I say, "Anything."

"I have not been fair to you," she says, "but I need you to let me explain, and then I need you to be the person that I know you are, and I need you to help me and Atreo."

"Calla," I say, taking her hands. "You're scaring me. What's going on?"

She screws her eyes shut and takes a deep breath.

"I'm—" Before she can say anything, there's a deafening crack and a flash of light. The entire house shakes as if there's been an earthquake.

"Was that a—" The entire house shakes again, knocking vases off tables, and a cascade of library books falls from the shelf. There's the distinct smell of smoke and the sounds of yelling in the distance. Something is wrong. In a second, both our demeanors change.

"We need to make sure everyone is safe and figure out what's going on," I say. There's another flash of light, and the house shakes so hard that cracks shoot up the walls.

"Let's go," she says. Now that we're running towards the front of the house, I can hear voices outside shouting, but can't make out what they're saying. I can hear pounding on the doors to the front hall.

"Tyre!" My mom screams and throws her arms around me as she barrels into the front hall.

"I'm alright, Mom, we're both alright," I say. "Where is everyone else?"

"They're up here!" Aydin calls from the top of the stairs as the yelling and pounding on the door from outside intensifies. "They're in Maddie's room. The teenagers won't come out, they think it's Meltair!"

"Is it Meltair?" I yell. Aydin is about to answer when another blast sounds, and I hear a scream that I can now discern as Maddie from upstairs. We bolt upstairs to Maddie's room, where she, Pax, and Hugo are all sitting with their backs pressed to the wall, looking wild-eyed and trying to cling to Bevin and to Hugo's parents. Hugo's parents look as petrified as the teenagers, but Mr. O'Reed is looking up defiantly with one arm wrapped around Hugo and one arm around his wife.

"You can't let him take us back!" screams Maddie.

"That is never happening," I say.

"No indeed," says Mom, with an edge to her voice that makes me smile in spite of the fact that we're clearly under attack.

"I'll open the weapons safe," I say. "Bevin, stay with the kids and Hugo's parents?"

"Not like I have much choice," she says, looking down at her arm that somehow all three teenagers have their hands latched to. She even manages half a smile, and I give what I hope is a smile back.

"I'm coming," says Mr. O'Reed, standing up.

"Dad, no!" shrieks Hugo.

"We need you here," I say gently. "Bevin's great but . . . "

"I'm not exactly the muscle of this group," she says. He looks like he might argue, but slowly sets his face and nods.

"Let's go," I say to everyone else. I lead the way past my bedroom and Mom's to the room with our weapons collection. I sling a sword around my waist, as does Aydin. My mother picks up a bow and a set of arrows that I know belonged to her mother. She used to love bragging about never having had to use them and what that says about peace in Thiaghal, and I realize with a pang that she may not be able to say that anymore after tonight. When I glance over to Calla, she has a crossbow slung across her back, and she's adding a third dagger to a holster on her leg.

"We need to think about this," says Aydin. "It sounds like there could be a lot of people out there."

"I sent a pigeon to Sheriff Murchad for help as soon as the first blast sounded," says Mom. "They're not as reliable as Holpies, so I sent them to the rest of the council as well for good measure. We should have backup soon. We just need to hold them off if they get inside." Just as Mom finishes speaking, we hear the splintering of wood and the roar of the crowd intensify. We're almost to the top of the stairs when I hear a voice I recognize, and my stomach drops to my feet.

"Check every room! Open every secret passage! He's here somewhere!" It's Sheriff Murchad.

"No," I whisper, desperately trying to get my head around what's happening. It's only then that I realize I can make out the shouts from the crowd downstairs.

"Kill the beast! Kill the beast! Where are you, monster?"

"This," I stutter, "this can't be happening."

"Tyre, you need to leave," says Mom. Her voice breaks me out of my daze, and I can feel my shock hardening into rage.

"No," I say. "No way. Murchad wants a monster, I'll give him a . . . "

"They're up here!" We look up to see someone has rounded the corner from the stairs into the hallway.

"We need to move!" says Calla. She's right, we're backed into a corner with no exit in this upstairs hallway, and we're drawing the mob right to where Bevin and the O'Reeds are protecting Maddie, Hugo, and Pax.

"Only way out is through," says Aydin. As soon as the man sees he's outnumbered, he turns and runs back toward the stairs, but the damage is done. By the time we reach the staircase, the mob is already surging up.

"There!" yells Murchad as soon as I'm visible. The next few minutes are a blur. I jump over the banister and land on the first floor. The mob surges towards me in seconds, but it draws enough people away from the staircase that Aydin, Mom, and Calla can fight their way down. For a few seconds, I think I'm holding my own, but there are too many people and, no matter which way I turn, someone is swinging at me with a sword or an axe. Even though we're outnumbered, luck must be on our side because everyone seems to just miss us somehow. That is, until I suddenly feel a burning pain in my calf. As I fall, I see an arrow lodged in the back of my leg. Someone raises an ax, I assume intent on severing my head, when an arrow pierces the ax-wielder in the eye. Calla and Aydin are both next to me now, Calla slinging her crossbow back over her shoulder.

"You need to run!" yells Aydin as the three of us grapple with the surging mob.

"I'm not leaving you!" I yell.

"Tyre, they're mostly ignoring us unless we engage them; they want you!" he yells. "Get out of here, and we'll hold them off! We've already got some backup for our side arriving." In between parries, I follow Aydin's gaze and see that Brogan from the bar and Colwan are fighting through the front door with another group from town.

Brogan is swinging the largest axe I've ever seen and screaming, "WHAT IS ALL THIS?!" I put my weight on my right foot, feel the pain shoot through my calf again, and lose my footing. It's already healing, but it will still take a minute, and I won't be able to move quickly until it does. Calla catches me while Aydin kicks back a middle-aged woman wielding a kitchen knife.

"Go!" he yells. Before I can say anything else, I feel Calla, somehow, dragging me backwards. We limp into the ballroom where she locks the doors behind us. The quiet in the ballroom amplifies the echoes of our feet, and my ears are left ringing after the clamor of the entryway. I can already hear the mob pounding at the doors.

"That won't hold," I say.

"Come on," says Calla. I lean on her as we make our way out to the terrace. We both take in lungfuls of the cold night air. "We can probably find a way to climb down," she says, looking at the stonework and latticing on the house's side.

"I wouldn't count on it," a voice says from the shadows at the other end of the terrace.

"Sheriff Murchad," says Calla. She sounds calm, but she steps in front of me and takes out one of her daggers. "I take it you saw us head down the hall and went around to climb up the terrace. Excellent. If you climbed up, we can certainly get down."

"You won't be going anywhere," he says, looking at me.

"You." I stand and try to charge at him, but the pain in my still-healing leg sends me to the ground. Murchad ignores me and turns to Calla.

"You," he says, pointing at her, "I don't have a problem with. Although I don't much care for your taste in men. Unless, of course, you're being held here against your will; but somehow, I don't think that's the case."

"Hm," says Calla, "so you are capable of seeing past appearances to someone's true nature when you want to. How surprising." For a second, he looks like he's on the verge of asking Calla what she means by that, as am I, to be perfectly honest, but he seems to decide against it.

"Like I said," he continues as if Calla hasn't said anything, "I have no problem with you. Stand aside now, and no harm will come to you." In response, Calla throws a knife. It flies through the air but misses its mark and catches Murchad right on the palm of his hand. He screams more out of surprise than pain and clutches his hand. It's bleeding a decent amount, but, unfortunately, it probably isn't that deep.

"Calla," I say, "just do what he says, it's alright. I've got this." All I can think is that I need to get her out of this unharmed and in just another few seconds, when I can stand, Murchad is an easy fight. She glares at Murchad for another second, and then her shoulders drop.

"Alright," she says. "Alright." She sets down her crossbow and raises her hands. Murchad approaches her as she stands in front of me.

"Now, stand aside," he says. His face is just inches from hers.

"I just need to ask you something first," she says. "Just one thing."

He looks like he's just going to shove her aside when she says,

"How's your godmother?"

Before I can comprehend what's happened, he slaps Calla clean across the face with his injured hand, leaving a trail of blood over her cheek and mouth. For just a second, I swear I see a smirk flit across Calla's face. I know this particular expression well, because it's the same way she looks when she knows she beat me when we play cards. Then, another second later, I'm sure I've imagined the smirk because she looks horrified as she drags the back of her arm across her face, wiping off the blood.

Murchad reaches again to push her aside, and she latches on to his arm. Suddenly, Murchad is screaming. He drops to the ground, pulling Calla with him. She screams, but it's drowned out by Murchad's shrieks. I have no idea what's happening, but I need to get Calla away from whatever it is.

"Calla!" I say running towards them. "Get away from him!"

"What's going on?!" she screams. She pushes him off her, but keeps one hand locked on his wrist and the other on his face, trying to catch his eyes.

"Murchad, look at me!" she yells. "What's going on?"

He just continues screaming and is somehow . . . shrinking? It's like watching an apple left out in the sun for too long. He's shriveling before our eyes. Calla is still screaming, until suddenly she's the only one screaming. Murchad is a silent, shriveled husk on the ground.

"Calla, get away from him!" I manage to pull her backwards onto my lap. She's shaking and burning up like she's running a fever.

"What was that? What was that?!" she yells.

"Hey, look at me!" I yell. I turn her to face me and look into her eyes. "Are you hurt?"

She calms down and shakes her head 'no.'

"Alright," I say, "Calla, Murchad is gone. The rest of the mob is still here, and my presence here puts everyone in danger, especially when they see what's happened to Murchad. We need to go."

This seems to snap Calla back into action.

"Right. You're right. Let's find that way down the terrace," she says. We make our way down slowly, my leg finally working as it should, and then we're running into the night with the shouts of the mob, and our family, fading behind us.

18

It's about an hour before either of us feels like there's enough distance between us and the angry mob that we can stop and make a plan. The next town is another hour's walk, but we're exhausted. Although there are willies on the road this time of night, it might be just as unwise to stay put, even for a short rest. Calla, being Calla, could knock at any one of a couple of country houses that we can see in the distance and probably find a bed for the night. Me— not so much. Although at the moment, Calla looks ridiculous enough that someone might actually think twice before inviting her into their home. Obviously, neither of us had time to grab a cloak before fleeing an angry mob, and Calla has my shirt draped over her head and shoulders so her glowing doesn't become a beacon for any overzealous members of the group who decide to come looking for us.

"Won't the mob just follow the Holpie if your family sends a message?" says Calla as we sit down on a boulder by the side of the road to rest our feet.

"A Holpie would never allow itself to be used for that purpose," I say. "They take too much pride in their role as deliverers of messages."

"I like the Holpies," Calla says, forcing a laugh, "I wish we had more of them in Andestine. We only ever see them when they bring messages over to and from Maradal. We have pigeons, but those are, you know, just pigeons."

At the word pigeon, I scan the skies again. I'm getting more nervous by the minute. Surely with me gone, Mom, Aydin, and our allies have everything back under control by now? I'm about to suggest we keep moving when I hear hoofbeats and see a shape galloping in the distance. I stand and pull Calla behind me just in case, but I let out a sigh of relief when I see it's a Holpie. Even though Holpies aren't huge fans of affection, I throw my arms around its neck after I take the letter from its back and see Aydin's handwriting. The Holpie trots off looking offended while I read the letter in the light of Calla's glow.

Tyre, I'm making Aunt Laurel let me send this letter so she actually sits down instead of writing it herself. She would like me to tell you that the coast is clear and you can come back. As your friend, though, I have to be honest with you, I don't think that's true. The mob is gone, and the council is meeting tomorrow to appoint a new acting sheriff, but until then, no one who was part of the mob tonight can be arrested or detained. Honestly, I'm worried they'll try again. I would go on to Ger and get a room for the next few days until the new sheriff can get everything settled down. We are all safe with only minor cuts and bruises. Teenagers are all fine too. Hugo's parents are terrified and want to leave for home in the morning, and Hugo is refusing to separate from Maddie and Pax, so I'm not sure how that will go.

Also, I need to let you know, Murchad is dead. I'm not sure if you saw what happened to him. We'll talk when you get back. It's like he was shrunk, I guess? Shriveled? That's not the best way to explain it. I know that sounds crazy. I can explain more when I see you in a few days. Like I said, all safe. I'll send you the all clear in a few days.

I watch Calla's face after I hand her the letter. I know she's thinking that we're going to do as the letter says, go to Ger and then head home when the coast is clear, re-group, and then leave for Andestine and Atreo. At that moment, I decide we're not going home. We're already headed in the direction of Andestine. We're going to keep going.

"Are you sure?" she whispers when I tell her.

"Yes," I say, "we've put this off long enough. Let's head on for another hour to Ger. Once we have a place to sleep, I'll write to Aydin and ask him to send a Holpie with money and clothes for the trip. We don't really need anything else. Unless you need something?"

"We could use some of your dad's old books," she says, frowning in concentration. "We don't really have a plan for taking on The Inimical."

"We'll work on it on the way. It's a long journey," I say, hoping that I'm projecting confidence I don't feel. "It will be alright." I reach out and put my hand on her shoulder.

"Liar," she says, smiling, reaching up and taking my hand.

"Come on," I say, "let's get going. There's a mist setting in, and I don't want to get found by any willies out here."

It takes longer than expected to reach Ger, and I'm not looking forward to convincing the innkeeper at The Trechend Inn to rent us a room on credit.

"I've got it," says Calla as we approach the desk.

"You've . . .?" but before I can finish speaking, she pulls a roll of bills from a hidden pocket on the underside of her dress.

"You carry a roll of bills in a hidden pocket?" I ask. I turn with raised eyebrows to Aydin, and remember with what feels like a punch in the gut that he and Bevin aren't here for this adventure.

"Not always, but this isn't the first time I've had to flee with just the clothes on my back, remember?" she says. "Plus, I didn't bring any money on our last adventure, and now I owe you a round of drinks."

The woman at the check-in desk, to her credit, takes this all in stride and offers us a room key with a face that's shockingly free of confusion or judgment. Calla takes the key and heads toward the stairs as I follow, but the hidden pocket in her dress and the reminder of how she came into my life unsettles me for some reason, as does being alone with her on a journey. Our last solo adventure to the Clocks campus in Lytwist brought with it the realization that she had withheld a major detail of her life.

The pocket is yet another Calla secret, and this time, away from home and the protective bubble of my family, I can't quite shake the unease. Why did she leave Andestine? Why does she glow? Why is she always warm? Why does she smell like roses? Why can Maddie electrocute her without killing her? Why didn't she tell me about Atreo? Why did she leave out the fact that Atreo was her brother? What is the mysterious hold The Inimical uses to make her sick? Finally, my mind flashes back to seconds before Murchad withered in front of me and the memory of Calla's smirk.

As frustrated as I've been with Calla's secrets, I remember the feeling in the library earlier today when I realized that those secrets have also felt a little mysterious and exciting; a welcome break from my previously monotonous life in Thiaghal. As I watch her toss her hair over her shoulder and tuck the wad of bills back into her hidden pocket, I can't shake the memory of that smile, and something about her feels . . .dangerous.

"You alright?" she says, turning to look at me. Has her stare always been this intense? I tell myself that I'm paranoid, confusing anxiety with being attacked and chased from my home for anxiety over Calla. Was I just projecting all the trauma that I just experienced onto the nearest, safest person?

"Yeah," I say, "just a little bit in shock, I think."

Her stare softens, and she loops her arm around my waist while taking my arm and tossing it around her shoulders. I lean into her warmth as we make our way towards our room. Finally, we fall into bed exhausted. I start to feel my uneasiness slipping away, but even the simple act of resting my hand on the small of her back as she sleeps next to me suddenly fills my brain with doubt again. I stare down at my claws, a reminder that I'm still a monster and that our love story didn't break the curse. Is that because Briowney is a liar or because this isn't the love story I thought it was? Briowney's voice echoes through my mind.

Love cannot live where there's no trust.

Have I never really trusted Calla? Thinking about Briowney reminds me that Calla isn't the only one who can have secrets. I reach into the satchel that I wear under my shirt and take out the fairy knife and candle from Briowney. I've been carrying these with me since Briowney gave them to me without letting myself think too hard about why. Now, as I look at them, I wonder, did Briowney think that I'd need protection from someone? The Inimical, maybe? Surely that was it. She gave them to me so that I'll have a better chance when I face The Inimical. If I really believe that, though, why haven't I told Calla that I have them, and why am I only taking them out now that she's asleep? I consider the candle and feel the urge to light it, but a second later, I tell myself I'm being ridiculous, and it will wake Calla up for nothing. Still, when I consider putting them away in the satchel and putting the satchel in a cupboard like I usually do every night, I find myself sliding them under my pillow instead.

***

The next morning, I wake, as usual, to Calla wrapped in my portion of blankets with her hair spread across my face. Before I'm fully awake, I wrap my arms around her and pull her on top of me out of habit. She swats at me for waking her up, but lets me pull her so she's lying on my chest, facing me. I pull her close and lean into her warmth. By the time I remember my paranoia from the night before, she's already propped herself up on her elbows and started talking to me about what we should have for breakfast. In the cold light of day, I can't for the life of me remember what felt so sinister about her a few hours ago.

I had written to Aydin as soon as we checked in last night, and by noon today, a Holpie arrives with our supplies from home and another letter from Aydin. I scan it quickly, seeing that it says basically what I thought it would: Mom is apoplectic regarding my intention to continue on to Andestine. Aydin and Bevin wish me the best of luck and assure me again that they're fine and will handle everything until we get home.

***

On the road that afternoon, I pull an apple out of my bag and take a bite before offering a bite to Calla.

"We should plan," I say.

We're walking along the main highway through Maradal towards Diereanach, the last town before the Andestine border. It's a full day at least before we're there, so we'll have to stop along the way as needed. There aren't too many people on the road this time of day, but occasionally a group with a wagon or horses trots past us. Most are friendly and wave, but some give me a glare or a suspicious glance. Calla nods and takes a bite of the apple before handing it back.

"What can you tell me about The Inimical?" I ask, feeling a seed of unease from yesterday settle into the pit of my stomach.

"Let's start with the Fog," she says, "since that's the first thing we'll need to deal with."

The knot in my stomach twists even farther. I can't help but think that this is just another question dodged, but at least she isn't still outright denying having any knowledge about The Inimical.

"I know the Fog will let me in," she says. "We, that is, the people who live in Umbra, have managed to figure out that it recognizes us and always lets us back in."

"Always?" I ask. "I thought no one could get through the Fog?"

"There are weak points," she says. "When you live in The Inimical's shadow for a while, it's possible to get a sense of how the magic works, and it isn't foolproof."

"That's excellent," I say. "Tell me everything."

"Well," says Calla, "this is also based on what I know from Clocks, but ongoing magic requires constant energy expenditure. It's not like once someone magics something, it's set and just keeps going. If you want to keep it in a magical state, it requires a constant flow of magical input to maintain. Take you, for example; even now, Briowney is putting a small amount of magical energy into keeping you the way you are. Not nearly as much as to create the initial transformation by a long shot, but a small bit. Changing you back would be just a matter of stopping the flow. Of course, she allegedly set up the spell so that her magical connection to you would be automatically severed if someone fell in love with you. It obviously wasn't true, but things like that can be done. Since Briowney seems to see herself as an arbiter of justice, it wouldn't have felt fair to her to leave you no escape clauses."

"So, what does this have to do with The Inimical?" I say.

"The Inimical is human," she says, "not a magical creature. So, unlike a fairy, let's say, The Inimical's supply of magic is limited. It needs to 'recharge', so to speak. The Fog varies in strength depending on how fully charged The Inimical's magical abilities are on any given day and how much magic The Inimical is able to pour into the Fog to sustain it. On a weaker day, you can push through the fog with sheer force of will. It's actually amazing how much magic can be broken by willpower, but it helps when the magic is weak to begin with."

"So, will we need to wait for a weak day in the Fog so I can get into Umbra? Because the Fog keeps outsiders out, as well as the people of Umbra in?" I ask.

"Maybe, but I'm hoping it works the way things worked at Clocks. That you're covered in enough fairy magic that the Fog will recognize you as part of itself," she says, "and recognize me as someone who was supposed to be in Umbra all along. We never have a problem getting back in. It's just getting out that's hard."

***

When we finally approach the outer neighborhoods of Diereanach days later, I find myself getting excited despite everything that's happening. I feel Calla nudge me as we're walking into town.

"What's up?" she says. "You look very happy for someone who has just left on an impromptu quest to confront the entity who has been trying to capture you for months."

"It's silly," I say, "but I've just always wanted to see Diereanach. It's one of the biggest towns in Maradal. I mean, sure, it's nothing compared to Lytwist or probably Umbra, but my parents used to tell me stories about visiting here. They've always got music and festivals, and it's so close to Andestine that supposedly the food has some Andestinian flavors, and it's a little bit warmer here and . . ." I stop when I realize how much I'm talking. "Sorry," I say, "I just, I guess I'm realizing for the first time how much I like traveling. Seeing the world."

Calla nods and gives me a sad smile.

"You sure you're not just in shock given what just happened in Thiaghal?" she says.

"Oh, I'm sure I am," I say. I am. I'm somehow aware that the horror of what I've just experienced is lurking in the back of my mind, and I know I'll have to process it at some point. "I think I'm in shock. Until the shock wears off, I can't feel it."

Calla looks skeptical but decides not to address it.

"Well," she says, shrugging, "then we should make the most of our one night here." She shakes her head, like she's trying to clear it of whatever she'd been thinking. "What does the perfect evening in Diereanach look like?"

"Come on," I say as I take her hand.

The first thing we do is check into The Hotel Diereanach. I've stayed in hotels and inns more in the past few months than I ever have in my life, but this hotel, I've always pictured. Just like my parents described, its entrance faces a huge town square. There is a fountain in the center of the square, and each side of the cobblestone square is lined with shops and carts selling food, clothes, or souvenirs. It's also more colorful here than in other parts of Maradal— again, probably because of its proximity to Andestine. All different shops and stalls are painted in bright greens, reds, yellows, and blues. The air smells like a mixture of pot roast coming from the pubs and sweet smells from the carts. If I close my eyes and breathe deeply, I can even smell the flowers from the florist at the opposite end of the square.

"Pastries," says Calla, spotting a bakery cart. Without another word of explanation, she heads for a cart selling crispy, sugary treats. We're licking sugar off the tips of our fingers as we check into the Hotel Diereanach.

"Are you in town for the festival?" asks the woman at the front desk. Her smile is plastered on her face, and I can tell she's trying incredibly hard not to look uncomfortable with me, which I appreciate.

"Just passing through, actually," I say. "What festival is today?"

"Lafuar," she says, smiling. "The last day of cold. Of course, we can't really predict when the last day will be before a warm front moves in from Andestine, but we estimate, and we celebrate."

As the woman finishes talking, I notice Calla looking out at the square. The pastry cart is closing up shop and wheeling away to make space for tables and what looks like a stage. Calla's eyes light up as she watches musicians come out and start warming up.

"Is there dancing?" she asks, spinning to face the woman.

"Of course!" she says. "Dancing and music, and even more food than usual. Games and drinks . . ."

At this point, she stops talking because Calla has actually started to vibrate with excitement. I guess one of the pros of marrying someone I'd only known for a few weeks is the joy of constantly learning new little things about them. Including, apparently, that Calla loves festivals. I wrap my arm around her shoulders and kiss the back of her head.

"Hey, Calla," I say, "I'm sorry, we've just had such a long trip. I just don't think I'm up to going to a festival tonight."

She whirls around to face me, and I can't help but laugh at the look on her face.

"Tyre!" She smiles and shoves me. "Come on! Let's go drop off our things!" she says, pulling me up the stairs towards the room.

***

The sun is totally down by the time we step back outside, the festival now in full swing. Calla laces her fingers through mine and pulls me from cart to cart, looking at food, games, and handmade items. With the exception of a strolling bard who she finds "irritating", she's so delighted by everything that I don't even care that people are staring at me. When she's happy like this, it reminds me of the party Mom threw right after Calla arrived in Thiaghal. As I watch her looking down at a cart of handmade jewelry, I reach over and tuck a strand of hair behind her ear. I start to think maybe everyone here has actually been staring at Calla, not me, all along. When she's finally explored every inch of the square, I gently tug her towards the center of the space where people are dancing. It's a slower song now, and mostly couples swaying to the tune or families with their young kids dancing on their parents' toes.

"This is where I always said I wanted to live when I was a little kid, before my dad died," I say, as we sway in unison with the other couples on the dance floor.

Calla lifts her head from my chest and looks up at me.

"It always sounded like this magical place, but after seeing Lytwist, who knows how many magical places there are in the world?"

"Lytwist is nothing compared to some of the cities in Andestine!" she says. "You should see . . ." Suddenly, the light in her eyes goes out, and she stops talking.

"Calla," I say, "if I ask what's wrong, will you tell me?"

"Yes," she says, shooting me an annoyed glance. "Well, actually—"

"Calla."

"Alright, fine." She wraps her arms further around my back and leans her head against my chest again. "I had the completely morbid thought that we're headed into a fairly dangerous situation with The Inimical and that I hope that Umbra isn't the last city you see."

"It won't be," I say, as I lean down to kiss the top of her head. "And," I say as she tilts her head up to look at me, "I know we've gotten out of the habit, but just out of respect, I think we should start calling him Mark again." This gets Calla to crack a smile.

"Don't you think he's Meltair?" she says. "Or actually, that he's three brooms in a giant coat controlled by Meltair?"

"Honestly," I say, laughing, "wouldn't that be the best case scenario? I took out one magical broom, no problem at all. Two of us together could definitely take three, especially after what you did to Murchad." I don't know what makes me say it. I didn't even realize I thought it until it was already out of my mouth. Calla freezes, and I feel a shiver down my spine as she turns to look at me.

"What?" she says.

"Nothing, forget it," I try to backtrack.

"No way," she says, "there's no putting that salt back in the shaker. You think I did whatever that was to Murchad?"

"Calla, I don't know what made me say that. I don't even really know if I think it."

"Well, you clearly think it because you just accused me of it!"

"How else do you explain what happened back there?" I ask.

"I can't explain it any more than you can!" she says.

"Calla," I say, "I'm not as smart as you, and I realize that in so many ways I don't know you as well as I'd like to, but there are some things about you that I've figured out by now. If you really couldn't explain it, you would just say that. You chose your words very carefully and said you 'can't explain it any more than I can.' However, I can at least offer a theory. Which means you probably can too."

"Tyre, to be honest, I have no idea what any of that means," she says, "and you're not offering a theory, you're offering an accusation."

"Am I wrong?" I ask.

"Are you wrong? About your implication that I turned Murchad into a raisin? Yes," she says. We don't separate, but I can feel Calla's muscles have gone rigid in my arms, and I imagine mine feel the same. I let out a long breath. She settles her head against my chest again, but I think it's just to avoid looking at me.

"Calla," I say.

"What?" she asks.

"I would still love you, you know."

"What?" she says again, lifting her head to look at me.

"I would have questions," I say. "I mean, I would have a lot of questions. So many questions . . ."

"Tyre, focus."

"I would still love you," I say, "if you had turned Murchad into a raisin." Some of the tension leaves Calla's shoulders, and she reaches up to cup my face in her hand.

"Tyre," she says, "you're just . . . you're a good person. And I know that. I want you to know that I know. I do. I know it so much, every second of every single day. I—" Her words are getting more and more rapid, and she sounds like she's on the verge of tears.

"Hey, hey," I take her hand in mine. "Thank you, but what does that have to do with anything?"

"Nothing, I just— I love you, too," she says, "please believe that."

Before I can say anything else, the musicians start playing a faster song, and more people flood the square to start spinning and gliding to the tune.

Calla raises her eyebrows, and her question is clear: *Do you want to leave and keep talking?* We could step away, keep talking, leave the lights and music behind, or we could keep dancing and consider the subject closed. I hesitate for a second before I spin her, and we're off twirling with the rest of the crowd. Calla is still a terrible dancer, and it's still like dancing with the sun.

Later that evening, as Calla sleeps next to me, I can see the lanterns in the square out the window from bed. I watch them flicker and remember how many times I've compared Calla to warmth between the glowing and her literal physical warmth. I've always thought of her as sunshine, but as I watch flames flickering in the lanterns, the uneasy feeling that's been following me since we left Thiaghal sinks back in.

19

A sense of surrealness washes over me again as I look down at my sleeping wife. Calla. *My wife*. It doesn't seem possible that I'm actually married to the woman asleep beside me. I feel so close to her, and yet the events of the past few days remind me how little I know her, how short a time I've known her. Her breath rises and falls. Even though she's sleeping, she doesn't look peaceful. I don't think I've seen Calla look truly at peace even once in the months that I've known her. When she sleeps, I watch her, the gentle movement of eyes behind closed lids suggesting a vivid dream that I know she won't tell me about.

Calla, I'm learning, has endless secrets. For just a second, I have a horrible feeling of dread as I watch her that makes my entire body run cold. At the same time, I gently brush some of her long brown waves out of her face and set one of my hands on her bare shoulder, the tips of my claws just barely resting on her shoulder blade. Some of my inexplicable dread fades away at the solid feeling of her body under my clawed hands, and the gentle rise and fall of her breath.

Not for the first time, I think that Calla may be the most beautiful woman in the world. A woman of constant contradictions, she nestles into the comfort of my body as if she's cold; her skin, meanwhile, radiates a feverish warmth. I tell myself that whatever danger I think I'm sensing right now is foolish. I try to tell my muscles to unclench, to relax, to go back to sleep, to stop staring at her and trying to unravel the thread of her sleeping thoughts. I will Calla's muscles to relax, too.

I never realized before we were married, before Calla slept against me every night, that her muscles always felt coiled and ready to snap. She sleeps with her arms curled close to her body, bent hands tucked under her chin. I drag the nails of my claws gently up and down her arm and feel her muscles relax just the tiniest fraction as she lets out a long breath. I try to relax my muscles just the tiniest bit, too, but as I fall asleep, I can still feel the whisper of dread burrowed deep in my stomach.

***

I wake up the next morning feeling groggy with a cloyingly sweet taste stuck in my mouth. I sit up and drink the entire glass bottle of water by the bedside table in one gulp and realize Calla isn't next to me anymore. She wanders in a few minutes later with pastries wrapped up for the road.

"You alright?" she asks when she sees me rubbing my head.

"Fine," I say, harsher than I mean to. She perches on the side of the bed and stares at me, and for a second, I consider bringing up Murchad again and starting a fight just so all the feelings from my terrible night's sleep have somewhere to go.

"Andestine today," she says and holds the wrapped pastry out as a peace offering. Hearing her mention Andestine reminds me that this will be the first time in months that she's been in her home country, let alone her home city. I reach back to take the pastry.

"Andestine today," I echo while I squeeze her hand. We cross into Andestine by midafternoon. Calla is asleep on my back, but I wake her before we cross into the country. At first, there isn't much to see along the main highway. Gradually, however, little houses and neighborhoods start to populate the side of the road. There will be no major cities until we reach Umbra, and that's still a while away. Calla chatters about the landscape and how it will become more and more dense with buildings until, at last, we reach the crowded streets of Umbra. The houses are a mix of what looks like small stone castles and brightly colored cottages. It's chilly, but warmer than Thiaghal, and my clothes are starting to feel a little bit heavy for the milder air.

"Should have brought lighter clothes," I say, shrugging off my coat. "Although, to be honest, I've never been totally clear on whether or not I need to wear clothes, given all the fur."

"Probably not," says Calla, "I say get rid of them." I feel myself grinning despite my uneasy feelings toward her.

"Yeah, you'd like that, wouldn't you?" I say, attempting to flirt back.

"I'm just offering a practical solution," she says.

"I will if you do," I say.

"Believe me, I wish I could," she says. She reaches up and brushes sweat away from her hairline. Come to think of it, Calla doesn't look very comfortable. There's still a nip in the air, and she's wearing her usual white shift dress, but I can see places where sweat has slicked her dark hair to the back of her neck.

"You alright?" I say. I reach over and lift her brown waves and fan cool air onto the back of her neck.

"Yeah, I guess I've just gotten used to Thiaghal temperatures."

"How long until our first stop?" I say. Just a short time later, the first stop turns out to be a small roadside inn along the highway with terrible food but comfortable beds. Calla and I lay awake for a couple of hours leafing through some of Dad's old books, not that anything seems useful. She falls asleep slumped against me with a book on magical herbs open in her lap.

The next few days pass by much the same, walking, chatting, reading, and sleeping. In any other circumstance, this would have been such an adventure. Sometimes, just for a minute, I forget the reality of what we're facing and all the questions that have been crowding my mind about Calla. I'll catch a glimpse of her with her eyes closed and face upturned towards the sun as we walk. In those moments, I have an urge to grab her and kiss her the way I did when she told me that she would help me rescue Maddie, or the day she rescued me from the miserable ball Mom threw right after she arrived. In those moments, I'm overwhelmed by the fact that despite whatever she's hiding, I love this woman. I love her as much as my family and my home. When I stand near her, there's a constant magnetic pull to touch her, hold her, pull her close. *Calla*, I think to myself, *what have you gotten me into?*

In the inevitable moments of silence as we travel, I have the occasional thought, what would have happened if I'd never met Calla? Would this have turned out differently? I suppose not. With or without Calla and Atreo, my story was always linked with The Inimical. The image of his shadowy presence fills my mind and sends a shiver down my spine. I instinctively move closer to Calla, and she takes my hand, which just reminds me that I would make the same choices all over again.

20

As much as I wish my love for Calla would dull the uneasiness that settled in after leaving Thiaghal behind, it doesn't, and I find myself caught in a cycle of affection and suspicion that's exhausting my mental stamina before any actual encounter with the enemy we're here to face. I'm grappling with this when we finally see the Fog for the first time. I feel it more than I see it. As I stare into the distance, I see what at first appears to be an ocean on the horizon.

"There it is," says Calla, eyes fixed forward.

It's then that I realize that the wall of gray in front of us isn't a sea extending outwards, it's a wall of Fog. I let out a long breath.

"You ready?" says Calla. I can't respond at that moment, so I just set my face and nod. We walk silently until we're standing centimeters from the Fog, our noses practically touching it.

"So," I say, "we just walk through then?"

Calla nods, although she seems much less confident than I'd like her to be.

"Any way of telling how strong a barrier it is today?"

"No," she says, "it looks the same no matter what. Just remember, willpower, alright? Focus all your will on getting through to the other side."

I don't point out to Calla that, per her theory, my willpower should be irrelevant since the Fog shouldn't detect me at all with my fairy magic. Then I remind myself that she's making this up as she goes along just as much as I am. She may even be risking more. After all, I'm the one with a personal invitation from The Inimical, and once she sets foot through this barrier, she has no way to know for sure she'll be able to push through again. Given the power that The Inimical has had over her, being trapped this close to him couldn't be an appealing thought.

"Together?" I say, looking over at her. She blinks quickly, and I can't tell if it's because of dust or tears.

"Together," she says. She reaches out and takes my hand as we step into the Fog.

The feeling of passing through the Fog is hard to describe. It's like being squeezed from all angles, which is uncomfortable but not intolerable. Worse than that is the feeling of being watched. It's the most intense sense of being watched I've ever experienced, like standing naked (and furless) in front of a crowd that's not at all pleased by what they see, circling me to decide their next move. That feeling alone makes me very nearly bolt backwards the way we came.

"I feel it too," she says, as if reading my thoughts, "just hold on, we're almost through." I grit my teeth and push forward. Just when I think I can't stand it anymore, I catch a breath of cold air and pitch forward onto the ground. I hear a thud next to me that I assume is Calla and reach out towards her.

"You alright?" I say, putting my hand on her shoulder.

"Yup," she says. "You?"

"Yes, that was horrible, though. I've never felt anything like that."

Calla pushes herself up, and I slowly do the same. I take another breath and realize that something is wrong. The air tastes freezing cold and stale. Andestine is a warm place; it shouldn't feel like this.

"The weather," I say to Calla, "is it because of the Fog?"

"We think so," she says, "it lets limited sunlight through, so we don't all die in here, but not enough for it to be warm. I think the air feels stale for the same reason. Very little in or out."

"But why?" I say. "Why is he doing this?"

"You'll get to ask soon enough, I guess," says Calla, her mouth set in a grim line.

"How long until we get to Umbra?" I ask.

"A couple of hours? We might want to stop somewhere for the night, and we should get to Umbra early tomorrow."

"Staying in inns seemed like such a glamorous part of travel as a kid," I say.

"A little homesick for our own bed?" she asks.

"More than a little," I say.

She gives a wry laugh and rubs her hand over her face. I lose track of how long we've walked before I take a second to really look around. I can tell that in its natural state, this place is beautiful. I can make out little clusters of houses in the distance, and even further away, slightly taller buildings that must be the beginning of Umbra proper. Unlike Maradal, where the mountains are jagged peaks, the mountains in the distance are loping, rolling hills. Bushes and wildflowers line the sides of the road. I can tell that, without the Fog, the landscape here is supposed to be green and vibrant. The flowers and shrubs are meant to be purples, pinks, and reds, but it's all been muted somehow, as if we're looking at everything through a dirty, grey window. The effect is vaguely nauseating.

"How does anyone live here?" I ask as we start walking towards the first cluster of houses in the distance.

"It's amazing what you can get used to when you have no choice," says Calla. After what seems like hours, we approach the first little village. In structure, the houses look just like the other Andestine style houses we passed, but the gray haze of the fog gives them an eerie look, rather than looking like miniatures from a fairytale like the other houses we've seen. Despite the oppressive environment, the village sounds very alive as we approach. I can hear children running, yelling, and playing. People are hanging laundry to dry or chatting in their yards as we pass by. At first, I think I'm imagining it, but all activity seems to stop as we pass, and all eyes turn to us. I should be used to this, but it somehow feels different than what I've experienced outside of Andestine.

"Calla," I ask, keeping my voice low, "have these people ever seen someone like me before?"

"I doubt it," she says, "but neither have most people in Maradal or Burne. You're fairly uncommon." She's right, but still.

"Have they ever even heard of someone like me? This just feels different. I guess I'm used to suspicion, but this feels like. . ." I let my voice taper off. I don't exactly have a word for what this feels like. The best I can come up with is a combination terror and. . . admiration, maybe? As if to accentuate my point, a father gardening in his yard goes pale as he notices us. He drops his gardening tools, snatches his daughter from where she's playing a few feet away, and disappears into their house. He gives a quick, polite wave before slamming the door behind him.

"People are scared here," says Calla. "Their daily lives have been impacted by magic in a way that most people can't understand. They're bound to be more fearful, I think." It makes sense, but the more people disappear into their houses and the quieter the town goes, the more unnerved I feel.

Calla is trying to act nonchalant, but I can tell from her body language that she's as focused now as she was the day we broke into Clocks.

"Does he ever leave his estate?" I ask. "The Inimical?"

"Sometimes," she says. "It's more of a castle, though, and not a very well-kept one. It's called Fowler's Keep. When the royal family lived there ages ago, there was apparently someone who was fond of raising chickens, and for a while, the place was overrun with them after the royal family left. The chickens are gone now, but the name stuck. The entire thing is a bit of a ruin. Atreo and I actually used to play around there as kids a lot. Anyway, when I think of an estate, I think of your home, somewhere warm and maintained." I know what she's doing; she's trying to take my mind off this cold, eerie place by filling my head with memories of home, and I'm grateful for it in spite of trying to remain focused myself.

"*Brujita,*" A voice hisses from somewhere nearby. Whoever it is isn't close, but in the stagnant air, the hiss carries like it's been whispered in my ear. From the way Calla tenses, I can tell it feels the same for her. I whirl around looking for the source of the voice and finally see a pale face in the window of one of the houses we just passed. It's a woman, perhaps a few years older than Calla and I. Like Calla, she has long dark waves and dark eyes with pronounced dark circles under them, but everything else couldn't be more different. Where Calla glows, whatever light this woman might have had, internal or otherwise, was snuffed out long ago. She raises a hand and curls a finger, beckoning us over to her. I feel goosebumps erupt on my skin and have to fight the urge to bolt. I tighten my grip on Calla's hand.

"Come on," I say, pulling her forward along the road, but she untangles her hand from mine.

"Just give me a minute," she says, and starts to walk toward the house.

"Why?" I say. "So you can talk to a strange woman, hissing nonsense at us?"

"It's not nonsense," says Calla gently, "it's our old language, from before we agreed to a common language with Thiaghal and Burne."

"Oh," I say, "Calla, I'm sorry. I'm such an oaf, I didn't mean to call your language nonsense."

"I know," she says. She gives me a quick, reassuring smile as she moves towards the woman again. I fight the urge to pull her back. The woman's eyes stay glued to me, only briefly flicking towards Calla as she approaches the window. Her stare makes my skin crawl. What does she want? Does she think I'm going to hurt Calla? Is she trying to offer to help Calla because I'm a monster?

As Calla approaches the window, the woman reaches out and latches onto Calla's arm so tightly that she's yanked forward. I'm about to sprint for the window, but Calla turns and holds up a hand to stop me. I can hear the sound of urgent hisses and whispers, but not well enough to make out what's being said. The woman's voice becomes more frantic, and she starts to cry, glancing back over her shoulder into the house. She seems to be gesturing for Calla to come inside. Calla shakes her head 'no' and tries to pull her arm away. The woman points at me, and something angry takes over Calla's expression, as she hisses something back to the woman. I'm inching closer to trying to hear when the woman starts trying to pull Calla into the house again. Calla finally yanks her arm away and tosses her hair over her shoulder as she strides back towards me. The woman is crying in earnest now, yelling after us in ancient Andestinian. As we hurry down the road, away from the woman's screams, Calla's face crumbles, and she starts crying. I wrap my arm around her shoulders as we walk.

"Calla, what was all that about?" I ask.

"She wanted me to come in and take a look at her daughter," she says, taking a shaky breath. "She's sick. She has an illness that people in Andestine call—"

"Senzicaria?" I ask, my mind flashing back to the emergency council meeting from weeks ago.

"Senzicaria," she says. "I forgot, you'd know what it is from the medical briefs that our government will have sent you."

"The emergency council meeting as well," I say. "I don't think I ever really got a chance to explain what made Murchad turn on me so completely." I briefly explain the role Senzicaria played in the council meeting and in Murchad's attack on the estate.

"Hm," says Calla, "well, I guess a simple disagreement about a foreign aid policy was as good an excuse as any to act on years of misplaced fear and hate."

"Why would she want you to come in and look at her daughter?" I ask, referencing back to the woman from the village we just passed.

"Because she knows I went to Clocks," says Calla. "Not many people in these smaller places outside the cities have any training in healing."

"They teach healing at Clocks?" I ask.

"They teach poisoning," she says, "and most treatments are just poisons in varied quantities. Unfortunately, I'm pretty out of my depth as far as being able to help her. I did what I could for her daughter before I left Umbra last year. There isn't much more I can do for now, but that obviously wasn't easy to hear."

"Her daughter's been sick for over a year?" I say. "Doesn't Senzicaria have a timeline?"

"That's what I did before I left," says Calla. "I managed to stabilize her. She's stuck in the phase of the illness she was in when I first met her, so about a week in. It won't progress, but I can't make her better."

"What did you use to stabilize her?" I ask.

"Oleander mostly," says Calla. I nod, realizing that it was pointless to ask since I don't know anything about medicinal (or poisonous) plants.

***

We continue walking into the night and it's late when Calla says, "We're here." I'm shaken from my thoughts and realize we're standing in front of a small door in a little row of houses. The buildings in Umbra so far aren't as grand as the ones in Lytwist; they're shorter and simpler, but they have more character somehow. They're all built in adjoining rows, and there are gas lamps lining the cobblestone streets.

As we make our way through the city at night, it's easy to see people tucked into the little houses sitting in front of the fire with their families or sitting down to dinner. I'm thinking about my family and wondering what they're doing right now when Calla's voice pulls me back to the present. We're standing in front of a worn wood door with a large metal door knocker. Calla takes my hand as she knocks twice. The door immediately flies open to reveal an old man, his hair completely gray. He's leaning on a cane and wearing a simple brown shirt and pants. Before I can register much else about him, he says, "Calla," and throws his arm around her.

"Grandad," she says. She buries her face in his shoulder and hugs back, and they stay like that for several seconds. When Calla finally pulls out of his embrace, her grandfather turns and faces me, with his hand still on Calla's shoulder. I can't read his expression. Is he horrified? Skeptical? It's hard to imagine he's thrilled with the man, or monster, that his granddaughter decided to marry. His face doesn't give any feeling away. Calla opens her mouth to introduce me as I hold out my hand, but she's halted by the scurry of little feet echoing down the long front hallway.

"Aunt Calla!" A little girl flies through the open door and launches herself towards Calla.

"Ameri!" Calla yells, hugging her back. Two boys, a little older than Ameri, tumble down the hallway too, closely followed by a man with a dish towel slung over his shoulder.

"Welcome home, Calla," he says, reaching out to shake her hand.

"Thanks, Uncle Ramon," she says. She opens her mouth to introduce me again, but her grandfather cuts her off.

"Well, come on," he says, "no reason to be having this conversation on the porch. Come inside, come inside. Any bags?" He quickly surveys Calla and I and gives a sharp nod when he sees that I've got our bags settled on my back. Calla turns and gives me an encouraging smile as we follow her family into the house. The house has a long hallway that eventually branches off into a small room that seems to be a kitchen, where something smells amazing, like simmering tomatoes and garlic. Ramon disappears into the kitchen as we make our way down the hallway, and I can hear him laughing and chatting to a woman in ancient Andestinian.

Despite the light pouring from the kitchen, the hallway itself is dark, and the sense of unease that has been following me this entire trip settles over me again. Although I can't rule out that it's just nerves at meeting Calla's grandfather, who so far seems determined to ignore the fact that I exist. Some of the feeling evaporates as we round the corner to the light-filled kitchen and see Ramon lean over to kiss a short woman who looks very much like an older, rounder Calla simmering something on the stove. Calla's grandfather sits down at a small, cluttered table in the corner in front of a huge fireplace. The three- no, four now- kids all settle around him, chattering to each other.

"Tyre," says Calla, pulling me towards the wood stove where Ramon and the woman are cooking, "this is my second cousin Ramon and his wife Cecilia, and these," she says as she snatches one of the four kids running by into a tight hug, "are their kids Ameri, Linso, Phillipe, and Marvin."

"Nice to meet you all," I say. I extend my hand, and Ramon shakes it and smiles. He doesn't seem fazed by me at all, but he and the youngest three kids are the only ones who don't. The oldest boy, Cecilia, and Calla's grandfather, have yet to as much as look at me. If Calla's bothered by this, she doesn't show it. She releases her little cousin and takes my hand again.

"We're going to get our things situated for the night, then we'll come back and help with dinner," she calls as she pulls me from the room.

"Nice to meet everyone," I call after her. As we leave the warmth of the kitchen, the uneasiness grows again, and I fight the urge to turn and make eye contact with Aydin or try to catch a reassuring smile from Bevin, knowing that obviously it's no use.

"We'll have to sleep in the sitting room," says Calla. She gestures for me to hand her our packs. She leads the way further down the hallway, which ends in a small sitting room with worn sofas and another fireplace, although it isn't lit at the moment.

"Calla," I say, "did your grandfather ever write to you to tell you what he thought of us getting married? You did tell him, right?"

"I told him," she says. "Just give him some time. Trust me, it has nothing to do with the fairy magic and your antlers. It has everything to do with him not being able to be at the wedding, not getting to meet you before, and me disappearing for a year in general."

"Calla, you know he could have been at the wedding? We would have arranged for transportation."

"I know," she says, giving me a sad smile, "but he still couldn't have."

"Why not?" I ask.

"Well, remember I wasn't exactly on vacation when we met," she says. "I was hiding."

"So, your family traveling," I say, pieces sliding into place, "would be a surefire lead to you. Hiding from?"

"The same thing we're now running towards," she says.

"I thought you said that you didn't know The Inimical?" I ask, as I feel a surge of anger at her.

"It's complicated."

"You don't say," I say, my voice dripping with sarcasm. "Now that we're literally walking into his clutches, are you finally ready to tell me what your connection is?"

"The Inimical will tell you soon enough anyway," she says without offering anything further. I'm too tired to pry secrets out of Calla right now.

"You scared?" I ask. She does a double-take like she'd expected me to ask anything except that.

"Yes," she says. "I am."

"Me too," I say. She reaches for me, but one of her little cousins careens into the room from the hall.

"Calla! Mama says dinner is almost ready!

***

That night, Calla and I lie side by side on the floor of the sitting room. We've pulled cushions onto the floor to make a makeshift place to sleep. I'm not sure what time it is when I hear a rustling in the room. Calla is dreaming fitfully next to me when my eyes flutter open. I'm suddenly sure someone is walking in the room. Slowly, I turn over and am confronted by a face inches from mine. I gasp and yank my knife out from under the pillow before I realize that it's Marvin, the oldest of Calla's younger cousins. He's staring at me with a finger to his lips, gesturing for me to be quiet.

"Marvin, what . . . ?" I tuck the knife quickly back under my pillow. He holds up his finger to his mouth again and shakes his head 'no'.

"Alright," I whisper, "alright, I'll be quiet. What are you doing in here?"

"You should leave," he says.

"Marvin," I say, letting out a breath. "I'm not going to hurt your cousin. I know I can look scary, but—"

"No!" Marvin whispers. He glances at Calla to make sure she's still asleep. "You need to leave."

Before I can say anything, he scampers away and back up the stairs. For obvious reasons, I struggle to fall back asleep. I must fall back asleep eventually, but I don't realize it at first, so it takes me a moment to realize I'm dreaming. I just think that I've woken up and plan to go to the kitchen for a glass of water. The sense of something uncanny washes over me, but I've felt that way so much recently that it doesn't register until I hear my dad's voice.

"Look," he says. I turn and see him standing down the hall in front of the opening to the kitchen. I look down and see myself sleeping, but no Calla, and I hear voices coming from the kitchen. I walk towards my dad, but he doesn't speak again. He just watches me round the corner into the kitchen. Calla is sitting with her grandfather at the table, holding a warm drink in her hands. The fireplace has been re-lit, and gone is the cold man I met earlier. This man radiates warmth. He leans in towards his granddaughter, his hand over hers as she clutches the mug.

"How sick are you?" He leans forward and places the back of his hand on her forehead as if checking for a fever.

"I'm fine, grandad," she says, gently nudging his hand away.

"Hmph," he says. He begrudgingly lowers his hand back to her's wrapped around her mug.

"You could have at least said 'hello' to him, grandad," she says.

"Calla," he says, "I'm sorry. I couldn't. I tried."

"It's not as if you didn't know," she says.

"I know," he says, "but seeing it, seeing him . . . I just . . . " Calla pulls her hands away, and a tear slides down her cheek.

"Calla, I'm sorry. It's not your fault. None of this. If I had never been stupid enough to send you to that cursed excuse for a school—"

"It's not your fault either," she says. "You didn't know."

"It's not your fault," he says again with even more emphasis. He reaches back over and squeezes her hand again, and she lets him. For a second, it looks like she's going to argue, but she slumps her shoulders and deflates at the last minute.

"It is, though," she says, "not all of it, but some of it."

"If it wasn't for you," her grandfather says, "Atreo would be dead, and so would a great number of other people in Umbra."

"But it's still getting through," she says, "and I can't find the antidote. I'm trying but—"

"You will," he says, "you just needed more time, and now you have it. You will, *Brujita*." On the last word, the same Old Andestinian word that the woman had yelled at Calla on the walk here, he reaches up and cups her face. I wonder if it's a childhood nickname. "Why are we sitting here debating fault when we all know the fault lies with that bastard Meltair?" says her grandfather, sitting back in his chair. This gets Calla to let out a laugh. I want to listen more, but I hear my dad calling my name from the hallway, so I turn and walk back out toward his voice.

"Don't touch her, Tyre," he says.

"Little late for that, Dad," I say.

"No," he says, shaking his head, "don't touch her after the blood."

"Blood?" I feel a warm, crawling sensation on my arms. I look down and see blood. It coats my hands and slides down my arms. I feel my heart race as I raise my hands to my face to look. A single drop falls to the floor, and I wake with a start. Calla is asleep next to me, tense but completely still. There is no light coming from the kitchen, and I hear the distant snores of the rest of her family asleep on the second floor. I look down at my hands and arms. How likely is it that, for once, one of my dreams was just a dream? It's hard to ignore the warm burn of the medallion around my neck.

***

"Remember, the goal is stealth," says Calla the next morning. We bid her family a tearful farewell, and I even got a passing moment of eye contact from her grandfather. He explains something to Calla in rapid, hushed Old Andestinian, and she rolls her eyes and hurries us out of the house before her younger cousins wake up. When I asked her what it was about, she explained that Marvin apparently didn't want her to leave and was planning on challenging her to a "duelo de destino" or duel of fate on the condition that if he won, she would have to stay. Just like people in Thiaghal tend to be extra superstitious when it comes to fairies, the people of Umbra have their own quirks. Apparently, it's considered highly inappropriate in Andestine to refuse a duel of fate, although in the case of Marvin challenging Calla, it sounds like this duel would have consisted of a round of rock-paper-scissors rather than an actual fight.

We've finally managed to scrape together what feels like a workable plan for rescuing Atreo, which mostly relies on Calla's knowledge of the castle layout. The castle was apparently abandoned and easy to access before The Inimical took up residence and made Umbra his base of operations. In a way, this is starting to feel very similar to the plan we used to get Maddie out of Clocks. At least it feels like we've had a dry run. Hopefully, it won't take us two tries to get Atreo. What's murkier still is whether I'm actually going to confront The Inimical. Stupid as it may be, I want to. Even if The Inimical has fairy magic, I've got my medallion, and there are very few people I can't physically overpower, but Calla seems hesitant.

"Let's just get Atreo out before we decide if you go barging back in to challenge Mark to a duel," she says. Understandably, Atreo is her first priority, but I have Thiaghal and myself to think about. The Inimical has been a lurking threat for too long. I'm going to challenge The Inimical one way or another. Calla has enough secrets that I don't feel too bad keeping this one from her.

"Right," I say, "stealth. In through the front wall is the garden, and The Inimical lives alone, so unless he's staring out the window when we come through the gate, it should be fairly simple to hide from hedge to hedge, statue to statue until we reach the front doors."

"Once we're in," says Calla, "I'll lead the way to Atreo, and you'll use a combination of muscle and magic to get through the barrier, hopefully similar to the Fog when we entered Andestine. The magic will let you through because you're part of it, and then?"

"We get out of there," I finish. I feel a tiny twist of guilt in my gut knowing I plan to hunt The Inimical after we get Atreo out, but I'm still going to do it. Calla has her crossbow, and I've got my sword at my hip and the fairy knife tucked under my shirt as always.

"This is it," says Calla when we're finally standing outside the gates to Fowler's Keep. She wasn't kidding when she said it was run-down. "The royal family used to live here centuries ago," she says, "until they moved their residence to Delante de Bosque." She stares up at the old gate. It's covered in ivy, and a huge wall of bushes surrounds the rest of the garden. The only way in or out is through this gate.

"Ready?" I say, taking her hand. Calla takes a shaky breath and swallows before giving one short nod. I take a deep breath and push open the gate. It isn't locked. Why would it be when The Inimical thinks he's untouchable? We step through, and I find myself in the garden from my nightmares. The very same dead garden where I've met The Inimical every time he's haunted my dreams. I shake off the shock of being here in person as Calla, and I scamper from old statue to old bush, staying out of sight of the windows. She yanks me back from the last bush before the door.

"Rosebush," she whispers. I'm reminded of her bizarre reaction to me reaching for a rose the night of the party, but I don't have time to ask her why this matters before she's scurrying towards the front doors. I follow as quietly as I can, and again, I take her hand and count to three before pushing open the front door as silently as possible.

Just like that, we're inside. I don't bother to close the door, not when we'll need as quick an exit as possible. I quiet the voice in my head that tells me this is too easy. It's easy because The Inimical is overconfident, and this can only work to our advantage. The entry way is huge, breathtaking even, with tall ceilings and a grand stone staircase leading to the upper floors. Without a word, I start moving towards the staircase as quickly as I can, knowing from what Calla says that Atreo is being held upstairs. I feel Calla following close behind me. Suddenly, a huge clanging noise echoes across the silent entry hall. I spin to see the door slamming shut.

"Shit," I rush back toward the doors and tug on them, but they're locked. "Calla," I whisper frantically, "we might be in trouble."

"We're not," she says, her voice unbothered, and at full volume.

"Calla," I say, slowly turning to face her, "come on. Help me with these doors." Something is not right. I can't make sense of the sudden shift in Calla.

"No need," she says. She doesn't sound scared or frantic. She sounds sad.

"What are you talking about?" I ask.

"I closed them," she says.

"How?" I ask. "You were right behind me on the stairs. How could you have closed the door?"

"Magic," she says, shrugging her shoulders.

"Humans can't use magic," I say, swallowing a lump in my throat.

"One can," she says.

I'm an idiot.

21

"No," I say. I keep tugging on the doors. "No, no, no." I hear myself still talking, but my head is making a whirring noise.

"Tyre, just . . . "

"NO," I scream, pounding both my claws against the door. I spin to face Calla. She's so maddeningly calm. So beautiful and glowing like she's lit from within. Liar. Liar. Liar.

"Liar!" I scream out loud. She clamps her jaw, and I can see her eyes start to tear up. How dare she? How dare she have the audacity to cry in this moment? She doesn't try to speak again, and I'm glad of it because I don't think I can stand the sound of her voice right now. "I trusted you!" I scream. "I mean, I really trusted you. Stupidly, blindly. All those times you asked me not to ask questions about all the secrets and asked me to trust you, and I just did."

"It's because you're a good person," she says. The glare I give her finally breaks her composure, and she takes a step back.

"Any of it?" I ask.

"What?" she says.

"Any of it . . . " I stumble over my words, trying to get my thoughts together. "Was any of it real?" She scoffs. "I'm sorry, what was funny about that question?" I yell.

“It’s not a real question,” she says. “You’ve already decided the answer. So, it’s not a question, just an accusation.” My brain can’t process the rush of emotions whirling through my body. The ghost of affection at first, because it’s such a typical Calla answer. Then, when my brain catches up to the situation, rage and pain. I realize that all Calla’s double-talk and dodging and weaving with her words was never the defensive habit of a traumatized damsel. It was a stupid game she played with an interesting mouse. *‘How much can I hide from Tyre and still have him follow me right into a trap like a lovesick puppy?’*

“I hate you,” I say. She shrugs, wraps her arms around herself, and starts walking towards the stairs. “So that’s it?” I yell. In my anger at Calla, I haven’t had a chance to feel scared. I don’t want to admit to feeling scared now, but I’m trapped. Whatever I thought I’d be facing when I finally met The Inimical, I was very wrong. “Why am I here? Why is he, or you, why are you taking people like me? Just answer! Don’t pose another question or make some broad statement about the world. Tell me! You owe me at least that!”

She pauses and turns back.

“You remember Murchad?” she asks. “I know it’s a question, but the answer requires some explanation.”

“Do I remember Murchad? The man who, until this moment, held the record for the most successful attempt on my life? Yes, I think I remember Murchad,” I spit.

“He had a fairy godparent. I guessed because of how much he hated you. People gifted things by fairies hate magic more than anyone because of how much trouble the ‘gifts’ cause. They seem to find it and anyone impacted by it, themselves included, grotesque and unnatural.”

“Fine,” I say, “so maybe Murchad had been gifted something by a fairy godparent. So what?”

"So," says Calla, "I can use magic, but I can't generate it. I need to siphon it from somewhere. People touched by fairy magic are an excellent source. If I touch them, I can absorb it, and then I can use it. That's what I did to Murchad."

"You're going to do to me what you did to Murchad?" I say, feeling my body go cold.

"It's not that simple," she says.

"Is that why you brought me here?" I ask. "It's not complicated; it's a simple answer. Did you bring me here with the intention of doing to me what you did to Murchad?"

"Tyre . . . "

"Calla if you don't answer me, I swear . . . "

"Oh, you'll what?" she snaps. "What are you going to do, Tyre? You're not exactly in a position to set terms here." There's silence for a beat as we both react to what she said.

"I'm sorry," she says.

Now it's my turn to laugh. I turn back and start banging on the doors again.

"Tyre!" she yells. "Stop! No one will hear, and no one will care if they do!" I don't listen. I pound and pound on the doors until I feel a sharp tug around my waist and skid backward along the floor away from the doors. My medallion glows warm on my chest as if telling the magical tug to back off.

"Don't!" I scream at Calla. "Do not use magic on me!" She holds her hands up and steps back in a gesture of surrender. I'm breathing hard from my fight with the doors, and trying to fight the urge to panic.

"So I ask again, what now?" I say. "How long do I have until you turn me into a raisin?"

"I'm not going to kill you if I can avoid it," she says.

"Well, that's just great, Calla," I yell, throwing my hands in the air. I feel like I'm on the verge of a complete mental breakdown. "Let's have someone bake you a cake. It will say, '*not as big an asshole as you could have been.*'"

"Tyre, just let me explain!" Hearing those words, something inside of me finally snaps.

"No," I say, through clenched teeth. I cross the room to her and wrap my hand around her throat and shove her backwards until her head slams the wall behind her. I squeeze her throat, and I wonder if I could actually kill her, but I realize it's irrelevant. Calla can use magic to throw me backward anytime she wants. She just feels bad for the stupid fly that flew right into her web. "No," I say, "you had your chance to explain. If I'm going to die, I want you to know that I died not understanding how you could do something like this. You don't get to use me to ease your conscience." I snatch my hand away from her neck and back away. She reaches up to massage her neck, and we both stare at each other, breathing hard.

"I'll show you to your room," she says.

***

I follow Calla silently up the decaying grand staircase to a somehow even grander and even more decayed upper floor. Everything in this place whispers 'used to be.' There are carpets that used to be plush and soft, paintings that used to be bright and vibrant. I wonder how The Inimical, *Calla*, I remind myself, ended up here. Especially now that I know The Inimical is apparently welcome in her family home just down the hill. I feel another wave of nausea as my brain tries to consolidate everything I know about The Inimical with everything I know about Calla. As I follow her down the hall, there's a part of me that still thinks she's going to turn around and say, 'It's all a joke!' Then I'll get to be mad at her for her twisted sense of humor instead of her year-long plan to kill me. As we walk down a new wing of the castle, she pauses and opens a door.

"You can stay in here," she says. The room is fine as far as rooms to be held captive go. There's a warm fire, a clean bed with soft-looking pillows, and a broom sweeping on its own in the center of the room. "Oh," says Calla, seeing it, "I make all the brooms go around on their own. It helps with both cleaning and loneliness." The broom drifts over to her, and she scratches the top of the handle the way someone would a favorite cat.

"Calla, get out," I say.

***

I have no idea how I sleep, but I wake with a horrible taste in my mouth and a feeling of panic. I sit up in bed with my heart pounding and reach for Calla next to me. When she isn't there, and I remember the events of the past several hours, I finally throw up. Thankfully, the room is attached to an adjoining bathroom because the last thing I'm doing is going looking for Calla to ask where I can wash vomit out of my sheets. I drag myself back to bed and collapse until the nausea almost passes. When I feel like I can move again, I rub my face and sit up. Time to get to work.

The Inimical has another thing coming if she thinks I'm going to sit here in this room and wait for her to kill me. My first task is to take inventory of what I have with me in the room. Thankfully, I still have Dad's medallion, although The Inimical knows about that, so I have to imagine at some point she'll try to take it from me. It's what saved me from her the first time. I push away the memory of Calla the night I told her about the medallion, yelling, 'How? Because no one escapes The Inimical! Not ever!' Safeguarding the medallion has to be a high priority. I'll need to think about the best way to do that, but for now, I tuck it under my shirt. I've also still got my fairy knife and candle under my shirt, which I count as my second most useful items right now.

The room is next. When I look around and take stock, there's a bedside table and a large dresser, but no other furniture in the room besides the bed. I open the dresser, which is stacked with piles of clothes that look about my size. How thoughtful. I don't know why she'd take the time to pack all these clothes if she's just going to kill me. The only other place to look for anything useful is in the bedside table, where I find a few empty notebooks and some pencils. In case I want to sketch or journal, I guess.

With the inventory taken, I move on to looking for escape routes. I hesitate, but grab one of the notebooks to write down anything that might be useful. There's one window in the room, but when I reach for it, I find my hand can't even touch the glass. I hit a barrier that suddenly pulses the same golden glow Calla emits, which leads me to believe she's magicked the windows so I can't get to them. I had assumed that I was just trapped in the castle, but now I wonder if I'm actually trapped in this room. I'm about to walk to the door when it slowly opens on its own. I jump back to the other end of the room, but it's just a broom. It wanders in and starts sweeping dust into a little pile in the center of the room. I watch it blankly for a few minutes before slipping around it as quietly as I can. I don't know why I bother since it completely ignores me and just keeps going about its sweeping.

I gingerly approach the threshold of the door, but I don't hit a barrier, so I slip out into the hall. I pause and listen, but the only sign of movement is the little broom swishing inside the bedroom. I'm not sure what I'm looking for as I pad down the halls, but I keep a mental inventory of anything that could be useful. There are empty places on the walls where old, decorative weapons might have hung, but Calla has pretty well taken everything down. I follow the hall back out to the grand staircase, keeping my ears pricked for any sound of movement. The grand entryway is still and quiet as when we arrived, except for another broom quietly making its way around the hall.

I have to fight the impulse to try to wrench open the front doors again. Instead, I walk the perimeter of the room looking for any other entryways or exits. There is a small door to the right of the staircase that I didn't notice before. I slowly push it open to find it leads to a damp hallway lit with gas lamps that is, if possible, in even more disrepair than the other parts of the building. It ends in another wooden door. When I make my way down the hall and push that door open, it leads to a steep downward staircase. The draft from the stairs makes me shiver even with my fur, but I'm cautiously optimistic that maybe this leads to an exit. I keep following the stairs down, but the farther I go, the less convinced I am that it will lead outside. The air is becoming colder, but also staler. A few rats scuttle by my feet as I step into what seems like a basement. As my eyes adjust to the dim light, I see a series of bars demarcating cells.

"What do you want?" A voice I don't recognize right away spits from the corner of the room, making me jump.

"Hello?" I call. "Who's there?"

"Hello?" says the voice. I realize it sounds familiar. I move towards the corner of the room where the voice seems to be coming from.

"Hello!" I call back.

"Here!" The voice yells. "I'm over here! Hurry!" I reach the last cell in the row and finally see a human shape, but as my eyes keep adjusting, I realize it's not a human at all.

"Briowney?" I yell.

"*Tyre?*" she yells back. She slumps down against the wall behind her with a groan. "I tried to tell you." My mind flashes back to the night she appeared at the manor house with her cryptic warnings and her knife.

"Calla is the one who took you," I say.

"Looks like she got you, too," she says. "Quick, give me back my knife and let me out. I think I can kill her if we move quickly enough."

"Wait, what?" I say as my brain races to catch up.

"Knife," she says, holding out her hand. "I only gave it to you because you had more access to her at that point. Regular weapons won't kill her; she heals too quickly because of the magic."

"Why did you give me the candle?" I ask, still disoriented. Briowney rolls her eyes.

"It shows things as they are," she says. "If you had lit it in front of her, you would have known she was The Inimical. It's fairly useless now. Now, quick, let me out of here. Calla is smart, and once she realizes you're exploring the castle, I doubt she'll waste any time before checking on me."

"I'm not killing Calla," I say, surprising myself. Apparently, I'm not killing Calla.

"What?" screeches Briowney. She throws herself against the cell bars and reaches for me so quickly that I need to scramble backwards to avoid her grasp. "You can't be serious. She'll kill you, I've seen it. She'll kill you like she did all the others."

"The others?"

"The others like you. All of the ones who have disappeared; they're all here."

"I thought you said they were dead?" I say. She rolls her eyes again like she can't believe how dense I'm being. "They may as well be. Look in the door at the end of the east wing. Then let me know if you want to let me out of here. Until then, stop wasting my time."

"Do you know why she's doing this?" I ask.

"Your lovely wife? No. She doesn't exactly confide in me." With that, Briowney turns and stalks to the back of her cell. She flops down facing the wall, and it seems clear she's done talking to me, but as I make my way back to the door, she calls out.

"While you're at it," she says. "I should tell you, I used to be free to roam around like you with my very own room. I wasn't always in here. Then one day, I went somewhere I shouldn't have. I think she thought the door was blocked with magic, but I'm sure you know from getting through the fog that no magical barrier is foolproof, especially to creatures like me. I ended up in the room with a sleeping boy in a golden glowing case. I wasn't so interested in the boy, although he didn't look so great, but in another golden case next to him, she's got a Claret Rose."

"A Claret Rose?" I say. "Like from the story?"

"Yes," says Briowney, "like from the *history*. That rose belongs to my kind. She has no right to it, but she stopped me right as I was about to take it. Since then, I've been in here. No more wandering."

"Why are you telling me this?" I ask.

"Because," says Briowney, "if you're feeling squeamish about killing her, but you want to hurt her, I would take that rose."

"Really," I say, "and why would I want to do that? And why are you telling me this? What's in it for you?"

"I want to hurt her too," says Briowney, "and I'm trying to garner some goodwill. If we want to get out of here, you and I can work together. Think about it."

"I'll think about it," I say. As I make my way back up the stairs, I can't help but think that if there's someone just behind Calla for "person I trust the least," it's Briowney.

22

The rest of the morning is uneventful, but when I come back to my room, there is a tray of food on my bed. I wonder if Calla dropped it off or if two brooms worked together to carry it. As much as I want to reject it out of spite, growing weak from starvation won't work in favor of my escape plan. Part of me wants to immediately go looking for the rooms Briowney described, but I need to be smart and careful, so I decide to move methodically throughout the rest of the castle.

The second half of my day is spent on the rest of the downstairs. There's another door on the other side of the grand staircase in the front hall. When I push it open, instead of cool air, I'm greeted with a blast of warmth and the smell of baking bread. I almost turn around because the smell of something baking means that a baker, most likely Calla, is nearby, but if this is the kitchen, it's potentially one of the most useful rooms in the castle.

She didn't lock me in my room, so she shouldn't be surprised that I'm walking around. The smell of bread gets stronger and stronger until I round a corner into a large kitchen. This is so far the only room in the castle that doesn't look run-down. All the cookware and surfaces look new and shiny, and the stonework on the walls has been repaired. When I enter the room, there is Calla sitting at a tall stone table in the middle of the room, sipping a warm drink. There are several brooms bustling around the room, and Calla is watching them with a wan half-smile. The rings around her eyes tell me she's probably been up all night. As I step into the room, the smell of roses mingling with the smell of bread is so strong and sweet that I almost gag. At the sound of the cough, Calla's shoulders tense, and she turns.

"I assume that since I'm not locked in my room, I'm free to walk around," I say.

"I've magically sealed anywhere you're not supposed to be," she says, tilting her head in agreement. "You won't be able to go anywhere you shouldn't."

"Don't be so sure," I say. I don't know why I say it. I should let The Inimical think that I'm terrified and compliant, but I'd replied to Calla before my brain could remind me that she's The Inimical.

"You want a coffee?" she says.

"No, Calla. I do not want a coffee." She rests her head in her hands for a second before speaking again.

"I wasn't lying about one thing, well, actually, quite a few things that you've barred me from explaining- but there is one thing you'll want me to explain." I ignore her and start walking around the kitchen, taking stock of items and looking for exits. There are quite a few knives, pots, and pans, all of which could be useful, but as far as I can tell, the only way out of the kitchen is the way I came in.

"I really might be able to help Maddie," she says.

"How dare you," I say. "How dare you even say the names of any of my family members, especially Maddie!" Then I have a horrible realization. "Stay away from her," I say.

"I'm not going to hurt Maddie," she says. "I've had plenty of chances to, and I haven't."

"You haven't been alone with her since Pax made the prophecy about her killing you."

"I'm not a big believer in prophecies," she says, "and I meant what I said when I said I don't hurt kids. I put some major plans on hold to go rescue Maddie, remember?"

"Yes, thank you so much for waiting until we rescued Maddie from a murder school before kidnapping me."

"Tyre, go away," she says.

"Me go away?" I yell. "*Me?*"

"Yes," she says.

"No," I say, "I'm sorry you have to be a little bit perturbed by my presence, but if you're so bothered, then trust me, I'd be happy to return home and never see you again." She stands up from the table and walks toward the kitchen door.

"Wait," I say, cursing internally. She pauses but doesn't turn back around. "What makes you think you can help Maddie?"

"I have a workshop here, of sorts," she says, sighing and slowly making her way back to the table. "For magic. I've got supplies and herbs. I could try to make something to help her stop the bursts of electricity. It would help if she were here—"

"No way," I say. "Never going to happen."

"Then I'll try to make something," she says. "A potion or an item. Something that I can send with a Holpie back to Thiaghal.

"I don't know if I'm comfortable giving Maddie anything you make," I say.

"I know," she says, "but I'll try anyway."

***

It's early morning again, from what I can tell, and I've decided to finally go looking for the rooms Briowney described. I can feel my emotional shock starting to wear off, and I'm worried that my frantic productivity will collapse, leaving me to fully acknowledge Calla's betrayal, so I need to make the most of this time. Logistically, starting with a room in the east wing makes the most sense, so I take out my notebook and caption a page '*east wing*'.

The east wing is mostly bedrooms, not very different from the one I'm sleeping in, although most don't have any linens on the bed. I don't see anyone as I walk except for an occasional broom. Finally, there's only one door left in the wing. I slowly push open the door and can't quite figure out what I'm looking at. I clamp my hand over my mouth to get myself to be quiet and try to slow and steady my breathing. There's a split second where I'm convinced that I'm looking at mannequins before realizing I'm in a room full of monsters, or rather people, like me. There are at least 14 or 15 monsters; people I can only assume were turned with fairy magic, all with varying degrees of wrinkles on any skin that's visible for some reason. They're seated on cushions with their backs against the walls of the room, eyes open and blinking, but all staring straight ahead, expressionless.

"Hello?" I say, stepping into the room. "Hello, my name is Tyre. Tyre Sylvan, Governor of Thiaghal in Maradal. I'm here to help you." They all remain perfectly still, staring ahead.

"They can't hear you," says a voice behind. I don't have to wonder who it is. "I knew you'd find them eventually," she says.

"What did you do to them?" I ask.

"They're asleep, kind of," she says. "They can't be totally asleep because they need to walk, but they're not aware of anything."

"This is disgusting," I say.

"I'm not overly fond of it myself," says Calla.

"You're doing it!"

"You won't let me tell you why," she parries.

"There's no reason good enough."

"Don't be so sure," she says. "By the way," she holds up a bottle with a glowing yellow liquid inside, "say that word, and we send this to Maddie. I can't be sure it will work, but it's a potential antidote for the electric shocks. Courtesy of magic, courtesy of . . ." Instead of finishing the sentence, she gestures to the room of comatose monsters.

My stomach twists uncomfortably. I tell myself that it's because I'll need to decide whether I trust Calla enough to send the medicine to Maddie, but really, it's because she makes a point. If I send that antidote to Maddie, is it an endorsement of what Calla's doing? My stomach twists even more when I realize it doesn't matter. If I were sure it would help, I would send it to Maddie in a heartbeat. I might even go round up more monsters myself.

"You wouldn't do what I've done," says Calla, gently.

"I'm sorry, can you read minds now?" I ask.

"No," she says, "I just know you. Let me know about the antidote."

"How did you make it so quickly?" I ask. "You didn't seem to know how to help back in Thiaghal."

"It isn't the first time Meltair has used a crackler for training," she says. "While I was at Clocks, everyone who faced off against one died, but there were rumors passed on from older students about the best ways to ease electric burns from them. The herbs are rare, but I've got them here. Just not in Thiaghal. From what I've figured out, the key to medicinal magic seems to be a real base and then infusing it with sheer force of will. So, for example, if I wanted to cure a cold in a day, I would take something that would actually help with a cold, like garlic, and infuse the will to completely cure the cold, and it would cure it instantly."

"Interesting," I say begrudgingly.

"Anyway," she says, smiling slightly, "it's time for their walk." She waves her hand, and in unison, all the monsters stand. I jump backwards.

"What are you doing?" I say.

"The only thing I can't seem to figure out with magic is bedsores," she says. "If they don't walk at least once per day, they start to get sores from sitting too long." In an eerie parade, the monsters file out of the room one by one. We follow them out to the grand staircase and then into the main hall, where they start to walk in circles around the room. I'm feeling sick again, watching them walk mindlessly. "Why are some of them more wrinkled?" I ask, swallowing back bile.

"I've siphoned different amounts of magic at different times," she says, "It doesn't kill them if I don't siphon all of it. Eventually, the wrinkles go away, and they're good as new, and I can siphon again, but it takes a while. I would estimate that before you got here, I had about a month left of magic at full charge without risking killing one of them. Although our run-in with Murchad actually bought me, and you, significantly more time."

"Have you started?" I ask. "Siphoning magic from me?"

"You'd know if I had," she says. "I can't just do it; I need to drink some of the person's blood first."

"Excuse me?" I say.

"Blood," she says. "Once I drink even a drop of the blood of someone who has had fairy magic used on them, I can siphon magic from them. Actually, I can't *not* siphon magic from them after that if I touch them."

"Why blood?" I ask, my head spinning. "Does it work with other body fluids?"

"Didn't have a way to test it until recently, but apparently not," she says. I can feel her fighting back the urge to wink at me, and for just one horrible second, I feel like I've been punched in the gut by how much I miss her.

"So," I say, shaking the feeling off as best I can, "without me, and before you killed Murchad, you're out of magic in a month. Maybe a few months if you're willing to kill for it."

"Seems that way," she says, "but it's a non-issue because I have you." I feel Iike I've been doused with a bucket of cold water. I have to be more careful. I can't chat and joke with Calla. I can't get complacent even for a second. If I let my guard down, if I forget for even one second that all my efforts need to be going towards an escape plan, I may never escape. I'm not going to die here.

23

"Tell me again about the room where Calla's brother is," I say. It's early morning the next day when I make my way back to Briowney's cell.

"The sleeping man is her brother?" says Briowney.

"Yeah, Atreo. Unless she lied about that, too," I say. "She told me that he was injured and captured after Meltair sent him to destroy The Inimical. Of course, now I have no idea what actually happened."

"Did she tell you anything about why she has a Claret Rose?" says Briowney.

"No," I say, "I only knew about Atreo." I'm reminded again that Briowney's and my interests here are just barely aligned, but she's my only option for an ally. I touch the hilt of the knife under my shirt out of habit, and I feel her eyes watch the movement.

"If you're not going to give me the knife, at least let me out of here," she says.

"Won't Calla just put you back?" I ask. "I assume you can't push through the magical barriers around the exits, or you'd be long gone."

"I could if I had enough time," she spits. "Your wife always finds me too quickly. Cut off from any humans to do magic on, I'm not at my full strength."

"How did you get to me in Thiaghal?" I ask. She winces at the question.

"With her gone, I thought I would try to gather enough energy to use my magic to disappear and reappear outside the Fog. Fairies can do that, disappear and reappear. I realized quickly that it didn't work because the magic here kept trying to pull me back, and Calla's little gag spell made the stunt useless anyway. I shredded my wings for nothing." She looks mournfully at the tattered wings folded behind her.

"Why didn't you magic Calla when she first captured you?" I ask.

"Why do you think I'm here?" she says. "I came here in the first place to put her in check and turn her into a newt or something. I wasn't anticipating the scope of her abilities." It looks like it pains her physically to admit that Calla had overpowered her. Suddenly, an idea occurs to me.

"Change me back," I say. "Calla has no use for me if I'm just a human man."

"You think she'll just let you go skipping home to tell everyone she's The Inimical?" she scoffs. She's right, I know too much, and there is a part of me that's relieved. I'd happily change if it meant getting out of here, but there's still a significant part of me that likes the way I am now. "And," continues Briowney, "the conditions haven't been met. No one has fallen in love with you."

"Thanks for the reminder," I say. "You'd seriously hold that line now if changing me back could get us out of here?" Her silence tells me that she would. In the twenty minutes I've been down here, I've rethought this alliance five different times.

"What do you need to get us out of here but not kill Calla?" I say.

"May I recommend we kill Calla?" she says.

"Your preference is noted," I say, "have a great however long she keeps you in here." I stand and walk towards the door.

"Wait!" she says. "Fine. Fine, I'll agree to your ridiculous condition of not killing Calla."

"Do I have any reason to believe you'll keep your word on that?" I ask.

"If you want to get out of here, you'll just have to trust me," she says.

"I'm not giving you your knife," I say. She glares at me. "What else do you need?"

"Well, first," she says, "I need you to let me out of here."

***

I tumble into bed later, wondering if I've made a horrible mistake. I double and triple check that the fairy knife is still pressed against my chest before setting my dinner tray outside the door, lying down, and closing my eyes, hand still wrapped around the hilt of the knife.

"Well, I see you let Briowney out." I open my eyes, and for a single second, I think I've somehow sleepwalked outside to the desolate front garden before I realize I'm dreaming.

"You have got to be kidding me," I say. I turn and see 'The Inimical' standing on the other side of the garden, a massive black cloak wrapped in shadows. "Knock it off, Calla," I say. 'The Inimical' lifts two skeletal hands from inside the cloak and snaps. Suddenly, the scene changes. The garden is healthy and lush with sun streaming down. When I look up, Calla is standing across the garden wearing a shining, golden gown with a flower crown in her hair.

"Better?" she says.

"Better would be out of my head," I say. She drifts toward me, her golden gown dragging behind her, catching flower petals as he walks.

"I figured you'd let her out at some point," she says, "but it's interesting that you didn't give her the knife."

"We're not all killers," I say.

"Briowney is less capable of killing me than you are, and for her it's a skill issue," she says.

"Alright, fine," I say, "I'll give her the knife."

"Fine," says Calla, "I'll take your medallion." I ignore the jolt that goes through my body when I realize she hasn't forgotten about the medallion.

"Yeah, why haven't you?" I ask, stalling for time as I figure out a compelling way to deter her. She looks away and shrugs. Something clicks into place.

"You don't want to take it because you know it's important to me," I say. She rolls her eyes and scoffs, but I know that I'm right.

"You wouldn't answer my question when we first got here because it wasn't all fake, and you don't want to admit it."

"Tyre," she says, "I'm sorry, you're a good person, and I'm sorry to hurt you, but I really needed you here to extend my magic."

"Huh," I say, watching every move her face makes, "liar."

24

I lay staring at the ceiling as light starts to creep in through my window the next day. Realizing that Calla might care about me on some level can't change anything, and there's a large part of me that wishes I didn't even know. The door creaks open, and I look, expecting to see a broom.

"Let's go," Briowney's voice rings out through the shadows.

"I'm surprised Calla hasn't found you yet," I say as I swing my feet over the side of the bed.

"I haven't underestimated her this time, which is something I recommend you don't do either," she says.

"I think I've clearly learned my lesson with that as much as you have," I say. Briowney keeps talking like I haven't spoken.

"Just distract her long enough for me to get the rose," she says. "Calla has a limited supply of magic, and creating the case around the rose and Atreo took a lot of it the first time. Once she realizes the rose is out of its case, she'll have to pull all her magic from the windows and doors and pretty much everywhere else in the castle to try and reseal it. That's when we run." I roll my eyes internally. Briowney clearly has no plan other than to steal the Claret Rose, which I can't let her do. Based on every account I've ever heard, the Claret Rose is incredibly dangerous, but I've got my own plan.

"Why are you so fixated on this rose?" I say.

"It belongs to my kind," says Briowney, "and after what you've seen, do you really think Calla should have access to a dangerous magical plant like the Claret Rose?" I don't have an answer to that, so we continue our walk in silence.

As we walk, I swear I see Briowney's eyes stealing glances toward the place where I have the knife hidden under my shirt. She leads the way to the only place in the castle I haven't managed to explore yet, which is the highest floor. We climb a spiral staircase onto a landing of sorts with only three doors. Standing in front of one of them is Calla.

"I see you've finally made it to cataloguing the last floor," she says.

"Stand aside," says Briowney, glaring at her, "you're outnumbered."

"You think if I thought the two of you joining forces was a threat, I would have let Tyre find you at all?" says Calla. Briowney lifts her hand, but Calla is faster, and Briowney's hand freezes as if Calla has physically grabbed her wrist. With a flick of her hand, Calla lowers Briowney's arm back to her side. Briowney glares at her.

"Calla," I say, "we are going into that room, whether you like it or not."

"Can't let you do that," says Calla. We look at each other for a split second before I move towards her. I wonder if she'll continue her penance of not using magic on me, but I don't have to wonder long as an invisible force holds me in place. I see Briowney next to me struggling against the same hold. Calla stands in front of us with both hands raised.

"Come on," she says, sounding weary, "everyone back downstairs." Briowney turns, but I don't. Suddenly, I realize I have more wiggle room than Briowney does. The medallion glows warm against my body. It's figured out that magic is being used on me against my will. I feel the magic's grip loosen a little bit. I turn and pretend I'm under the same amount of control as Briowney and wait. Right as Briowney starts walking towards the stairs behind me, I turn as quickly as I can, imagining breaking the invisible bonds. I can almost hear a snapping sound as the magic comes loose.

"Ow!" Calla doubles over, holding her hand as if she's been burned, and I rush forward to loop my arm around her and swing her away from the door.

"Briowney, now!" I scream. Briowney only has seconds before I'm slammed to the floor with arms pinned to the carpet below me, but it's enough for her to dart into the room. Calla runs into the room after Briowney, leaving me unpinned and forgotten on the carpet. I stand up and follow after her, finding myself in the room that, until now, I've only seen in Calla's mirror. There's a small window letting in the morning light above the bed of a young man. He's sleeping, but clearly ill, pale, and covered in beads of sweat. Atreo.

I think about how I pictured this moment so differently. Emerging into the room where Atreo is being held as a rescuing hero, not a captive. Just as he was in the mirror, he's encased in a golden, glowing dome that I now recognize as Calla's magic. I don't have long to look at Atreo and wonder what that might mean before my attention is drawn back to Calla and Briowney.

Briowney looks murderous and is trying to push her hand through the golden dome surrounding the rose on the table in the corner of the room, but she's caught in both the barrier of the dome around the rose and in Calla's magic grip.

"Tyre," says Calla, "there is nothing in this room to help you. Please leave."

"Can't do that, Calla," I say, slowly edging toward them. I see Calla slowly lifting her hand, and before she can decide whether or not to use magic, I grab Briowney from behind and hold my knife to her throat.

"Take the barrier off the front door," I say. Calla looks shocked. Not as shocked as I would imagine Briowney looks, but there's no way to know. Briowney is struggling to get out of my grip and kicking my shins. I can even feel a tiny tug of what I assume is Briowney's magic on my arms and fingers, and I'm shocked at how faint it feels compared to Calla's. Briowney wasn't kidding when she said being trapped here has made her weak.

"Tyre," says Calla, sadly, "we both know you're not going to kill Briowney."

"Probably not," I say, "but if I did, I would turn back into a normal man. No use to you at all. If you let me go, there's a chance you could recapture me, antlers and all."

"I taught you that trick," says Calla, the ghost of a sad smile tugging at the corners of her mouth," *'Why take those odds when you could take the ones I'm offering you?'* That day outside the pub, remember?" I fight to keep my face neutral because I do remember that day. The first time we kissed. That first day, I should have known she was a traitorous liar, because the curse didn't break. Anger and sadness wash over me in waves.

"Are you willing to bet weeks of magic on the chance that I won't kill Briowney?" I say.

"Take it as a compliment," says Calla, "but yes, I am." I glare at her. Angry at her for calling my bluff, angry at the world for putting me in this position, angry at myself for being stupid enough to be tricked. I release Briowney, who falls to the ground sobbing, and I'm vaguely aware of Calla pulling her out of the room. I assume she's taking her back to her cell in the basement. I don't care. I'm still standing in the room, fuming when I hear Calla come back in behind me.

"Tyre," she says. The sound of her voice triggers a new wave of rage, and my gaze lands on the Claret Rose. Suddenly, Briowney's voice comes back to me. *'After what you've seen, do you really think Calla should have access to a dangerous magical plant like the claret rose*?' The answer is no, I don't. Before I can consider the potential consequences of such an action, I gather all the willpower I can and bring my hand holding the fairy knife crashing down onto the Claret Rose.

"Tyre, no!" screams Calla. As my fist hits the golden dome, I hear a cracking sound like glass breaking, but I'm thrown backward before I can make any contact with the rose. "No!" screams Calla again, and the sound makes me sick to my stomach. It isn't the angry yell of someone whose evil plans have been ruined. It's the cry of someone in pain.

The Claret Rose is now on the bedside table, looking like an ordinary rose, but I realize that my attempt to destroy the Claret Rose has also damaged the golden dome around Atreo. It seems to be melting away.

"No, no, no," Calla says, running over and falling to her knees next to his bed. She grabs his hand. "No," she sobs again. She's gathering a golden glow from everywhere in the castle and using it to try to repair the dome over Atreo. She's crying as hard as she did the night outside Lir Haven. "Atreo, please, hold on," she says.

"Calla," I say. "I didn't . . . this isn't what . . ."

"Get out," she sobs.

"Calla I . . . "

"Get out! Out of this room, out of this castle, out of this country. Get out!" On the last 'get out', I feel myself thrown backward through the door, and it slams shut behind me. I stand frozen for a second before I find myself sprinting for the front door. I pause halfway down the spiral stairs. *Maddie's antidote.*

I hesitate for only a second before running back up the spiral staircase. There are only two places I could think to check for the potion, and those are Calla's room and her workshop. Since I haven't come across those rooms yet, I have to assume they're the other two rooms at the top of the stairs. I open one door and quickly search the bedroom, not allowing myself to think about how this is the first time I've seen Calla's bedroom and how many times I've wondered what her bedroom at home was like while she slept next to me in Thiaghal.

When the potion isn't anywhere in the bedroom, I open the door to the second room, Calla's workshop. I'm struck by the same overpowering smell of roses that defines Calla and turn to see an entire terrarium of roses behind a glass case. Besides that, there are empty glass bottles, small gas heaters, all kinds of dried herbs, and an array of crystals. Sitting on one of the shelves, I see the yellow elixir Calla showed me days before, and quickly put it in my pocket. As I arrive back on the landing, my hand hesitates over the doorknob of Atreo's room. I can still faintly hear Calla crying, and for one ridiculous second born out of an entire year of loving her, I almost go back inside. Then the moment ends, and before I can change my mind, I turn and run for the front hall.

When I emerge into the front hall, I'm overcome by an even more eerie stillness than usual and see all the brooms lying on their sides. Whatever Calla is doing to re-contain the Claret Rose and Atreo, it's taking all her magic just like Briowney said it would, which means . . . Just as I think it, I push the front doors, which swing open without any resistance. I take deep gasps of cool air as I run through the garden and, as fast as I can, towards home.

25

The journey home is a long one. I don't keep track of days or nights. I only stop and check into whatever inn is closest when I absolutely can't keep running or walking anymore. When I finally see the manor house in the distance, I choke back a sob. I haven't even started to think about how I'll explain the events of the last few weeks to my family. All I can think about is seeing them again and sleeping in my own bed. Everything else can wait.

"Mom!" I call as I push open the front doors. "Aydin, Bevin! Mads!"

"Tyre!" My mom is the first one to respond. She comes into the front hall from the sitting room, closely followed by Aydin. She takes one look at me and rushes to pull me into a hug. She's sobbing and hugging me for what feels like an eternity. "When Aydin told me what you'd gone to do, I thought I'd never see you again."

"It's alright, Mom," I say. "I'm here, I'm right here, I'm alright."

When she finally lets go, Aydin pulls me in for a hug, but before he can say anything Mom speaks up again.

"Did you . . . The Inimical . . . Is he . . . ?" she asks. She stops and looks around. "Where is Calla?"

"Where is Bevin?" I say. "I'd rather only tell this story once." As if on cue, Bevin rushes down the stairs.

"Tyre!" she says, throwing herself into a hug just as tight as Mom's.

"Hey, Bev," I say, squeezing back.

"Tyre," says Mom, "just tell me, is Calla alright?"

"Calla's physically fine," I say. "Mentally, she's deranged, but . . . Come on, let's sit down." I make a move towards the living room, but Aydin puts his hand on my shoulder.

"Tyre," he says, "before you sit down and fill us in, there's something you should know." Is it my imagination, or is Bevin glaring at Aydin and my mom? Since when does Bevin glare at anyone? Much less Aydin and Mom? And where is Maddie? Before I can ask, I hear another voice call out from the living room.

"Everything alright out here?" Then Delanum Meltair walks into my front hallway from the living room, sipping tea in his pajamas.

"Let's sit down," he says. "It seems like we have a lot to talk about."

The End

Acknowledgements

I could never have done this without so much support!

Thank you to my husband, Chas, for listening to me read every chapter out loud as I finished it.

Thank you to my mom, Kate, and Katelyn for their work reading, reviewing, and editing the first drafts of this book.

Thank you to Emily, for being the first person to ever read one of my books.

Thank you to my little brother, Peter, for making the first ever character art for one of my characters.

Thank you my wonderful cover artist Brittany Evans of BE Designs.

Thank you to @MsMorbid on Instagram, the artist who brought my main characters to life with character art.

Thank you to Rosemary of Heartfelt Editing for being such a thorough and caring proofreader for this book.

Finally, to all my readers who reached and signed up to read ARCs of this book and to everyone who spent their time and money on my writing, I truly can't thank you enough!

About the Author

Ashley is a clinical psychologist and a lifelong lover of folklore and fairytales from around the world. She used to love going to the library in her neighborhood and curling up for hours in the folk and fairytales section, so in all her work you'll find threads of a lot of classic folklore. She also loves mysteries and figuring things out! She and her dad used to sit together every night when she was growing up and read two chapters of a Boxcar Children mystery, then spend several minutes "discussing the case"

and coming up with theories. Her love of mysteries has never gone away and you'll also always find a puzzle to unravel in her books.

She lives in the Northern Virginia area with her husband.

www.ingramcontent.com/pod-product-compliance
Lightning Source LLC
LaVergne TN
LVHW091256150826
845673LV00006B/1441

9798995362210